THE MARQUESS METHOD

KATHLEEN AYERS

Copyright © 2021 by Kathleen Ayers

All rights reserved.

No part of this book may be reproduced in any form or by any electronic or mechanical means, including information storage and retrieval systems, without written permission from the author, except for the use of brief quotations in a book review.

Editing by Midnight Owl Editing

Cover by Covers and Cupcakes

PROLOGUE

The Barrow, Duke of Granby's estate, 1840

Lady Theodosia Barrington hurried down the tiled floor of the hallway. The strains of a waltz were just reaching her ears as she scurried in the direction of the Duke of Granby's ballroom. Cursing under her breath, she envisioned Lady Meredith, *eyelash-batting viper*, taking advantage of Theo's absence to sink her gloved claws into the Earl of Blythe.

"Bollocks," she whispered to herself.

In the future, it would be best to watch her intake of punch. Perhaps stop sneaking wine from the Duke of Granby's servants. Her goal was to have Blythe escort her into the cool night air for a walk about the terrace and to steal a kiss, not take yet another inconvenient trip to see to her personal needs.

A kiss. From Blythe.

"Drat," she hissed as her toe made contact with one of the ornate, overly large candlesticks decorating nearly every inch of The Barrow. The return journey to the Duke of Granby's ballroom was fraught with a multitude of obstacles, most of which Theo couldn't see. At least not clearly. The fault of poor lighting and her decision not to wear her spectacles to the house party. Better to be clumsy, though, than to have Blythe see her in that blasted bit of metal and glass.

Blythe's opinion of 'bespectacled bluestockings' was less than positive. At Lady Ralston's ball, he had disparaged the looks of one such lady within Theo's hearing. She'd vowed at that moment that Blythe would never see her wearing spectacles and promptly put the loathsome frames away. Far better to be thought a tad awkward than hideously unappealing.

Theo wore her bruises, scratches, and resulting embarrassment as a badge of honor. A courageous fight to maintain what attractiveness she possessed. During her week at the house party, she'd so far stubbed her toes at least a dozen times, waved enthusiastically at a selection of Grecian statues in the garden thinking them other guests, and tripped over a mop plus the maid wielding it.

Then there was the unfortunate incident involving Lord Haven and a glass of ratafia.

Ill-mannered. Uncouth. The Marquess of Haven was *very* unlikeable.

Despite the marquess's presence, when Cousin Winnie had received an invitation to attend a house party given by the Duke of Granby and his aunt, Theo had jumped at the chance to attend.

Lord Blythe and the Duke of Granby were close friends. His attendance was assured. Granby's friendship with the golden, sunny earl was really the only thing Theo liked about Granby. His friendship with Lord Haven, on the other hand, didn't recommend him at all.

The Marquess of Haven was disreputable. Impoverished. Prone to fistfights and gambling. Fond of making unkind comments about young ladies who couldn't see well. In short, there was *nothing* Theo liked about Haven. He reminded her of a brigand or a thief. At the slightest provocation, she thought he'd pull out a pistol and rob a coach. If one liked the appeal of, say, a highwayman or some other nefarious gentleman, Theo supposed a woman *might* find Haven attractive. But one would have to overlook his annoying sarcasm, unpleasant personality, and short temper.

The very first day at the duke's estate, Theo had ruined Haven's coat by spilling ratafia on him. Ratafia, unbeknownst to her, was an impossible stain. No amount of gentle dabbing or brushing had restored his coat. His *best* coat, Theo was certain. She had begged forgiveness. Most gentlemen would have graciously accepted her pretty speech.

Not Haven. He had thus far spent the whole of the house party glaring at her with his moss-colored eyes, flinging caustic comments at Theo whenever she had the poor fortune to come near him.

'That elongated bit of marble isn't what you think it is,' Haven would whisper to Theo as he passed her in the garden or, *'I'm not a coat rack, but a marquess,'* as her shawl touched his arm accidentally. And her personal favorite, uttered into her ear as she sat for dinner, *'As you feel your way around the other guests, aren't you terrified you'll ruin yourself?'*

"Ow." This time it was her shin banging against a marble podium holding the bust of one of Granby's ancestors. A rather ugly one. At least as far as she could see.

"Stay in the middle of the hall," she muttered to herself, determined to avoid the monstrous candlesticks with their ornately carved leaves of iron. The candlesticks mocked her, reaching out to grab at the skirts of her gown. A slight tug halted her progress rather abruptly as one of the blasted leaves succeeded in catching her. Blythe was sure to be dancing the waltz with Lady Meredith by now.

Theo tugged gently at her skirts.

The rush of air was instantaneous. The metal stand

teetered dangerously in her direction. A candle dropped to the floor with a small thud before rolling away into the dark recesses of the hall. She struggled to grab at the heavy iron with one hand while attempting to untangle her skirts with the other.

The stand tipped wildly. Unlit candles pelted her arms and shoulders. She waited for the heavy stand to make contact with her head. Perhaps it would knock her to the floor and leave her unconscious. There Theo would lie on the cold marble, injured and unable to move, her absence unnoticed until another guest ventured out and tripped over her prone body.

"Drat," she whispered.

A gloved hand, masculine in size and shape, caught the iron in a firm grip, surprising Theo and saving her from being bludgeoned. Due to the poor lighting and her bent position, Theo couldn't make out her rescuer, but she recognized the buttons on his coat.

Her heart thumped in anticipation.

Blythe.

Every one of the handsome earl's coats possessed buttons with the same distinct design: a bird about to take flight. There was a reason behind the bird, but when Blythe had related the story, Theo hadn't been paying attention. She'd been too fascinated by the movement of his lips as he spoke.

"Lord Blythe," she breathed, her eyes fluttering down as she carefully freed her skirts from a jagged iron leaf. "What a most timely rescue."

Fingers wrapped firmly around her elbow. His touch warmed her entire arm.

"A moment, my lord. I'm almost free." A playful, flirtatious laugh escaped her. "Much like our first encounter in the park when you came to my aid. Do you recall?"

A masculine sound of agreement came from above her.

Once her skirts were freed, the hand on her elbow pulled Theo up, even as his other arm settled around her waist. Fingertips pressed into her skin.

Theo kept her eyes focused on the buttons decorating his coat, overcome with shyness, an emotion she rarely exhibited around Blythe. Not knowing what was expected of her, she counted the small line of birds, afraid to take a breath lest this moment end.

He dropped his nose to the side of her neck, gently gliding his hand through her hair before taking a breath against her skin. A low rumble came from his chest as his fingers trailed along her cheek and down her jaw, tipping up her chin.

Theo's eyes fluttered closed. She'd dreamt of this exact scenario for months. The press of Blythe's mouth on hers. The tender adoration of his lips. The sheer romance of the act. Perhaps he'd even whisper poetry to her. Blythe adored poetry.

This kiss wasn't at all what she'd imagined.

There was no hesitation or asking for permission before his lips caught at hers. The kiss was gentle but demanding. Lazy in the decadent exploration of her mouth. A nip at her bottom lip coaxed her mouth to part, and she did, unfurling like the bud of a rose. The sensual flick of his tongue, the subtle luring of her senses, filled Theo with such wicked thoughts.

She couldn't even hear the musicians playing in the ballroom anymore, only the sound of her pulse beating in her ears.

A warm hand skimmed up the length of her spine, the spread of his fingers stopping when he reached the back of her neck. He squeezed ever so softly. A gentle warning for her not to move, only to surrender.

Her hands flew up to grasp the lapels of his coat, fingers

sinking into the luxurious fabric. She pulled him closer until her aching breasts flattened against his chest. She sagged against him, hanging on for dear life, her legs no longer capable of holding her upright.

A low growl vibrated beneath her fingertips.

Mouth moving to the line of her neck, he cupped the underside of one breast in a tender caress.

A whimper left her.

The thick strands of his hair brushed seductively along the exposed skin of her shoulder, trailing over the tops of her breasts as his tongue trailed along her neck.

Theo gasped, eyes popping open in horror.

Blythe's hair was *short*. Closely cropped to his skull. His hair would be unable to trail against her shoulder or anywhere else. And there was the aroma of spice in the air, not the citrus scent Blythe favored.

Theo turned her head, fingers curling into fists as she pushed back against the man who held her, so shocked, so *outraged*, she could barely speak. "You—"

"The Marquess of Haven," he supplied.

"I know who you are. I've eyes." Her mouth, still swollen, could barely form the words.

"Yes, and lovely eyes at that. But you should wear your spectacles, Lady Theodosia. I'm told you own a pair." Haven's hand still cupped her breast as if it were of no consequence. "I could have been one of the footmen."

Theo smacked his arm, his chest. Basically, any part of Haven she could reach. "Release me. This instant." Heat flamed her cheeks. *My God*. The audacity of him. What if someone had come upon them? "How dare you pretend to be Blythe."

"Pretend?" His hands released her. "I did not. It isn't my fault you can't see anything. I could have left you to be hit in the temple by this"—he motioned to the towering candlestick—"but I very gallantly did not. Though it might have knocked some sense into you."

Theo's lips and body were still throbbing from Haven's kiss. Which did nothing to improve her mood. "That's Blythe's coat," she accused.

"Correct. It appears you can see quite clearly when you choose to." He lifted his broad shoulders in a careless shrug. "He was kind enough to lend me a coat for tonight. Mine," he said, glaring down at her, "was ruined."

Haven was intolerable. "You—" She took a deliberate step back.

"You're having trouble speaking, my lady. Are you sure you didn't run into the wall on your way to me?"

"I wasn't coming to you," she spat, humiliated to the very roots of her hair. "I didn't even know you were here."

Haven. I've kissed Haven.

"Exactly. Much like the day you ruined my coat." He crossed his arms across his chest.

Theo's fingers tingled, remembering the feel of all that warm muscle. "It was an accident. I've apologized. Besides, the coat I *unintentionally* ruined would not have been appropriate for this evening, as well you know."

Another roll of his shoulders.

"I assumed you to be Blythe," she informed him again.

"No one else confuses the two of us."

Haven was a *horrible* person. He deserved his impoverishment. Even if he looked somewhat magnificent in Blythe's borrowed evening wear.

"You are a —" She choked, trying to find the appropriate word.

"Bastard? Rogue?" he supplied. "Personally, I prefer libertine. Has a nice ring to it." He cocked his head. "Come, Lady Theodosia, you can do better than that. Your brother owns a pleasure palace."

"Gambling hell," she corrected automatically. None of the Barringtons liked to acknowledge that the club owned by Theo's two brothers, Leo Murphy and His Grace, the Duke of Averell, was more than a place to play cards and roulette. A gambling hell was marginally more acceptable. "I should slap you for the liberties you've taken."

Haven turned so his cheek faced her, waving her forward. "Have at it." A bit of light bathed his roguish features and glinted on the dusting of dark hair along his jaw. "Won't change a thing."

He had a very strong jaw. Lovely lines. Lots of contrast. Interesting little details like the scar on his chin. He'd make a fabulous drawing in charcoal. Possibly a miniature. Though she couldn't imagine anyone wanting to cart around a picture of Haven in the pocket of their gown.

"You're only put out because you enjoyed it."

Heat washed up her cheeks. She *had* enjoyed it. Theo could still feel the press of his mouth against hers and the responding ache sliding down her midsection.

"*Did* I enjoy it?" Theo leaned forward before making a great show of wiping his taste from her lips with one gloved hand. "You overestimate your meager charms. Step aside, my lord."

The amusement faded from his roughly hewn features. Insults didn't sit well with Haven. One only had to count the number of fistfights and duels he was rumored to engage in. Theo's gaze took in the tiny bump on his otherwise perfect nose.

Probably where that came from. A fistfight.

"Wear your bloody spectacles, Lady Theodosia," he snarled at her. "Else there's no telling who else you'll mistake for Blythe."

"As long as it isn't you," she said. No one at the house party save her sister Romy knew Theo wore spectacles. Not even Cousin Winnie had ever seen her wear them. How in the world did Haven know?

They glared at each other, unmoving, as the air around them crackled and popped, thickening as if a thunderstorm would erupt in Granby's hallway.

His eyes drifted to her mouth.

Theo swallowed and took a careful step back. She had the most terrible urge to leap into his arms and allow him to kiss her again.

His fingers stretched out to her. "Theodosia." The soft whisper was like a wisp of smoke snaking along her body.

Theo danced away, shaking her head to dispel any notion of being close to Haven. She turned her back on him and fled in the direction of the ballroom. The intoxication of his kiss still lingered, though she willed it away.

For the first time since the house party had begun, Theo couldn't wait to leave.

1

London, Some months later.

Theo marched into the park just as the sun was beginning to pinken the sky, thinking how fortunate it was that the Averell mansion backed up to the rolling expanse of grass and trees. The park was easily reached through the mansion's garden gate, usually kept locked to avoid any unwanted guests from wandering onto her brother's property. Something that had never happened. The Averell footmen were incredibly vigilant.

When it came to someone slipping *into* her brother's garden.

No one spared Theo a glance as she left her bed before the sun was up and made her way down the double staircase. Or if they had, they'd chosen not to pay attention. Not an unusual occurrence. Theo was used to moving quietly through the house, unnoticed except by perhaps Pith, their butler.

Phaedra, Theo's younger sister, would have drawn notice immediately. She demanded attention. Olivia, her mother's ward, would *never* sneak into the park without escort at the crack of dawn.

If any one of them possessed an ounce of ladylike decorum, it was Olivia.

And Theo's elder sister, Romy? Now married, she no longer lived at the Averell mansion. Instead, Romy resided with the immense block of stone everyone in London referred to as the Duke of Granby. The newlywed pair had left only yesterday for an extended tour of Italy and wouldn't return for several months.

Theo tucked the bit of canvas she carried more securely beneath her arm.

Painting and contemplating the Earl of Blythe was how Theo planned to spend her morning. His birthday was next week. An invitation for the celebration, planned by his mother, had already arrived at the Averell mansion. Theo would be attending with Cousin Winnie and Rosalind. She'd already chosen the gown she would wear.

Blythe's gift from Theo, rather splendid if a bit improper, was finally finished and already sitting in a tiny wooden box decorated with a bow. The gift was sure to compel Blythe to offer for her, something Theo desired above all else.

Her fingers tightened on the handle of the rosewood box containing her paints and brushes. The blanket she carried shifted against her hip. Theo paused to tuck the blanket and the canvas more securely beneath her arm.

If Romy were in London, she would be quite distressed by Theo's plans. Horrified, in fact. Frankly, Theo herself was more than a little shocked. But nothing was ever achieved by being a milquetoast, according to Theo's mother, the Dowager Duchess of Averell. Still, before her departure, Romy had made Theo promise she wouldn't do anything impulsive. Or brazen. Blythe's mother was known to be a bastion of propriety. She wouldn't look kindly on a bold young lady attempting to ensnare her son.

Theo rolled her eyes as she trudged along, the rosewood box banging against her thigh. What did Romy know? Granby hadn't courted Romy properly. He'd ruined her and *then* married her.

Though Blythe hadn't asked permission to formally court Theo, he'd paid her a great deal of attention at Granby's house party. By his own admission, he regarded her highly. Blythe had also danced with Theo at Lady Cambourne's ball *and* at Lady Ralston's, two of the social season's most significant events. He'd called on two separate occasions. They had even read poetry together in the garden. And during Romy's wedding to Granby, he'd *winked* at Theo from across the aisle of the church, his golden beauty, clothed in a suit of peacock blue, nearly blinding her with its magnificence. A blush had warmed her cheeks at the affectionate gesture.

Until she'd caught sight of Haven sitting next to Blythe.

Theo stumbled over a tree root. "Drat."

Haven's eyes had lingered far too long on her bosom before reaching her mouth, a not-too-subtle reminder of the kiss he'd stolen from her at Granby's house party. What was worse, she'd enjoyed that kiss far too much. Embarrassing to admit, but true. Even more humiliating when she learned how competitive Haven and Blythe were with each other. Haven, poverty-stricken marquess that he was, envied Blythe his wealth and a great many other things.

Her first real kiss had surely only been done to anger Blythe.

Theo had little choice but to avoid Haven on principle. When Haven had called at the Averell mansion for Romy—as an ambassador of sorts on behalf of Granby and under the guise of friendship—Theo had made herself scarce. Fortunately, outside of Romy's wedding, Theo hadn't seen Haven at any of the events she'd attended, for which she was grateful. According to Cousin Winnie, Haven's interests were solely focused on Miss Violet Emerson.

Good riddance.

Theo forced her mind back to the task at hand and the entire reason for being in the park at such an ungodly hour. Olivia had issued Theo a challenge. Create something *other* than a miniature. Yes, miniatures showcased Theo's singular talent, but wasn't it time to expand her horizons? Try something different? A landscape perhaps, or a bowl of fruit.

Or a breast.

Theo bit her lip. Olivia would faint dead away even mentioning the word.

But Theo acknowledged it *was* time to move on. After all, the miniature she had painted for Blythe was by far her best work. Difficult to surpass. One of a kind. Incredibly improper. Perfect. She might not ever paint another miniature.

Earlier this week, Theo had finally yielded to Olivia's pressure and sketched out the small pond hidden in a copse of trees at the base of the hill she now climbed. Theo's pencil had scratched away while Olivia had perched on the blanket beside her, calmly paging through one of the dull books on gardening she found endlessly fascinating.

Hyacinths. Peonies. Soil fertilized with cow dung. An interest Olivia unbelievably shared with Granby, of all people.

Theo enjoyed a good book as much as anyone, but her tastes ran more to romance. Lately, she'd developed a taste for novels featuring pirates. Thieves. Dangerous highwaymen. Horrid villains. Not the proper way to prune a rose bush.

The sun was beginning to rise as she approached the top of the hill, soft morning light spreading out atop the slick surface of the water. She took bigger steps, hoping to get to the correct spot before the light changed and ruined the vision in her mind's eye. There were very few people in the park at this hour, which was a good thing. No one would remark on the reclusive, slightly odd middle Barrington daughter alone without escort, though Theo didn't consider herself quite so solitary or strange now, thanks to Blythe and his attentions.

She set down her artist's kit and the canvas before tossing out the blanket tucked beneath her arm. Spreading the blanket across the grass, she turned her gaze to the pond.

The mist was just starting to burn away, giving the water and surrounding grass a mysterious, otherworldly look, a mood she wanted to capture. Peering into the hazy morning mist, Theo tried to make out the cattails at the edge of the pond.

She squinted into the mist as a goose honked. Somewhere.

Theo refused to wear her spectacles when out in public, and this morning was no exception. Blythe still didn't know how vision-impaired she was, and Theo had no intention of him finding out. She *had* worn them when she sketched out the pond the other day, but *only* because Olivia had been beside her, promising to alert Theo if anyone of their acquaintance came by.

Settling herself on the blanket, Theo opened the lid and took out the easel, setting the small canvas against it. The palette was cleverly tucked away inside the lid of the box, and she placed it in front of her. Looking at the array of colors, each securely tucked in small glass tubes, filled Theo with a sort of giddy joy. Smoky greys. Pale pinks. Soft creams.

She loved, *loved*, colors. And pencils. Chalk. Pastels. All of it.

The tiny containers holding the paints were so clever. A fairly recent invention by Winsor and Newton, where Theo purchased most of her supplies. She supposed her adoration of the glass syringes was what had led her to decide not to use watercolors for this painting.

Carefully, she selected a glass tube, placing just a dab of cream—*Flemish White,* her mind whispered—on the palette. Next, a tiny drop of *Cadmium Yellow* which she swirled on the tip of her brush while watching the sun make its way above the horizon, bathing the pond with early morning light. Working quickly to capture the exact right hue, she hummed to herself, pausing only to squint at something she couldn't see clearly, which was nearly everything. She told herself the details weren't important. This painting was more about color.

"That's not right."

Startled, Theo's brush slashed across the canvas.

Drat.

"You've forgotten the green tinge to the water," the gravelly voice continued, acting as if he had any idea about art, which Theo sincerely doubted. "Pond scum."

Dear God. Where had he come from? Only moments ago, Theo had been hoping she wouldn't see him ever again. "Lord Haven, what an unexpected pleasure."

"Isn't it?" Haven's voice always sounded as if he'd just woken up, every word sounding utterly decadent. "A pleasure, I mean."

Theo turned to view him, noting the lovely coat he wore, the color of freshly ground nutmeg. Obviously new. She stifled the urge to flick paint in his direction. Paint was much more difficult to get out of a coat than ratafia.

"Can you even see what you're painting?" He gave her an innocent look, the mossy green orbs of his eyes sparkling in the early morning light. "I'm terrified you might poke yourself in the eye with your brush or miss the canvas and ruin your dress, which is very pretty, by the way."

Haven, despite his other faults, did have amazing eyes.

She'd give him that. The color of moss clinging to river rock. Close to *Mitis Green*, but a shade darker.

"I can see the pond perfectly well, my lord. It's quite large."

"So are servants. Candlesticks. *Me*. You've run into all of those with regularity, though I will admit, I did enjoy it when you stumbled my way."

Theo had hoped Haven would never, ever mention *Theodosia's Unfortunate Incident*, as she had labeled the kiss in her mind, but she should have known better. As grateful as Theo was that he'd never told anyone else, *especially* Blythe, it still didn't leave Theo feeling charitable toward him.

Pretending to misunderstand, she said, "I've apologized several times for spilling ratafia on your coat, my lord."

"You have," he agreed. Haven's hair, much too long for a proper gentleman, looked like it had been cut by poorly sharpened scissors. The color of the strands, which Theo likened to *Burnt Umber*, buffeted gently against his cheek. Strong jaw. *Glorious* cheekbones, like the bold slash of a knife across his face. Patrician nose sporting that tiny bump. The scar in the shape of a half-moon on his chin. Haven had none of Blythe's perfectly curated attractiveness nor an ounce of his friend's charm.

Theo's pulse fluttered madly at his presence, though she willed it not to.

Her fingers itched to paint him with all his delicious hollows and hues. But Theo would never ask him to sit for her. Haven was to be avoided. *Especially* by Theo. He needed to move along before anyone saw them together.

"Don't let me keep you, Lord Haven. I'm sure you'd like to be on your way." She turned back to the canvas and lifted her brush, hoping he would take the hint. "Good morning."

Haven ignored her less-than-subtle suggestion to leave, plopping down next to her on the blanket without asking permission. He studied her artist kit and the tiny vials of paint contained within. A forefinger trailed over the rosewood box, pausing only to trace her initials.

"TLB. What does the L stand for?"

She caught a whiff of spice and attempted to slide away, trying to put some distance between them.

"Louise. My paternal grandmother's name," she answered.

Haven traced the edges of the rosewood box holding her supplies, his fingers gliding over the letters of her name. Almost a caress. The same way his fingers had skimmed the length of her back when he'd kissed her. Inappropriate things began to fill Theo's mind. *Naked* things. Lips and mouths. Moans and whispers. All of them belonging to Haven.

The paintbrush she clutched in her fingers wobbled. She quickly pulled it from the canvas lest she ruin what little work she'd already done.

"Theodosia Louise." A smile hovered at his lips. "And a brother named Leo. Must get confusing around the dinner table. Leo. Theo." A small sound of amusement left him. There was a strange light hovering in his eyes, like fireflies sparkling in a field of summer grass.

"Are you acquainted with my brother?"

It seemed unlikely. She doubted Haven could afford a membership to Elysium.

"We've met."

Theo didn't know much about Haven, but what she did know had been supplied by Cousin Winnie. Haven's father had been a wastrel, drunkenly gambling away the family fortune. It was not a stretch of the imagination to assume the former Marquess of Haven had spent at least some of his time and coin at Elysium.

"It's a clever little box," he said. "Does the palette fit just here," he pointed to the inside of the lid, "when you're finished?"

"Yes." The longer Haven's large, broad-shouldered form hovered near hers, the more unsettled Theo became. His presence on the blanket gave the air around them an expectant flutter, the sense that something barely restrained would burst forth at any moment.

Very unlike the way she felt around Blythe.

She wished he'd go away. Why *was* he in the park so early? Haven didn't strike Theo as someone who embraced the morning. She pictured him quite clearly in a smoky tavern at night.

Her eyes flitted to the left and right. No horse, though admittedly there might be one near and Theo just couldn't see it. Nearly everything beyond the small cluster of trees a short distance away was fuzzy about the edges.

"I feel certain, my lord," Theo tried to keep the exasperation out of her words, "you've much better things to do than watch me paint. I don't want to keep you from your morning stroll." She threw another hint in his direction.

"I've a bit of time before meeting a young lady for a walk."

The color of his eyes deepened to emerald as he peered at her from beneath his lashes. It was difficult to discern if Haven was being truthful or not, though if he were meeting a young lady, it would explain the coat. But if that were Haven's purpose, he should have taken the time to have his hair cut properly.

Theo raised a brow, curious. "I know few young ladies who would be interested in such an early morning stroll, my lord."

"You're here."

"I'm *painting*." Really, he was infuriating. "At least, I'm trying to," she said pointedly.

"Are you acquainted with Miss Violet Emerson?"

"I haven't had the pleasure." Cousin Winnie was correct, as usual. Haven *was* pursuing the adored daughter of Viscount

Emerson. Petite, raven-haired with porcelain skin, Violet was renowned for her beauty and ladylike manner. She doubtless also possessed perfect eyesight.

Something curdled in Theo's stomach.

"I doubt you two would get on," Haven said casually as he drew a circle on the blanket with his forefinger.

Theo had no idea what he meant exactly, but it sounded like an insult.

"Besides," Haven said before she could speak again. "I find your creative process to be fascinating."

"You've no idea what my creative process entails. Or anyone's creative process. I'm doubtful of your appreciation for artistic endeavors." She dabbed her brush in another circle of paint, intent on capturing the glistening of the water as the light rippled across the surface, and deliberately turned her back.

The skin behind her ear tickled as Haven breathed over her shoulder. "I sense you don't like the thought of me walking with Miss Emerson."

Theo's entire back arched in his direction. To her utter horror.

"Relieve yourself of such a notion, my lord. With whom you walk in the park is none of my affair." Her brush hovered; she was more annoyed than she had been previously, and it would surely influence her work. Because Theo *didn't* care for the thought of Haven kissing Miss Emerson as he had her.

Turning her head to once more urge him to move along, Theo found his face mere inches from her own. If Haven so much as tipped his chin, their lips would touch.

"You forgot the green." His voice was a low hum against her skin.

"I didn't forget anything. Will you *please* go? I can't concentrate with you chattering away next to me, Lord

Haven. I'm sure Miss Emerson is impatient for your company."

"But I wish to see you work on your painting. It is a painting, isn't it? Despite the smaller size? Though not small enough to be a miniature. I understand you are quite good at those."

"I am." She nearly smiled back at him, thinking of Blythe's gift. Daring was what the miniature was. Bold. Painted to showcase both her talent and affection. It was meant to compel Blythe to announce his intentions. She refused to believe it would not work.

"Must have been what ruined your eyesight. All that tiny painting."

Theo's lips tightened. She came very close to stabbing Haven with the end of her paintbrush. "I'm experimenting with a larger canvas."

"You are? How interesting," he purred.

Haven probably sprang from the womb mildly debauched and rumpled, with a cheroot in one hand and the other reaching for a glass of scotch. But if he thought for *one moment* that Theo would be taken aback by his blatant attempt to insert impropriety into their discussion, he was sorely mistaken. She had two older brothers, both of whom were far more masterful at innuendo than the marquess sitting next to her.

"Where does one hang such a thing?" Haven finally said after pretending to study her canvas with great interest. "It's barely larger than a book."

"It is *much* larger than a book," she snapped, concerned with the stretch of Haven's fingers next to her skirts. "One hangs a picture such as this in their home. Perfect for a nook in the foyer or a study. Possibly a parlor."

"A nook?" Haven made a small grunt. "I can't imagine art specifically for a secluded, dark corner. Why would you bother? If one is in such a place," his voice lowered, "their intent is not to observe a painting." He leaned close again, the edge of his chin brushing lightly atop her shoulder. "Though the strokes are very fine."

Spice filled Theo's nostrils. "You know nothing about painting. Annoyance, however, is a different matter."

"You've missed the geese." He pointed first to the canvas and then the pond, the movement of his lips as he spoke grazing just over the curve of her ear. "You probably can't make them out clearly. Those blobs of white, just there."

"I know what they are," she said through gritted teeth, trying to steady herself. "I am not blind."

"Are you certain? Because you've missed them," he said.

"My lord, is your presence here this morning meant to punish me in some way? Perhaps because I insulted you at Granby's house party? After . . ." She moved her paintbrush in the air.

"After I kissed you?" he said in a solemn tone. "When you claimed you thought I was Blythe?"

"Yes."

"After you kissed me back?"

Theo didn't care to be reminded of her lapse in judgement. "I made it clear I didn't enjoy your attentions. I'm sorry if you found that to be insulting—"

Her words were cut off by a snort of derision coming from Haven as he waved away her excuse and sat back from her. "I'm only trying to help, my lady."

"Your help isn't required."

"Clearly it is because you've missed the geese. You really need to wear your spectacles. I can't believe you'd allow your art to suffer for vanity."

Theo wondered, if she screamed loud enough, if the Averell footmen would hear even from this distance and rush to her aid. Pith would certainly come barreling into the park. Better yet, Theo could simply lure Haven to the edge of the pond, pretend not to see him, and push him in. Haven, for whatever reason, seemed determined to irritate her with his presence and unwelcome comments. This had been the entire theme of their limited acquaintance. He wasn't at *all* like Blythe.

With a sigh, she took a rag from the rosewood box and wiped off her brush, resigned to having had her morning ruined.

"Aren't you going to finish?" Haven's eyes dipped to her bodice where a spray of freckles emerged from the very modest neckline of her dress.

Blythe often likened the line of freckles to a constellation in the night sky, though he'd never actually been able to name one. Theo still took it as a compliment.

"No," she replied tartly. "The light is no longer correct. You interrupted me, spoiling my work." She wiped the paint off her palette before stowing it away in the rosewood box and tossing the rag inside. Placing the easel atop the rag she said, "I hope you're pleased with yourself, my lord."

"I've angered you." Haven stood and offered her his hand. "Let me help you. I'll escort you home."

"Absolutely, positively no." She stood and smoothed her skirts. "I do not wish to be seen with you and risk my reputation. Go away."

"You're very hostile this morning, Lady Theodosia." There was a tiny smirk on his lips. The wretch was enjoying her discomfort.

"Perhaps the cause is the uninvited company."

He pressed a hand to his chest, where she guessed his heart might be. If he possessed one. "You wound me."

"Get off the blanket," she snapped. Really, Haven was the most trying person she'd ever met. If he annoyed everyone as he did her, it was no wonder the result was a punch thrown in his direction.

Stepping off with a small hop, Haven held his hand out again, which she ignored, opting instead to snatch up the blanket. Tucking the blanket under her arm Theo picked up the rosewood box and her canvas.

"You must allow me to help. You could drop your canvas."

"I managed to get everything out here on my own, my lord. And you've helped me quite enough for today. Good morning, Lord Haven."

"I should escort you." He kept pace with her easily as she headed in the direction of the gate to the Duke of Averell's garden. "You might run into a tree. Or bump your head into the stone wall surrounding your brother's house. What if you reach for the door leading inside and instead of the knob, one of the footmen is there and you grab—"

Theo quickened her pace before she could hear the rest.

2

There are times in a young lady's life when emotion overrides common sense, leading her in a direction where scandal lurks. She convinces herself that reckless behavior will gain a gentleman's attention. Perhaps impress upon the gentleman the depth of her feelings and force him to realize his own. And in doing so, receives an offer of marriage.

London was riddled with usually level-headed, intelligent young women who found themselves following their hearts instead of their heads. Society was *not* kind to them.

Tonight, Theo anxiously mused, scanning the crowd gathered at the Earl of Blythe's house to celebrate his birthday, she had allowed her emotions to dictate her actions. Impulsivity had won out over the common sense and manners which had been instilled in Theo since birth. It was as if she'd gone completely mad.

All week long, Theo had looked forward to Blythe's birthday celebration, choosing her shimmering turquoise silk adorned with rosettes at the shoulders with the utmost care. Cousin Winnie and her daughter Rosalind, who accompanied

Theo tonight, had arrived exactly on time for the carriage ride to Blythe's home. Theo had leaned back against the plush seats of her cousin's carriage grateful for the pocket in her gown, concealed amid her skirts. The outline of the tiny wooden box was well hidden beneath the silk. She'd become light-headed just imagining his reaction to her daring.

How many times had Blythe declared Theo incomparable? More worldly than most young ladies. Delightfully bold. Gorgeously bordering on impropriety. How often had he implied that he did not care for demure, modest misses, stating he found them bland? *Colorless*.

She, he'd assured Theo, was different.

Ironically, it had been Romy, who loved to toss out her opinions to everyone whether they wished for them or not, who was to blame for the anxiousness now gripping Theo. It was Romy who had given Theo the idea, all the while berating her for what she considered nitwit behavior over Blythe.

Shouldn't Blythe admire you for your talent as an artist? Romy had said. *More so than the curve of your bosom?*

Theo had taken Romy's advice to heart, her creation for Blythe a perfect combination of both her talent *and* her bosom. Creating a rough sketch and then painting a miniature while looking at oneself in the mirror had been challenging to say the least. A true test of her talent. The miniature was no more improper or less tasteful, Theo told herself, than, say, a painting by Rembrandt or Titian. Blythe was sure to be intrigued. Impressed. Totally captivated.

Her roiling stomach disagreed. Even her heart was no longer whispering what a grand idea it was to give the miniature to Blythe.

Glancing around the confines of Blythe's drawing room, Theo lifted her glass of punch to her lips but declined to take a sip. Overly sweet and cloying. Much like her hostess tonight, Lady Blythe. A woman for who the term 'overbearing' had been coined.

I did not think this through properly.

Swallowing down the dread which seemed determined to force itself up her throat, Theo slid closer to the wall, careful not to knock her head against a gilt-framed painting of ripened pears in a wooden bowl.

Trite. Boring. Exactly the sort of thing Lady Blythe appreciated.

Lady Meredith wandered past Theo, the skirts of her lavender striped silk fluttering about her ankles in a fetching manner so that a gentleman might catch a glimpse of her embroidered stockings. She paused with a smug look, waving at Theo with gloved fingers before gliding across the drawing room to flirt with the Earl of Blythe.

Blythe, oblivious to the gift Theo had painted him as well as her panic, stood amid a small group of guests, a half-filled wine glass dangling from one hand. Golden and beautiful in a way few men were, Blythe laughed at something Miss Cummings relayed to him before leaning to whisper his thoughts in her ear.

Miss Cummings twittered before lightly swatting Blythe with her fan.

The familiarity of the scene caused the glass of horrid punch to wobble in Theo's fingers. How often had Theo played the part of Miss Cummings while Blythe whispered something outrageous in *her* ear?

Upon her arrival tonight, while the sheer intoxication of bestowing her art upon Blythe still filled her mind, Theo had decided the best way for him to receive her gift would be in private, and with Lady Blythe in the room, it wasn't as if Theo could take him aside for a word. Instead, she had left it for Blythe in a spot where only he would venture. His study. She'd snuck away from Cousin Winnie and Rosalind, made her way to Blythe's study, and carefully placed the tiny box right on the chair before his desk.

It seemed like such a wonderful idea at the time.

The cup of punch in her hand trembled even further, spilling just a bit on her gloves as Theo watched Lady Meredith nearly push Miss Cummings aside to flirt with Blythe. And he, damn his glorious self, flirted right back.

Blythe was meant to see the box either later tonight or tomorrow. He would immediately be awed, compelling him to rush directly to Theo's side and offer for her in the most romantic way possible.

It all sounds rather foolish now.

Upon her entrance into the drawing room after leaving the miniature, Blythe had caught Theo's eye and come forward to take her hand. Several flirtatious comments had fallen from his lips. His gaze had lingered over her bosom.

The sheer excitement of her surprise had made a giggle burst from her lips. Nothing but raw anticipation had led Theo to mention she'd created something especially for him in honor of his birthday. His reply had snuffed out every bit of her enthusiasm.

'As a gentleman, I fear I am unable to accept such a token, as you surely must know.'

The air around them had become distinctly uncomfortable once he'd uttered his very polite refusal. Blythe, rather awkwardly, had looked away.

Theo had stared at the spectacular line of his jaw, her smile freezing on her lips. His response had not been that of a gentleman who returned the affection of the young lady before him. Or who even wished to encourage it. Instead, Blythe had firmly, properly, dismissed her. And as if to ensure his point had been made, he excused himself rather quickly and sauntered off to flirt with two young ladies who had just arrived.

Not once had he looked back.

Now, as she stood observing Blythe from her spot by the wall, Theo concluded, as Lady Meredith cooed over him, that she had *drastically* overinflated his affections.

Her stomach, already roiling with distress, didn't just pitch, it heaved. She might well retch into the punchbowl at any moment. The feeling was akin to being unable to discern an object across the room until she placed her spectacles on her nose and then marveled at how clear her vision had suddenly become.

Oh, dear God. I must retrieve the miniature.

"Theo, whatever is the matter with you?" Cousin Rosalind came up alongside her, gently nudging her with an elbow. "You look as if you've eaten something spoiled. Or perhaps Lord Blythe said something you didn't care for? Though I can't imagine such a thing."

"You can't?" Theo murmured back, remembering Blythe's rejection. She couldn't begin to describe how unpleasant that had been.

"You hang on his every word. I expect if he told you to leap off the roof of his home, you'd do so to please him." She leaned closer. "Your adoration and pursuit of him has not gone unnoticed, particularly by Lady Blythe."

How unwelcome. "I don't think Blythe's mother cares for me."

"Not in the least," Rosalind assured her with a smile. "But if it helps, she doesn't care for most of the young ladies in pursuit of her son. You are merely one of dozens."

"I imagine I am." Another wave of dread rose inside Theo at Rosalind's words. Her cousin had no idea how correct she was, as Theo had belatedly realized.

She tore her gaze from Blythe to glance at Rosalind, swathed in a diaphanous peach confection which did an excellent job of hiding her generous figure. "Did Romy design that for you?" Theo whispered lest they be overheard. The gossip that Romy, Duchess of Granby, played at being a modiste had finally faded. Mostly. There was no need to stir it up again.

"She knows exactly how to hide my deficits, something I appreciate, though no one else has noticed."

"You look lovely, Ros. Are you speaking of anyone in particular?"

"He hasn't looked once in my direction." Rosalind sniffed.

"I thought you didn't favor Lord Torrington's suit?" The older widower, some twenty years Rosalind's senior, had, earlier in the year, expressed interest in courting Rosalind. Theo's cousin had stubbornly rebuffed his efforts purely on the basis that her mother approved of him.

Rosalind's cheeks pinked. "I'm not going to marry him just to please Mother."

"Of course not." Theo thought Torrington smart to pretend disinterest in Rosalind. Because every time he did, she became that much more interested in *him*. "And I wouldn't jump off the roof to please Blythe. I'm not an idiot."

Rosalind gave Theo an incredulous look. "And yet, you won't wear your spectacles because you overheard Blythe decry their attractiveness." A frown crossed her lips as Torrington walked into the room, the voluptuous Lady Carrington clinging to his arm. "Instead, you walk around with bruises, destroying vases and tripping over servants. Ruining the coats of gentlemen with ratafia."

"I don't consider the Marquess of Haven to be a gentleman. And no one finds the spectacles I'm forced to wear attractive. It isn't just Blythe." That much was true. Theo had burst into tears the day she'd first looked in the mirror, staring back at herself through those tiny panes of glass.

"I see Blythe's appeal, Theo. Honestly, I do. He's rather spectacular, but —"

"But what?"

Rosalind pursed her lips, her brow wrinkling. "You've been very impulsive since meeting Blythe. I know you have a rather romantic nature."

Theo scowled back at her.

"And I know you imagine him to be—well, I only don't wish you to be hurt. Or do something reckless to garner his attention. A regretful something. Promise me you won't."

Far too late for such a vow with a half-naked miniature of herself sitting in Blythe's study. "You worry needlessly," she replied to Rosalind.

Lady Meredith's dark head turned intimately toward Blythe, her hand on his arm while Lady Blythe, clothed in a bright shade of yellow, watched, lips pursed, like a giant, disapproving canary.

"Will you excuse me, Rosalind?" Theo needed to get to the study. While Blythe and his mother were occupied with Lady Meredith. The last thing she wanted was to be caught wandering around Blythe's home by his mother.

"Why must you desert me? Now?" Rosalind gave a long-suffering sigh and nodded in the direction of Cousin Winnie, who was making her way across the drawing room toward her daughter and Theo. "She's sure to be angry I haven't spoken to Torrington."

Theo had no desire to have a conversation with Cousin Winnie, not when it was imperative that she collect the miniature from Blythe's study *before* her impulsive idiocy was discovered.

Theodosia's Magnificent Mistake.

Ignoring Rosalind's puff of frustration at her departure, Theo took a tentative step into the swarm of guests assembled for Blythe's birthday. In order to reach his study, Theo needed to be on the other side of the drawing room. With so many guests in such a small area, it would take every bit of concentration not to run into someone, spill a drink, or trip over a gentleman's foot.

But she had little choice but to press on. The sense of urgency to reach Blythe's study was rapidly turning into a screaming panic. Her breath came in spurts as she started across the floor, bobbing politely to those she knew. But Theo didn't stop. Couldn't risk being waylaid.

What if Blythe decided to retreat to his study?

Taking a deep breath, Theo reminded herself that there was no reason for him to do so. His house was filled with guests. Lady Blythe was busy shooting scornful looks at any young lady who got too close to her son. Both were well occupied. And outside of the people crowding the drawing room and the smaller, adjoining parlor, Theo was in no danger of tripping over a table or breaking something valuable as she made her way to the other side of the room. The rugs had been rolled up for dancing and the furniture pushed back against the walls because Blythe's home didn't possess a ballroom.

When Theo finally reached the entrance to the hall, she congratulated herself on not having stumbled or stepped on anyone's toe. She had in no way drawn attention to herself. She would be able to make her way to Blythe's study hopefully unseen. The miniature would be retrieved. All would be well.

She lifted her chin, ready to marshal forward.

Theo had been raised to be confident. Steadfast. Brave in the face of adversity. The Dowager Duchess of Averell insisted that not one of her girls be weak-kneed nitwits whose only goal in life was to marry well. While both of Theo's sisters and Olivia were self-assured, possessing little timidity, those same traits caused others in London to view the Barringtons as far too bold. Too daring. Entirely too adventuresome.

But none of them, not Romy, Olivia, or even Phaedra, would have ever presented such an inappropriate gift to a gentleman. Not only out of common sense and good breeding, but because none of them would have needed to resort to such a drastic measure to compel a gentleman to confess his feelings. Romy, Olivia, and Phaedra were all so . . . *spectacular.*

And Theo was bespectacled. Solitary. Hopelessly romantic.

When compared to the rest of the Beautiful Barringtons, Theo was horribly ordinary, at least in her own estimation. Yes, she painted, as did dozens of other young ladies, so nothing special there. Only the fact that she did miniatures made her the slightest bit interesting. When the physician specializing in eyesight, an oculist, had determined the need for spectacles, Theo had expected him to also say in the same breath that the middle Barrington daughter was destined for spinsterhood.

Theo's sisters sparkled like the most brilliant of diamonds. Olivia flared softly, like the flames of a banked fire. But Theo's own light was so *dim,* none could even see it. Until Blythe had noticed her. The bolder she'd become in his presence, the more attention he had showered on her.

Theo had felt as if she *finally* . . . sparkled.

All of which had led to poor decision-making.

Theo turned in the direction of Blythe's study. Being reckless wasn't nearly as fun as Phaedra made it out to be. Theo only took one more step before she was stopped in her tracks by a tall, slightly mannish form in skirts.

"Good evening, Lady Theodosia. How lovely you look. I thought you might be here this evening. I've only just arrived."

Drat.

"Lady Mildred." Theo fixed a polite smile on her face. "How wonderful to see you as well. Might I say your gown is stunning," she lied, taking in the blue silk cut low across Mildred's broad shoulders. Feathers decorated the upper sleeves of the gown, a tragic fashion mistake Romy would never have allowed. Mildred resembled a giant bluebird.

She tried to sidestep the other woman with a small nod, but Mildred took her elbow.

"Is Mr. Estwood in attendance?" Lady Mildred's brows lifted hopefully.

Theo hadn't seen the businessman and financier, an associate of Granby and Blythe's, among the guests, but that didn't mean he wasn't here. Though based on what she knew of Lady Blythe, she couldn't imagine Estwood had made the guest list. "I'm not certain."

"Lord Haven, perchance?" Mildred asked.

The name sent a ripple down her spine. "Lord Haven?"

"I've heard of his interest in Miss Emerson." Mildred's lips twisted. "But I am far wealthier."

And much more desperate for marriage, Theo knew. Poor Mildred. "Please excuse me, Mildred."

Mildred didn't release her arm. "I suppose I shall look for Mr. Clinton as well. Increase my odds, so to speak."

"All right," Theo stammered, looking up at the calculating gleam in Mildred's eye, having no idea who Mr. Clinton was. "I wish you happy hunting. I'm sure Haven is floating about somewhere, as well as Estwood."

Theo hadn't yet seen Haven in the press of guests packing Blythe's home. The very thought of encountering the annoying marquess, especially under her current panicked circumstances, was more than she could bear. His appearance in the park beside her last week had been unsettling enough.

"Now that I think on it, Mildred, I'm certain Haven is about. Miss Emerson is here, but she doesn't seem happy. Perhaps they've had a falling out. Now might be the perfect time to ingratiate yourself with Haven."

Mildred nodded slowly before giving a pat to her hair. "Perhaps you're correct. I should hurry." She sped away from Theo without so much as a goodbye.

Theo resumed her journey, finally reaching the door of Blythe's study.

Placing her hand on the knob, she twisted the cool metal, relieved to find the room still unlocked. Stumbling in, Theo shut the door quietly behind her. A fire flickered in the grate. The lamp on a side table was still lit. Blythe's ledgers were stacked neatly on the top of his desk. Everything was exactly the way it had been an hour or so earlier when she'd been so bloody sure of Blythe's affection and—

She stood for a minute, pressing a hand to her throat, and instructed herself again to breathe. Her reckless action could be remedied. Marching directly over to Blythe's desk, Theo took hold of the chair, pulling the piece of furniture back with one fluid motion. Her eyes fell to the leather cushion.

Empty.

Oh, no. No. No. No.

Theo's lashes fluttered down across her cheeks. She was merely overwrought. Her eyesight was poor. Possibly in her current panic, she was seeing things or, in this case, seeing nothing at all. Cautiously, Theo opened her eyes again.

The chair was still empty.

Bollocks.

She was going to be sick all over Blythe's perfectly neat stack of papers and leather-bound ledgers. The room tilted sharply to the right, and Theo grabbed the edge of the desk, fingers biting into the heavy wood as she tried to steady herself. There was an ugly paperweight in the shape of a bird sitting atop one of the ledgers. She thought it might be the same sort of bird displayed on the buttons of Blythe's coats. Was it a goose with abnormally long legs?

Oh, good Lord. Who cares?

Slumping in horror and defeat, Theo cursed out loud at her poor luck, every vile word she'd ever heard eavesdropping on her brothers spewing from her lips. She pounded on the desk in frustration, rattling the ugly bird.

This was very bad. *Anyone* could have the miniature. And while Theo hadn't *signed* the miniature, nor enclosed a note, she would be recognized all the same.

I'll be completely ruined. Perhaps banished. Dear God, when Tony finds out, he may even send me to a convent. In France.

She tried to picture herself as a penitent novice, head bent in contemplation and prayer. But at least she'd have plenty of time to paint. If convents allowed such things.

Breathe, Theo.

Looking down at her neckline, she tugged on the piping and lace edging her bodice, hoping to hide the spray of freckles. Impossible, as the small dots marring her skin stretched nearly to her collarbone. More noticeable than any birthmark. Thankfully, she'd brought a wrap with her tonight. A filmy thing that had been tossed about her shoulders by Mama only because so much of Theo's chest was exposed. She could claim to be cold. Chilled. Place the wrap around her to cover the freckles. Yes. She stood, smoothing her skirts, and nodded to the room before casting a glance to the empty chair once more.

Perhaps the small box fell to the floor when she pushed the chair in?

Hope burst in her chest. Falling to her knees, Theo sank her fingers into the thick rug beneath the desk, feeling about with her hands for the familiar shape of the box. She should have moved the lamp so she could see better. Gaze fixed on her hands, she turned in a semi-circle, reaching under the chair to check between the legs before stopping as her fingers slid over something hard and smooth.

Theo swallowed. Her hand moved a few inches to the left, not daring to look up.

Boots. Two of them. Scuffed. Worn. No matter the amount of polish they'd been given.

Dozens of excuses for being found in Blythe's study, on her knees, beneath his desk, during his birthday celebration ran through her mind. None of them sounded the least plausible.

The boots shifted as the gentleman they belonged to leaned down.

A spicy scent filled her nostrils.

Damn it.

"Looking for something, Lady Theodosia?"

3

Ambrose Collingwood, Marquess of Haven, looked down into the defiant, shocked face of Theodosia Barrington and wished he'd just compromised her in the park the other day as he'd meant to. Because clearly, if any woman was begging to be ruined, it was the gorgeous half-blind ninny crawling around the rug at his feet.

His fingers rubbed against the small box sitting in his pocket, remembering the contents. *Christ*, she might have already achieved ruination on her own.

Theodosia bumped her head on the top of the desk, and Ambrose winced in sympathy. If she didn't start wearing her bloody spectacles, she might physically hurt herself.

The moment Theodosia had arrived tonight in the company of Lady Richardson and her daughter, Ambrose's eyes had been drawn to her stunning form. Watching as she took careful steps because she couldn't see anything, his attention had stayed solely on her and not Miss Emerson, who was attempting a rather amusing story about a foxhunt. Miss Emerson was lovely. Wealthy. And very much the sort of woman who Ambrose should be pursuing for a wife.

However, she wasn't Theodosia Barrington.

Ambrose found himself unable to look away and not only because he lived in a constant state of terror she was going to go tumbling into a wall or down a flight of stairs. A wealth of emotions—lust, vengeance, jealousy, guilt—all flooded through him at the sight of her. The combination was a potent invitation for Ambrose to behave badly around Theodosia, which he always did. Relentlessly teasing her. Kissing her at Granby's. Stalking her through the park intent on ruining her and then at the last moment, finding himself unable to do so.

In truth, he'd wavered because he was unsure if his desire for her was *because* Theodosia was Leo Murphy's sister, or in spite of it.

"Lord Haven." Theodosia looked up, blinking at him, perhaps hoping he was a hallucination. Or possibly she couldn't see him clearly. He'd no idea how terrible her eyesight really was. Despite being so impaired, Theodosia had the loveliest eyes. Shards of blue with a darker circle of indigo around the pupils.

Exactly like her prick of a brother, Leo Murphy.

"So, you *can* see me." He reached down to help her up, and she batted his hand away in annoyance.

Ambrose had the urge to pull her up, toss her over his knee, and spank Theodosia until she promised not to go around painting highly erotic, *naked* miniatures of herself. A coil of arousal slipped around his legs as he thought of her plump bottom, bare, and her body spread across his legs. His hands on all that silken flesh.

"What are you doing here?" She floundered about a bit, bumping her elbow before standing as gracefully as possible. The luscious globes of her breasts rippled deliciously as she pulled herself upright.

Christ. He pushed the pads of his fingers against his thighs trying to still the sharp press of desire. The very second Theodosia had appeared on the terrace at Granby's house party, tripping over a servant and bumping into a table, Ambrose had wanted her well before finding out she was a Barrington.

When he'd finally spied Theodosia sitting oh-so-primly in the park, paintbrush in hand—a scene he'd found blatantly sexual for some reason—Ambrose had forced his way into her presence. He'd lied and told her he was in the park to walk with Miss Emerson because it was better than mentioning he'd planned on compromising her.

But he hadn't.

Compromising Theodosia on purpose, no matter Ambrose's need for justice, had never sat well with him, though it would solve all his problems. Because had circumstances been different, and were she not so enamored of Blythe, Ambrose thought he might have courted her. Properly.

"I'm waiting for Blythe," he informed her. "A private matter."

Theodosia froze in front of him.

Ambrose watched the muted terror make its way across her lovely features. She wildly assumed his meeting with Blythe had something to do with the miniature which was searing a hole through his pocket. Ambrose did nothing to reassure her. What in the world would cause Theodosia to paint a scandalous miniature of herself *and* gift it to Blythe? Why not just put an item in one of London's gossip columns announcing they were lovers?

A rush of anger filled him at the thought of Theodosia and Blythe. At the very least, he assumed his friend had taken liberties with her. Honestly, was her brother, the fucking duke, just not paying attention to what his sister was up to? Or perhaps Averell, like his bastard brother, was too focused on stripping drunk, grief-stricken noblemen of their wealth.

"Did he say what he wished to discuss?" Her lower lip, luscious and begging to be pulled between his teeth, trembled. She glanced at the chair, then back at Ambrose. It took her longer than he expected to draw the likely conclusion. "You opened it."

"I did."

No more than a quarter-hour ago, Ambrose had come into the study and headed straight for the sideboard, sitting behind the desk. The annoying, mindless conversations he'd been subjected to in the other room, as well as Lady Blythe's censure, demanded a moment of quiet before Blythe joined him. He'd seen the box sitting in the middle of the chair as he started to pour a scotch. Admittedly, it was bad form to open another's gift. It was Blythe's birthday, and the box was obviously meant for him, but Ambrose's curiosity had won out.

Once he'd opened the box, staring at the contents while the clock ticked in the background, Ambrose had poured himself a *much* healthier portion of scotch. The freckles were a dead giveaway. And it was a bloody miniature. Something Theodosia Barrington was known to paint almost exclusively.

"You had no right to do such a thing." The tops of her cheeks turned an alarming shade of red.

Nor did she have a right to present such a thing to Blythe. At least in Ambrose's opinion, which was admittedly colored with more than a hint of possessiveness. Jealousy was such a complex emotion. Fraught with peril for all involved. Especially Theodosia.

"It's exceptionally detailed." His gaze traveled over her bosom. "Every curve and *peak* clearly defined. You're very talented."

At the word *peak*, Theodosia's luscious mouth popped open.

He couldn't seem to tear his gaze from her lips. Rose-colored. Plump. Like tiny pillows. Ambrose still dreamt of her mouth, the way she'd surrendered to him so beautifully when he'd kissed her at the house party.

"You are easily recognized, my lady." His forefinger reached out, gently tracing the spray of freckles above one breast. The pattern reminded Ambrose of the Corona Borealis, a constellation his father had once pointed out to him long ago, before Edmund Collingwood had become a miserable sot.

A slight arch of her back in his direction betrayed her before she stepped away.

Theodosia was a bloody magnificent creature, absurd and yet so beautiful. Clumsy yet graceful. Bold yet shy. Ambrose wanted so badly to touch his tongue to the line of freckles, taste the warm smell of lemon emanating from her skin, bite—

Theo's hand shot out, disrupting his thoughts, her fingers wiggling beneath his nose. She was gulping deep breaths of air, agitated and annoyed at him, the tops of her breasts pushing against her bodice.

The movement fascinated Ambrose, especially because he now knew what lay beneath the silk.

"Haven," she sputtered. "Give it back to me. Bad enough you took it upon yourself to open it. Gazed upon it. But it isn't meant for *you*. It wasn't addressed to *you*." The color of her cheeks deepened further.

"In all fairness," Ambrose replied as calmly as was possible with the object of his erotic imaginings standing before him, "it wasn't addressed to Blythe either." A strand of dark, silky hair fell from her coiffure and bounced against the rounded curve of one breast, teasing the spot where he knew her nipple must be.

Pink. Like the underside of a seashell.

His mouth went dry thinking of that partially hidden peak so artfully depicted on the miniature. Ambrose struggled to remember what he'd been saying. Finally, he said, "How was I to know it wasn't meant for me? Or for Blythe's butler, for that matter?"

A small cry of outrage left her. Theodosia slapped a gloved hand atop the desk, knocking aside a paperweight Blythe kept atop his ledgers. A hideous bird of some sort. It fell to the floor and landed on Ambrose's foot.

"Ouch. What is that thing anyway? A stork?"

"I came here because I changed my mind." She stuck her fingers out again. "I'm not giving it to Blythe. So you may return it to me."

"Are you and Blythe lovers?" The words erupted from him before he could stop them. Envy made his voice sharp. "Or are you just stupidly impulsive?"

Theodosia peered at him from beneath her lashes, possibly attempting to appear worldly. Or she was simply squinting because she couldn't see. It was difficult to tell. "That, Lord Haven," her lips curled, "is none of your business." Her fingertips trailed suggestively along the edge of Blythe's desk as she shot Ambrose a coquettish look. "I know why you kissed me at the house party." She tucked the stray piece of hair back up into her coiffure. "You're as transparent as you are prone to fistfights."

Theodosia couldn't possibly know. She'd been so bloody tempting, stumbling about the dark hallway, in danger of knocking herself unconscious with a giant candlestick. And he did envy Blythe her affection. But there had also been a whisper in the back of his mind that Theodosia, desirable thing that she was, could be his solution. After all, it was far easier to compromise a woman you actually wanted than one you did not.

Unless you found you liked her. Quite a bit. Then things

became much more complicated.

"I doubt you are so intuitive," he replied. Theodosia smelled of lemons and an underlying slightly oily scent he didn't immediately recognize. Paint, maybe. The swell of her hips was barely discernable beneath the silk, the deep valley between her breasts beckoning him forward.

His trousers became entirely too uncomfortable.

"Blythe," she stated with assurance.

"Blythe?"

"Your jealousy of him speaks volumes. You covet everything that belongs to him. This house, for example." She lifted her hands. "The gift I painted expressly for him." She paused for effect. "*Me*." A smile crossed her lips at his stony silence as she allowed the word to sink in. "It's obvious. As blind as I am, even I can see it."

Ambrose *was* incredibly envious of Blythe and did a poor job of hiding it. There was also a competitive edge to their friendship, one that led to arguments and stretches where they didn't speak to each other. Blythe liked to bait him. Ambrose had a temper. Even so, he and Blythe were close friends, just not always in agreement.

"Does it bother you, Haven," Theodosia continued, eyes gleaming with satisfaction, "that the only reason I returned your kiss was because I thought you were Blythe?"

"You didn't think I was Blythe. At least have the courage to admit it."

Theodosia's mouth tightened. She took two steps in his direction before suddenly flinging herself at Ambrose as if she meant to tackle him to the floor.

Jesus. I underestimated her.

Her fingers grabbed at him, sliding beneath his coat, searching along his ribs and the inside lining. Another strand of hair fell down her shoulders as she pinched and prodded him with ruthless efficiency.

The entire lower half of Ambrose's body coiled, thrilled beyond belief at her touch. "Theodosia, stop this instant. While I find this delightful foreplay—"

A hiss of outrage was her response.

"— and your wrestling skills seem to be finely honed—" Ambrose's eyes widened as she pinched him again, this time hard enough to leave a bruise.

Good God, had the late Duke of Averell taught his daughters to brawl?

He grabbed her hands, attempting to pry them away from his chest. When that didn't work, Ambrose wrapped his arms around her, pulling Theodosia to him. Hugging her tightly, he heard her gasp for breath. "Stop," he insisted.

Theodosia's wrists, trapped against his chest, relaxed a fraction.

Small bits of lightning crawled up Ambrose's skin, sparking wherever Theodosia's curves molded to the length of his body. His cock, always thrilled to be in the vicinity of Theodosia, tightened to stone in his trousers. There was no way she could fail to notice, even through layers of skirts and petticoats separating them.

Christ, she's beautiful.

Her eyes, a vivid blue with their distinct ring of indigo, looked up at him. She wiggled against him, confusion and something much more tempting lighting in her eyes before her gaze dropped to his mouth. A ragged sound escaped her.

"Theodosia." The pull to her was like nothing he'd ever felt before. Despite having planned to compromise her for months, he wasn't thinking about vengeance or the fact that they were alone together as his head tilted, intent on covering her lips with his.

Unfortunately, Lady Blythe's scream pierced the air, sounding as if she were being attacked by wild dogs.

It completely ruined the moment.

4

It is one thing for a young lady to be compromised.

Quite another to be compromised by the entirely *wrong* gentleman while you are attempting to retrieve a half-naked miniature of your breasts which you painted for the *right* gentleman, who ironically is the witness, along with his overbearing mother, of your ruination.

Not even Phaedra, who had a flair for the dramatic, could have concocted such a scenario. It sounded like the plot of those lurid romances Theo was so fond of reading.

Lady Blythe's shrill cry of horror echoed through the quiet of the study, slid outside to the hall, and possibly made its way to the drawing room before her son pushed her inside the room, shutting the door behind him.

Theo's eyes had been closed, lips parted in anticipation of Haven's mouth on hers. She twisted her head to see Blythe and his mother, both equally horrified, as their eyes lingered on the tangle of Theo in Haven's arms.

"Well, this is unfortunate," Haven said beneath his breath as the moss green of his eyes shuttered, allowing none of his thoughts to bleed through. His hands slid along her waist before reluctantly releasing her.

Theo wanted to smack him. Didn't he understand what had just occurred? Her heart raced. Because she certainly did.

I'm ruined.

"Lady Blythe." Haven bowed, poorly cut hair falling in disarray. "Blythe."

Theo gazed with longing at the window, the fleeting notion that perhaps the very uncomfortable discussion in her future could be avoided if she simply tossed herself out the window into the street. Perhaps be run over by a carriage. Or two.

"Ruined," Lady Blythe announced to them all, her words cracking like a whip in the air. She sniffed at Theo in disdain.

"Mother, let us not jump to hasty conclusions."

Theo wobbled backward until the hollow of her knees bumped into the edge of the sofa. She sat with a very undignified plop, drawing another disapproving glare from Lady Blythe.

Her mind screamed out in shock. Horror. Humiliation.

There was no denying it. Even with a much more progressive upbringing than most young ladies, Theo knew well the consequences of being caught unchaperoned and alone with a gentleman. Not *just* alone, horror gripped her, but in an intimate embrace. No matter that such a position had begun merely as a struggle to retrieve a miniature. One whose existence she dare not speak of.

Haven had meant to kiss her. And worse, she'd wanted him to.

Her entire body still throbbed delicately from being so near him, heart fluttering at the press of that muscled torso against her breasts. In her search for the miniature, the hard planes of his chest had stretched beneath her fingers, making her exploration much more enjoyable than it should have been.

Oh, God.

She clasped her hands, wondering how on earth she was going to explain *this* situation to her brother. Because Lady Blythe, bastion of propriety, would *insist* the Duke of Averell be called to retrieve his errant, compromised sister. There was absolutely no chance Lady Blythe would put aside her stringent morals, not after seeing Theo in Haven's arms. Haven would be asked to do the honorable thing, and he would, regardless of his rumored pursuit of Miss Violet Emerson. Not because Haven was honorable, per se, or even because he liked her. But because Theo's dowry was enormous, easily dwarfing that of Miss Emerson's.

Theo inhaled sharply, the spicy scent of Haven still lingering on her skin and clinging to the silk of her gown. He was impoverished. Why didn't he smell of mothballs and worn clothing?

That somehow made things worse.

And she'd known full well what the hardness was scorching through the layers of her skirts. She'd seen a man's . . . *length* at Elysium once. Not purposefully, of course. She and Romy had been curious about the private rooms. Mostly they'd seen only piles of silken sheets, feathers, lots of scarves, most of which were tied to the bedposts—

A wash of heat hit her cheeks.

Admittedly, Theo was far more curious than most young ladies her age. Mama didn't believe any of her daughters should be raised in ignorance, oblivious to what took place in the marital bed. She knew the basics. Her mother had been descriptive. And Theo's brothers had often failed to close the door firmly when discussing certain matters. And then what she'd witnessed at Elysium . . .

"Ruined," Lady Blythe repeated in her precise, clipped

tones, sounding somewhat satisfied as her disdain landed on Theo again. "Send for the duke. Immediately."

Blythe watched Theo, a grim look on his angelic features, as if he were about to sentence her to prison and regretted it. She wanted to go to him. Explain, privately of course, that while things didn't look *good*, nothing untoward had happened. And while her recent realization of Blythe's feelings toward her hadn't been welcome, Theo couldn't completely diffuse her hope. She at least didn't want him to stare at her with such shock and disappointment.

Blythe turned and opened the door a crack, whispering to someone just outside before stepping back in.

He's sent for my brother.

"I came upon Lady Theodosia in the study," Haven finally said to Lady Blythe. "I fear we are all well acquainted with her clumsiness. She tripped and I caught her. That is what you saw, my lady. Nothing more."

Theo thought his defense of her, if you could name it as such, to be entirely too half-hearted.

"I'm not a fool, my lord." Lady Blythe puffed up like an angry hen. "I suspect Lady Theodosia meant to find *you* here," she said to Blythe. "And not Haven." A mixture of pity and scorn narrowed her eyes as she took in Theo. "It seems your plan failed. You 'tripped' into the wrong gentleman."

All hopes that the matter could be handled with discretion, perhaps allowing Theo to winnow her way out of the situation, immediately faded. Not that there had been much of a chance. Lady Blythe's dislike of her had never been more apparent. Nothing would sway her from her assumption that Theo had meant to entrap Blythe, but still she had to try. "It was an accident. I am often clumsy. Lord Haven kept me from falling and injuring myself."

Lady Blythe snorted in derision. "Did you trip all the way from the drawing room into my son's study?"

Theo looked back down at her lap. She could not give the reason she was here.

"Haven must do the honorable thing despite his consideration of Miss Emerson." Lady Blythe took in Theo on the sofa. "Another Barrington scandal, much like your sister."

"My sister is not a scandal. She is the *Duchess* of Granby."

"Yes, I believe all of London is aware of how your sister received the title, by enticing the Duke of Granby away from poor Beatrice Howard," Lady Blythe replied, her tone ripping at Theo's skin. "And now we must add Miss Emerson to the list of those injured by a brash and reckless Barrington."

"Mother, it would be best to keep this entire incident private. Our guests need not know. Lady Theodosia's reputation need not be harmed. If Haven says their meeting was accidental, I believe him."

But not Theo. Blythe didn't believe *her*. That was rather painful. Lady Blythe had judged Theo far before this evening. Too brazen. A lightskirt. A young lady with no decorum whatsoever.

"As long as Haven is willing to do the right thing," Lady Blythe said in a self-important tone. "I agree it is best to spare Lady Theodosia a dreadful reputation."

Theo sucked in a breath at the words. Lady Blythe wouldn't make her a pariah if Haven married her. How lovely of Blythe's mother. Her nails dug into her palms.

The room grew silent as they waited for Haven to speak. His handsome face had taken on a grim cast as if the thought of marrying Theo was abhorrent.

I don't want to marry him either.

Regardless of their almost kiss, as well as their previous actual one, Theo doubted Haven had any true liking for her. Everyone knew a gentleman's baser instincts could be aroused by the simple sight of a lovely bosom. Or a well-formed ankle. No affection was required to kiss or bed a woman.

When your brother operated a pleasure palace, you learned all sorts of things.

"I would prefer to discuss this situation with the Duke of Averell." Haven gave Lady Blythe a withering look. "Who will not wish his sister's reputation damaged in *any* way. If it will satisfy you to know, Lady Blythe, though it is not your affair, I do intend to do the right thing."

"I have a moral obligation to uphold society's rules," she snipped back, smoothing her bright yellow skirts. "It speaks well of you, Lord Haven, to make such a sacrifice to spare Lady Theodosia any further disgrace. *All* the Barrington girls are bound for disaster."

Theo bit her lip, stifling the scathing retort burning her tongue.

"I would make certain, Lady Blythe," Haven replied, his voice akin to gravel beneath carriage wheels, "that you do not relay your feelings to the duke when he arrives."

"I will ensure it," Blythe intoned, looking down on his mother. "Because she will be occupied entertaining our guests. And she will say *nothing*. When your nuptials are announced to Lady Theodosia, there will be no mention of how your match came about, will there, Mother?" He opened the door once again. "Please send Lady Richardson to the study," he said to a waiting footman.

Lady Blythe's chin jiggled, angered at her son's dismissal. "Lady Richardson? Yes, she performed her duties as well as she did at Granby's house party."

Blythe's mother was a horrid woman. How had she ever produced such a glorious being as Blythe?

"Haven and I will speak to the duke without your interference. I'll tolerate not another word, Mother. Should you speak ill of Lady Theodosia, I will send you and my sisters back to the country. Permanently."

Lady Blythe gasped. "You wouldn't dare."

Theo loved Blythe even more for his defense of her, if that were possible. Even if he didn't return her feelings. Nor wanted her gift.

"I would." He pushed her toward the door but held onto her arm, her plump form sputtering in indignation. "You will stay until Lady Richardson can join us."

"The duke will be at Elysium," Theo said, the words scratching against her throat. Tony was still managing the club in Leo's absence. He spent most evenings there. Receiving notice of his sister's disgrace was bound to put him in a terrible mood.

Blythe merely nodded. "I've sent one of the footmen."

Theo wrapped her arms around herself, refusing to so much as shed a tear at tonight's turn of events. She'd never imagined being forced to marry to save her reputation. Never even considered the possibility. Theo's parents had been married for love. As had Tony. And though Theo thought Granby as exciting as the stone wall surrounding her brother's London mansion, Romy and her new husband were madly in love.

Now she would be forced to marry Haven.

If he had just given her back the bloody miniature, none of this would have happened.

5

Theodosia, lovely and heartbroken, perched on the end of the sofa in Blythe's study, chin tilted down as she surely contemplated her future. Not so much as a sob left her throat. No tears cascaded down her cheeks. She didn't faint dead away like some fragile doll. Under the circumstances, it would be understandable for Theodosia to do all those things. Fall into a weeping pile of silk or faint dramatically while Blythe called for smelling salts. The only discernible sign of her distress was the twisting of her fingers in her lap.

How Ambrose admired Theo for refusing to give Lady Blythe exactly what that old bat hungered for.

Violet Emerson, wealthy and beautiful, *would* have made a fine marchioness, but she was never meant to be *Ambrose's* marchioness, despite what he'd allowed everyone to believe. Theodosia, glaring at him in obvious dislike from beneath her lashes, would be Lady Haven. A turn of circumstances which Ambrose was only too pleased about.

'Find yourself an heiress. That's what I advise.'

That had been Leo Murphy's advice to Ambrose just

before having him physically removed from Murphy's office at Elysium.

Heartless prick.

So, Ambrose had taken Murphy's advice and found himself an heiress. One he already wanted to bed.

'It isn't any of my affair, Collingwood, how your father chooses to bankrupt himself.'

Ambrose had been so bloody angry after that first discussion with Murphy, he'd immediately gone to confront his father. The resulting argument had led to Ambrose residing on the Continent for some time. When he'd returned, he found his father dead and nothing left of the Collingwood wealth.

Ambrose tamped down the anger he carried, always simmering just beneath the surface of his skin, boiling up at the mere thought of Leo Murphy. Murphy had taken undue advantage of an obviously grief-stricken man even after Ambrose had pleaded with him not to. The next time he'd seen Murphy, it had been to demand proof his father had signed away everything, including Jacinda's dowry. Ambrose had cursed Murphy, vowing to take back everything the prick had taken from him.

And now he would.

Pushing aside the past, his glance fell on Theodosia, the urge to comfort her so strong, Ambrose took a step in her direction. But he stopped. Remorse was a wasted emotion, especially in this instance. He'd already felt guilt over her for months as he'd waffled about when best to put Theodosia in a compromising situation. How he would use her to take back his fortune.

He looked up as Lady Richardson, pale and stricken, appeared in the study, her daughter trailing behind her.

Lady Blythe quickly explained to Lady Richardson what had transpired, making sure to impress her absolute disapproval on Theodosia before leaving the study to return to her guests. She nodded to Ambrose.

Self-righteous harpy. He bowed.

Blythe's mother didn't truly care for Ambrose. He had been in far too many fistfights and rumored duels for him to receive her mark of esteem. But she cared even less for the idea that Lady Theodosia Barrington might ensnare her son. Her posturing tonight had been as much for the rules that governed social etiquette as it had been to make sure she need never worry herself over Theodosia again.

'There's his signature. And his seal. He signed your sister's dowry away for a game of dice.'

Even having seen his father's bold script, Ambrose refused to believe it. If nothing else, Edmund had loved his daughter. He wouldn't have intentionally made her penniless, especially given—

Ambrose rubbed at the pinch in his chest. He refused to feel any more guilt over Theodosia. He'd done what he had to do, or rather, he hadn't had to do a thing. Even he wasn't so desperate as to ruin Theodosia at his friend's birthday party. But fate had decided differently. As if he were meant to have her.

A nudge from Blythe brought Ambrose from his musings. Lady Richardson and her daughter hovered over Theodosia protectively, both shooting him twin looks of dislike.

Ambrose wasn't the villain here. Lady Richardson should toss her disdain elsewhere.

"You could probably use another scotch." Blythe nodded to the half-empty glass on the sideboard Ambrose had left once Theodosia had burst into the room.

He nodded as his friend went to pour them both a drink.

"Here." He handed Ambrose one glass of the amber liquid before glancing in Theodosia's direction. "She must have been in the study because of me," Blythe said in a quiet tone.

"I'd no idea she'd be so bold as to try to speak to me in private. She'd said something about a gift earlier, which I dissuaded her from giving me."

"I didn't see any gift when I came in, and she never explained why she was here," Ambrose lied. The existence of the miniature was knowledge that would stay between him and Theodosia. No one else, especially Blythe, need ever know. He could spare her that much, at least. His friend had had every opportunity to claim her tonight, despite his domineering mother, and he had not. "I mentioned to the lady that she should return to the party. On her way to the door, Theodosia tripped, and I caught her."

"You are a victim of timing, I'm afraid. I knew you meant to court Miss Emerson, which is the only reason I brought my mother to the study. She is a close friend of Lady Emerson's."

Ambrose took a sip of his scotch, the alcohol burning away some of the regret he'd felt at lying to Blythe. He wasn't by nature a devious individual, not caring for subterfuge or false platitudes. That his dealings of late had been so dishonest bothered him a great deal.

"At least it won't be a hardship to wed Theodosia," Blythe continued, gesturing discreetly with his glass in her direction.

"No, I suppose not." An understatement.

Blythe nodded. "I expected you were more enamored of Miss Emerson's dowry than the young lady herself. Theodosia's will be far richer. I suppose it was a happy coincidence for you to find her here." There was a question in his friend's eyes, one Ambrose wouldn't answer.

Blythe could assume whatever he wished. All of London would speculate, especially if Lady Blythe didn't keep her gossiping lips shut, and he doubted she would.

"Did you never think to offer for Theodosia yourself?"

Blythe looked aghast. "No. Never." He took a sip of his

own scotch. "Theodosia is a delightful creature. I like her very much. She has no idea how beautiful she is, which is a great departure from many young ladies and quite refreshing. I do worry she'll just tumble into the street one day out of sheer clumsiness." He chuckled softly. "But the Barrington sisters are all too bold for my tastes. And my mother would never have approved."

"Indeed not." Lady Blythe had been nearly giddy with relief that Theodosia hadn't managed to ensnare Blythe.

A knock sounded at the door moments before it swung open to reveal a gentleman who diminished Blythe's magnificence to that of tarnished silver. His brilliant blue eyes scanned the room, lingering over Blythe before settling on Ambrose, lip curling in disdain.

"His Grace, the Duke of Averell," the footman intoned.

Ambrose choked on his scotch. He'd forgotten how much the duke looked like Leo Murphy, especially up close. Averell was probably just as much of a prick. He assumed. Ambrose had never been properly introduced to him nor had they ever spoken. Now was not the time for him to pretend to be anything other than an honorable gentleman, a victim of the same social rules as Theodosia.

6

Theo sat in the carriage, impatiently waiting for her brother as the future, *her future*, was decided. Cousin Winnie, silver hair forming a wreath around her head, lips trembling in shock, led Theo from Blythe's home to the carriage with nary a word.

Theo declined Cousin Winnie's offer to see her home, choosing instead to wait in her brother's carriage. There was no point in arriving at the Averell mansion, anxious and worried, only to sit on the edge of the sofa in the drawing room and wait for Tony to come home. Best to meet her fate head-on.

Giving a tired nod, one that told of her utter failure as a chaperone, Cousin Winnie merely pressed a kiss to her cheek.

Rosalind had grabbed Theo's hand before joining her mother. "I thought you promised not to do anything impulsive."

Theo could do nothing more than shrug and bid her cousin goodnight. There was little she could say. The entire evening had been a testament to reckless, impulsive behavior.

She pressed herself into the luxurious interior of her brother's carriage, trying and failing to remain calm. The accusations, hurled at her by Lady Blythe, had been incredibly hurtful. Everyone, including Blythe, assumed Theo had been in his study tonight with the sole purpose of trapping him in marriage. She'd be a laughingstock if word got out.

Only Haven, of all people, knew the truth, and she prayed he kept it to himself.

Her fingers curled into her skirts. Had he only given her back the miniature instead of taunting her, Theo would not have been forced to . . . *attack* him. This entire unfortunate incident would not have occurred, and she might even now be returning home with nothing more than a bruised ego from Blythe's refusal of her gift.

A sensation stung her fingertips. The feel of Haven's muscled chest beneath her hands.

Drat.

His eyes, as he'd lowered his mouth to hers, had darkened to nearly black, the depths swirling with something hungry and wicked. A promise which twisted between her thighs, conjuring up all manner of erotic thoughts.

Even now, those thoughts still lingered, making her pulse quicken. Theo blinked, willing them away.

The sound of footsteps outside the carriage heralded the approach of her brother, the Duke of Averell.

Tony climbed in with a grunt, displeasure coating his handsome face as he caught sight of her.

"You should have allowed Winnie to see you home."

"I wanted to wait for you."

He settled next to Theo as the vehicle rocked forward. Raking his fingers through his hair, Tony peered across the seat, looking her directly in the eye. "Did Haven coerce you to meet him in the study? Take liberties?"

"What?" Theo's mouth gaped open in surprise. "No. Of

course not." As much as she didn't wish to marry Haven, she wasn't about to accuse him of forcing himself on her.

"Were you having an assignation with him, Theo? Did you make plans to meet him in the study?"

"Absolutely not. I don't even like him."

"Do you know how many times I thought about the conversation I've just had?" Tony grimaced. "I assumed I'd be having it with Blythe, or maybe some other gentleman you decided to adore next."

Theo slid her eyes from him. "That's rather unkind."

"You used to have a great deal of common sense, Theodosia. It disappeared completely when you met Blythe. Or spotted him in the park." He waved his hand. "It really doesn't matter. Romy warned me after seeing the way you tossed yourself at him during Granby's house party."

Theo shrank back further into the squabs. "I'm not a dinner roll, Tony."

"You've been compromised, Theodosia."

"I realize that." She smoothed down her skirts. "I—"

"*Christ*, you were hiding in the study, waiting for Blythe, *hoping* for ruination. You were trying to compromise yourself with him. Well, it appears you got far more than you bargained for. Romy insisted you were unnaturally obsessed with Blythe. Swore that if I didn't put a stop to it, you'd do something dreadful."

Her mouth went dry. "That isn't exactly—"

Tony pinched the bridge of his nose. "You must have overheard him making plans to meet Haven in the study tonight. Decided to pop out and instead of finding Blythe, you found Haven."

Her face heated. What could she say in her own defense without mentioning that stupid miniature and making things worse?

"If you think I've been blind to your machinations, or too

busy at Elysium with Leo gone, I assure you, I have not been. I just hoped I was wrong." A deep sigh left him. "Phaedra has apprised me of the incident in the park."

"I wasn't conspiring to trap Blythe," she said, knowing he'd never believe her. "And that day in the park, well, it was merely an accident. As tonight was."

"You deliberately entangled yourself in Blythe's kite string while half of London watched. Lifting your skirts before he even asked so he could unwind the string which had mysteriously wrapped itself around your ankle. Your pursuit of him at Granby's house party was a study in brazen behavior. And it was only the beginning. You threw yourself at Blythe during Lady Cambourne's ball without a shred of decorum or dignity. We all witnessed it."

Shame etched itself across her chest. "Well, you *would* know about immoral behavior," she shot back, the fragile hold on her emotions finally snapping. Had she really behaved so poorly?

"As a matter of fact," Tony's voice raised, "I *do* know all about how to be improper. Do you know how many young ladies threw themselves at me in an attempt to be compromised?"

"Thousands, I'm sure," Theo bit out.

"At least. I suppose we should consider it lucky you didn't tumble over the sofa and break your neck in your determination this evening, given you won't wear your spectacles."

Dear God. Tony made Theo sound as if she were the most pathetic creature in all of England. And this was her brother's opinion of her. What must everyone else think? She was so horrified, she couldn't speak.

"Blythe—"

"Is a rake, Theo. He may reform one day, but it will not be for you." Tony leaned close. "Had Blythe been serious about you in any way, he most certainly would have offered for you immediately once you were compromised, not given you over to his friend."

Pain seared her heart, an echo of when she'd seen Blythe flirting with Lady Meredith and Miss Cummings. She'd only thought if she was different enough. Bold enough.

"Now, I will have the pleasure," Tony emphasized, words laced with more than a hint of sarcasm, "of having the Marquess of Haven in the family. A gentleman who was fortunate enough to *not* be Blythe. The recipient of a fat dowry which inexplicably dropped right into his lap. No wonder he didn't push you out the door the moment he saw you. The only person happier is Lady Blythe." He shot her a sideways glance. "There isn't a gentleman in all of London more desperate than Haven."

How incredibly hurtful. Even if it was true.

"I grew alarmed each time Haven came to call on Romy in Granby's stead," Tony said. "Your mother was convinced he'd steal an expensive vase by sticking it under his coat. After he ate the entire contents of our larder, of course. He's like a mongrel begging at the kitchen door for scraps."

"It was an accident," Theo whispered.

"Yes. It appears it was. Blythe assures me he asked Haven to come to the study to discuss a possible courtship of Miss Emerson and was caught in the midst of your scheme to compromise yourself with Blythe."

Theo swallowed. "You can send me away. I could meet Romy in Italy."

"Granby would send you back. And don't even ask to go to Leo in New York. Or to the country to wait things out. Lady Blythe has promised discretion over tonight's events given that Haven will do the right thing, but she's never liked us Barringtons overmuch. We will try to contain the gossip. Hopefully, it will dissipate after you're wed."

"You promised I would never be forced to marry. You

promised," Theo implored. "And marrying Haven is very much against my will."

"That promise did not have a stupidity clause, Theodosia. Did you really assume you could be discovered alone with a gentleman and not have this be the outcome? Even you can't be so naïve as to believe I can just wave this away. Or maybe you are. You actually imagined you could trap Blythe into marriage."

Tony's words cut her to the quick. Everyone whispered about the Barringtons, but this was very different. She'd made a scandal of herself. Destroyed her reputation.

"Theodosia." Her brother's voice softened. "You would become a pariah if you didn't marry Haven, with no place in society."

"It isn't fair. Nothing happened. Why should I be punished?" There really was no way out of the situation. Not even the Duke of Averell could fix it for her.

"You'd have to live your life disgraced," he said gently. "You need to understand what you would face should you not marry Haven. But I agree. It isn't fair."

It amazed Theo how much Tony sounded like their father just now. She loved her brother. Adored him, actually. But he was a poor substitute for the late Marcus Barrington. Theo fervently wished for Papa to appear across the carriage from her. Right now. For just a moment, she would be clasped in the warmth of her father's embrace, telling her all would be well.

A small cry left her.

"Oh, Theodosia." Her brother took her hand and pulled her close. "I will protect you as best I can."

"I'm so sorry, Tony. I didn't mean for this to happen. Truly."

"Possibly having Haven as a husband won't be as terrible as you think." His tone led her to believe otherwise.

"I'm sure it will be."

"Most marriages are not made because of affection," Tony said. "But that doesn't mean you can't be happy." His body tensed slightly as he lifted his head, peering at something outside the window. "Damn. That's Cousin Winnie's carriage pulling away. I told her to go straight home. I wanted to apprise your mother of what has happened. Come," he said as the carriage rolled to a stop. "We'll continue this discussion inside."

Tony helped her out of the carriage and kept her hand in his as the massive front door opened to reveal the unflappable Pith, as pristine and starched as he'd been at breakfast this morning.

"Your Grace," the butler intoned. "Welcome home. Her Grace awaits you in the drawing room."

7

The Dowager Duchess of Averell awaited them, her features pale and drawn, a glass of brandy sitting on the table before her. She looked up as Theo and Tony came through the door.

"Come, dearest," she said, patting the space next to her on the settee. "Poor Winnie is beside herself."

A disgruntled sound came from Tony. "I asked Winnie to go straight home." At least his annoyance was now directed toward their cousin and not Theo. "As usual, she completely disregarded my instructions. What is the use of being a duke if no one obeys you?"

Mama gave him a tired smile. "She feels responsible since Theo was in her care. I dare not even allow Winnie to take Olivia and Phaedra to Gunter's. They'd both be ruined before the ices melt."

Theo bit her lip and looked away. On top of everything else, her foolishness had hurt Cousin Winnie.

"I had to keep waving smelling salts beneath her nose just to keep her upright," her mother continued. "I didn't wish her as a guest for the night. Rosalind finally led her away."

Tony went to the sideboard and poured himself a healthy glass of brandy. "First piece of good news I've heard this evening."

Mama turned to look at Theo. "Compromised? By the Marquess of Haven? The very same gentleman who would call on your sister before she and Granby were married? The desperate gentleman in need of an heiress?" She shook her head. "I didn't believe Winnie at first."

"It was an accident, Mama."

"A happy one for him, I'm sure. I recall that on the one and only occasion we met, outside of seeing him at Romy's wedding, his coat was worn so thin, I could see clean through to the linen of his shirt."

"That's the one." Tony hoisted up his glass. "I'm thrilled." He paused. "Haven was at Romy's wedding? We weren't introduced."

"He arrived late," Mama said. "And disappeared promptly after the ceremony."

"Probably snuck about trying to pry the jewels from some of the statuary once we were all occupied. I should check to make sure the church wasn't sacked."

"Tony," Mama admonished.

Theo shut her eyes, wishing this entire evening to be over. Or that she'd awaken in her bed knowing it had all been some awful dream.

"I've only been concerned with Blythe, but it appears I should have looked further afield," her mother said.

"It was an *accident*," Theo whispered again, opening her eyes to face Mama's disappointment.

"Yes, brought on by your uninvited presence in Blythe's study. At least according to Cousin Winnie, who was informed by Lady Blythe." Mama's voice held a note of dislike. "It is my understanding that Haven was there awaiting Blythe and his mother to ask their help in speaking to Lord Emerson about courting his daughter. Were you invited to give your opinion as well?"

Her mother knew that wasn't the case. "No."

"I can think of no other reason why you would be present in Blythe's study during a party given in his honor, Theodosia. Except the obvious. We are very distressed by your lack of judgement. You've done irreparable damage to yourself."

We. Her mother at times spoke as if Papa were still with them. But she was correct. Papa would be terribly disappointed in her. He'd had such faith in her intelligence.

Tony took a chair across from Theo, his long legs stretching out before him as he sipped at his drink. "Lady Blythe claims she caught Haven and Theo in a torrid embrace."

"Yes, Winnie said as much. And what did Haven say?" Mama held up her hand when Theo tried to speak.

"Theo tripped, and he caught her. Nothing more, despite Lady Blythe's claims. Blythe confirmed that he did ask Haven to meet him in the study." Tony paused and looked into his glass. "I don't think he lured her there or took liberties."

"But?" Mama said.

"Haven is only too happy to do the right thing. I'd feel better if he'd made a squeak of protest. Or at the very least, mentioned he needed to speak to Miss Emerson. The situation only seems a bit convenient, I suppose. If I didn't know better, I'd assume he intentionally compromised Theodosia, except it would have been impossible for him to guess she was there."

"I agree, but we cannot condemn Haven for being impoverished. And it is Theo's own impulsiveness for seeking out Blythe which resulted in this mess." Mama turned to her.

"I—merely wished a moment alone. His study seemed convenient—"

Mama made a sound of disbelief. "Theodosia."

"Don't either of you care in the least that I'm being forced to marry a man I don't even like?" she said, looking up at them both. Self-pity threatened to overwhelm her. None of this was her fault. "That I love Blythe?"

Her mother set her glass of brandy down on the table with such violence, Theo thought the fine crystal might shatter.

"Tony," Mama said in a firm tone. "I'm sure you're exhausted with recent events, not to mention handling Elysium. I wish to speak to Theodosia alone. We can continue our discussion tomorrow."

Not many would dare to dismiss the Duke of Averell so casually, except his stepmother.

"As you wish, madam." Tony bowed politely, pausing only to press a kiss atop Theo's head before carrying his glass from the room.

Mama waited for the sound of Tony's steps to fade before picking up her brandy again. She took a sip, regarding Theo over the rim of her glass.

"I have had *enough*, Theodosia."

"But—"

"Do not dare interrupt me. I have stood by these past few months and watched you make a complete cake of yourself over the Earl of Blythe. Yes, he is charming. Handsome. Pays you an inordinate amount of attention, most of it directed toward your bosom. Not a bit of his behavior is that of a man with honorable intentions. Or a man with any intentions toward you at all. I think that despite your best efforts, there is little you could have done to induce him to offer for you."

"I'm not sure that is entirely true," Theo protested weakly, knowing that her mother was right. Hadn't she belatedly come to the same conclusion tonight?

"You are not a stupid girl, Theodosia, though you've behaved recently as if you've not a brain in your head. You were the one I didn't have to worry over. Romy was always marching about, declaring how she must lead and everyone else should follow. Olivia is kindness itself, so much so I've always worried her good nature would be taken advantage of. Phaedra," Mama's face took on a pinched look, "is destined for some sort of catastrophe. It is merely too soon to tell. But you? My reclusive artist? My lover of mysteries and romantic novels? My biggest worry has been you'd never leave your studio to associate with the rest of the world but would continue to live your life in the clouds. I thought Blythe a *phase*. A way to distract yourself because of," the words stumbled, and her mother paled, "your father."

Theo tried to take a breath, but it hurt far too much. "No." She shook her head. "That isn't the case." Blythe wasn't some sort of shiny distraction. "I love Blythe. Adore him."

"Listen to yourself, Theo." Mama shook her head. "How many times have I warned you and your sisters that it is one thing to be bold, another to be brazen? Did you assume behaving in such a flirtatious way would earn Blythe's admiration? He probably told you he found such behavior original. Becoming." Her fingers fluttered about her glass. "Or other such nonsense."

Theo looked away because Blythe had used those very words. She and her sisters had often mocked the flagrant ways in which young ladies tried to catch a gentleman's attention. Imitating the coos and chirps they made while batting their eyes and fluttering their fans.

Theo had become one of them. A nitwit.

"Has Blythe taken liberties?"

"No." Theo's gaze shot back to her mother. "Of course not. He has never been anything but a gentleman."

"Smarter than the average rake. I suppose I should be thankful. Is there any remaining idiocy I should be made aware of?"

Theo thought of the miniature, still in Haven's possession. That would certainly qualify as idiocy. "No, Mama."

"As I mentioned, I've met Haven," her mother said. "Briefly. He's certainly handsome in a rough sort of way. Charming when he chooses to be. Intelligent. We spoke about the stars, of all things. I can see why Miss Emerson found him so appealing. Perhaps having him in our family will not be as terrible as we all suppose. In spite of Tony's feelings, Haven can't possibly be any worse than Granby."

"I wouldn't be too sure," Theo murmured.

"You realize, Theo, that you do not have to like or live with Haven after a time should you find your marriage intolerable. If you decide you don't suit—"

"We don't."

"After a time, you might go your separate ways. Many marriages succeed in such a way. It isn't what I've wished for you, but perhaps you might agree to such an understanding with Haven."

Theo had never been more miserable in her entire life. Her future opened before her, empty of any love or affection. Her marriage reduced to nothing more than duty. A small whimper left her before she could stop it. This was all so unfair.

Mama took her hand. "What's done is done, Theodosia. You must now decide whether you will choose to remain bitter or find your own happiness. As a married woman, you are afforded greater freedom to do as you please, especially if you and Haven are of the same mind." She pressed a kiss to Theo's temple. "Now, I think I've given you much to consider. It has been a long night." Mama stood. "Don't wait too much longer to seek your bed."

She nodded, relieved to be alone with her thoughts as her mother shut the drawing room doors behind her.

Theo sat for a long time after, staring into the fire and

contemplating the strange, horrible turn her life had taken in the last several hours. She hadn't yet collapsed in a fit of tears. Or fainted. Both were points in her favor. Defiantly, she went to the sideboard and poured herself a finger of scotch, as she'd seen her brother do.

Bringing the glass to her lips, Theo tossed back the liquid, gasping as fire burned down her throat before warming her from the inside out. She didn't even cough.

Straightening her shoulders, Theo set down the glass and proceeded up the stairs, determined to shed not one single tear until she was in the privacy of her room.

8

Theo pushed her spectacles further up her nose and stared at her younger sister from across the breakfast table. It had been two days since the *Ruination of Theodosia Barrington*. The first night, after swallowing the glass of scotch, Theo had fallen on her bed, screaming and weeping into the pillows until she'd finally worn herself out.

Betts, her maid, had taken one look at her and quietly shut the door.

Last night, she'd merely tossed and turned. What little sleep she'd gained had been interrupted by dreams in which Haven walked into Blythe's party and showed her miniature to the assembled guests.

Everyone laughed, especially Miss Emerson and Lady Blythe.

The lack of sleep had made Theo irritable. Phaedra staring at her from across the table this morning as if Theo had grown a second head only worsened her mood. Placing her fork down, she regarded her sister. "Is there something you wish to say, Phaedra?"

Her brother had already met with Haven. Solicitors had

appeared. Contracts had been signed. The brief, private ceremony binding her to Haven would take place in a few weeks, after which they would immediately leave for his country estate. There were some vague suggestions about garnering support from Cousin Winnie and Lady Molsin before the wedding, but Theo had no idea what that entailed.

She was too upset about being banished from London. With Haven.

"No. I was only considering something." Phaedra pushed her thick braid of red-gold hair, the same shade as their mother's, over her shoulder. "You don't look *ruined*." She inspected Theo carefully. "I thought possibly you'd seem different. You know. Spoiled or something."

"Spoiled?"

"Like pudding that's gone bad. Or an apple with a worm at its center." Phaedra's nose wrinkled. "Or fish too long in the sun."

"I see."

Phaedra liked to provoke. Taunt. See how far she could push you. One day, possibly today, the trait would get her into trouble.

Theo glanced at Olivia who sat directly across the table.

Olivia pretended complete interest in her tea, drizzling a long strand of honey into the steaming depths. "I'm not part of this," she said without looking up. "Only having my tea."

"Has it driven you mad?" Phaedra blasted Theo with wide-eyed innocence. "The ruination, I mean."

Her sister was rarely innocent. Of anything. "Why on earth would the circumstances have driven me mad?"

"I don't know. You're an artist. Artists are given to fragile constitutions. Prone to insanity and fits."

"I'm not on the edge of lunacy, Phaedra. Not even a bit addled. Nor is my constitution the least fragile. How did you find out about my situation to begin with?"

"You mean your," Phaedra leaned across the table, "despoilment?"

"Were you listening at the door?" Theo couldn't imagine Mama or Tony had come right out and announced it over dinner last night. Though Theo couldn't be sure because she had taken a tray in her room.

"I overheard, quite by accident, Tony speaking to Mama and Maggie. And Freddie. Though I don't suppose he understands, so you don't have to worry about him gossiping. All he did was drool."

"I expect my nephew will have an opinion once he's older." He probably would, since Theo would likely still be living with her brother. She had no intention of residing indefinitely with Haven. If she had to go to his estate for appearance's sake, so be it. Then she was coming right back to London. Because she and Haven didn't suit. Would never suit.

"I'm a bit confused because I thought you liked Blythe." Phaedra blinked.

Theo's jaw hardened. Phaedra was also rarely confused.

"You went to all that trouble to tangle yourself up in his kite string, dragging me along to the park with Olivia. *And*," she drew out the syllables, "you forced Romy to go to that stupid house party. Then you have an assignation with Haven." She lifted her hands with a roll of her shoulders. "It doesn't make sense."

Oh, good grief. "I happened upon Haven in Blythe's study. I tripped. Haven caught me." Theo repeated the story Haven had concocted. It was as good as any, though nearly everyone, including her family, assumed Theo had been lying in wait for Blythe when Haven came upon her. There was simply no other explanation she could give. "Lady Blythe misunderstood the situation and screamed—"

"Was it *that* horrible? The sight of your ruination?"

Theo took a deep breath. She couldn't very well toss her cup of tea on her sister though she longed to. "No. Lady Blythe made much more of it than necessary. Much like you, she's given to dramatics."

Phaedra bit into her toast, crunching loudly.

"And you only found the house party stupid because you didn't get to attend," Theo added.

"Possibly. Romy didn't want to go at all. I remember quite clearly."

"Whether she wanted to attend or not is irrelevant. The result of the house party for Romy was marrying a duke."

"Yes, but the duke is *Granby*," Phaedra said. "The Frost Giant."

"I happen to like him." Olivia delicately nibbled at her own toast.

Olivia did everything in a ladylike, refined way. Floating about the house with her dark solemn eyes. Perfect curtseys. Hair never out of place. Just now, Theo found all of it annoying. "You would, Olivia. Your last conversation with him was about *worms*. And as for calling him the Frost Giant—"

"It's far nicer than the words Tony uses to describe him," Phaedra said, interrupting. "And I'm tired of Mama's Greeks. I've branched out to Norse mythology. Much more bloodthirsty. There's an entire race of giants who live in the north. I feel certain Granby is one. He's the look of," she lowered her voice, "a savage." She shivered. "I find him quite terrifying."

Phaedra wasn't afraid of anything, which in turn made the entire family fear for *her*. Theo's improper miniature would be nothing compared to what she was certain Phaedra would do someday. There was a reason Tony affectionately called her demon.

"I think it more possible Granby is terrified of you," Theo told her. "As we all are."

Olivia giggled, giving an incredibly ladylike snort into her tea.

Theo felt beginnings of a headache stir, her temples throbbing as much from this discussion as her impending doom. She had considered fleeing London. Running away to America. Or France. But in all scenarios, Theo risked hurting her mother, something she simply couldn't do. Nor did she want to resign herself to an estrangement from her family with a tattered reputation, leaving her no place in the world. Theo didn't want the likes of Lady Blythe and her daughters crossing the street to avoid coming in contact with her, as if she were a piece of refuse.

She must make the best of the situation as her mother had advised her.

"I quite like Haven. He's interesting. I liken him to Theseus." Phaedra paused. "The cat, not the Greek warrior," she clarified. "As I mentioned, I'm giving up on the Greeks. Possibly I'll even rename Theseus. I haven't decided."

"Haven reminds you of our cat at Cherry Hill? The one with half his ear missing, fur which is always full of mud, who keeps leaving Mama dead birds and such?" Actually, Theo could see the resemblance. Haven had the look of a feral cat lingering about, waiting for an opportunity to steal a bit of meat.

"They both have green eyes. Surely you've noticed."

Theo hadn't really made the connection. "I don't spend time gazing into the eyes of our cat, or Haven's, for that matter."

"I'm sure Theseus would wield a sword, much like Haven, if he could. He's quite brave. Loves a good fight. You see? They have much in common."

"I think you have given Haven attributes he may not actually have."

"You must like Haven a little to have been compromised by him. It's all right to admit it."

Theo looked up at her sister. "Wait, how in the world would you know if Haven wielded a sword or not?"

"He told me so when he called upon us. When Granby disappeared from town for a while. Don't you remember? Romy was secretly missing her Frost Giant, and Haven kept popping up to take her to the park."

Her mother had reminded her of Haven's visits only the other night. Since Mama had conversed with him, Theo supposed it wasn't a stretch to find out he'd also had discussions with Phaedra on weaponry.

"I've never seen anyone eat so many scones at one sitting," Phaedra continued. "Piles of them. And he ate all the sandwiches even though he claimed not to care for cucumber. Romy had to send Pith for another tray. You'll have to keep him from getting stout, Theo. At any rate, that is when we talked of swords." She waved about with her hand as if wielding one. "I may take up fencing."

"Perhaps you'll prove more adept at swords than the violin," Olivia said, still nibbling at her toast.

One had to be careful of Olivia. Theo had always admired her ability to strike when one least expected the attack.

Phaedra gave Olivia a hard look. "Not everyone takes to music as well as you do, Olivia. Mama says I deserve applause for at least trying." She frowned. "Perhaps swords will prove to be my passion."

"Perhaps," Olivia murmured dubiously. "Fencing is bound to bring you many admirers. The drawing room will overflow."

"Regardless," Phaedra continued while simultaneously flicking a bit of egg toward Olivia, "Haven always asked after you, Theo."

"How kind of him to inquire after my health." It surprised

her that Haven had asked after her, but possibly he was only being polite. Still, a bit of warmth settled in her chest at the words, refusing to be dislodged.

Olivia discreetly threw a tiny bit of honey-covered crust back at Phaedra. It landed just above Phaedra's ear, sticking firmly to her hair.

"He always wanted to know," Phaedra informed her, a bit gleefully, "if you were stumbling about blindly in the garden. He expressed his worry that you'd trip and fall out a window. Asked if the servants guided you about. Because, you know, he wasn't certain you were wearing your spectacles."

She should have known Haven's concern had only been an opportunity to find new ways to mock her eyesight. The warmth faded abruptly.

"Yes, but I'm wearing them now." Theo pushed the hated spectacles further up her nose. Phaedra was unlikely to notice the bit of toast stuck to her until much later. Served her right.

Theo shared a conspiratorial smile with Olivia. "Olivia, would you be a dear and pass the honey?"

9

"Lord Haven," Mama said, "perhaps you and Theodosia might wish to take a turn around the gardens."

Theo's fingers gripped her teacup before setting it down on the saucer with a slight clatter. She didn't *want* to be alone with Haven. Nor show him the garden. Especially after watching him demolish the contents of the tea tray. Most of her dowry would go to just keeping him fed.

Her mother had invited Haven to call without Theo's knowledge, choosing not to inform her until it was too late for Theo to come up with an excuse not to appear. And now here she was, trapped in the drawing room with an empty tea cart and a terrible disposition. Theo did find out several interesting things about her future husband over the course of his unwelcome visit. None of which made marrying him any more to her liking.

First, Haven didn't really care for tea. Oh, he made a great show of it, asking for sugar and stirring it around, but he only took two small sips, grimacing as he did so. He probably liked coffee. Or maybe his tastes were more basic. Theo caught him looking at the assortment of decanters filling the sideboard.

Secondly, Haven loved any sort of biscuit, scone, or sandwich. Food in general. Theo had nearly lost a finger attempting to grab the lone biscuit after he'd eaten nearly everything else. He'd graciously allowed her to have it, but she sensed his resentment all the same.

Third, Haven had a younger sister named Jacinda. The idea of Haven having a sister, or any sibling, had never crossed Theo's mind. He also possessed an uncle with the unfortunate name of Erasmus.

Lastly, and most importantly, Haven looked absolutely breathtaking today with his russet hair falling in waves over his cheekbones and the moss-green of his eyes glowing in the drawing room. Even if he was still in dire need of a decent haircut.

It was the last part that put Theo in such a bad mood. She didn't want to find him attractive. Or even remotely appealing.

"Certainly, Your Grace," he said politely to Mama. "I'd be delighted to see the duke's gardens. I've heard they are magnificent."

"From whom," Theo stood, not bothering to hide her derision, "would you have heard such a thing?"

"Lady Phaedra," Haven said, not the slightest bit nonplussed by Theo's thinly veiled hostility toward him. "She spoke very highly of the wisteria."

His absolute politeness grated on Theo's nerves. He was rarely so lovely to be around, in her opinion. But today, charm and pleasant conversation oozed from him.

The purpose in inviting Haven to tea today, along with Cousin Winnie and Granby's aunt, Lady Molsin, had been to ascertain what social event Theo and Haven should attend together to help stanch the gossip already forming about the announcement of their impending nuptials. The problem was solved when Lady Molsin agreed to play hostess to a small gathering. The trio of matrons was determined to combat whatever gossip Lady Blythe was circulating, no matter that she'd promised to remain silent. Many of the same gentlemen and ladies who had been at Blythe's party would be invited to Lady Molsin's.

Theo doubted any such efforts would help.

Standing to await her dubious escort to the gardens, Theo felt like a watch wound too tightly, a timepiece whose springs would snap and burst and never keep time again.

Or be happy, in her case.

Nonetheless, Theo led Haven out through the doors at the edge of the room and into the Duke of Averell's garden while Mama tilted her head in approval.

The sky above the garden shone brilliant blue and cloudless, the sun dappling in splashes along the grass. If one stood next to the large maple closest to the house and just looked across the expanse of trees and carefully manicured beds, the wall separating the garden from the park was barely visible. It gave the appearance of being in the country, which was lovely. Under normal circumstances, Theo enjoyed the view immensely.

Haven took her arm, the heat of his touch sparking up her elbow. "Show me the bloody wisteria." The low rasp of his voice licked against her ear.

Theo was unsurprised by his abrupt change in manner. Phaedra's assessment of Haven couldn't have been more astute. He was very much like Theseus the cat, forced to sit and be charming only because it eventually led to being fed.

She strolled beside him in the direction of the stone wall, listening to Haven's boots crunch on the gravel path. Ignoring the warmth where his hand touched her elbow, Theo focused instead on hurrying him through the garden.

The sooner this walk was over, the quicker Haven would leave.

"I don't wish to attend a party in your company," she finally said, needing to break the silence between them.

"It is a small event given by Lady Molsin. I think Granby's aunt was very kind to offer," came his reply.

Theo thought so as well, but that wasn't the point. "A celebration of our engagement? Virtually no one believes our marriage is anything but the result of me being compromised, including the hostess herself." She would have to smile and pretend to be happy when all of London knew what a farce this was, thanks to Blythe's mother. "Lady Blythe misunderstands the meaning of the word *discretion*."

"Hmmm." Haven gave a low purr.

Complete disinterest. Of course, the gossip wouldn't really affect Haven. His reputation wasn't being shredded over tea in drawing rooms and parlors all over London. No one judged him for being an impoverished title who'd bagged a fat dowry. The gossip was all directed at Theo. Pathetic, brazen Theodosia. The odd Barrington who paints miniatures and trips over everything.

The one who would never have Blythe.

Perhaps Theo might never have had him anyway, but now she would never really know. Meaning she'd made a cake of herself for nothing. Admittedly, her pursuit of Blythe hadn't gone exactly as she'd planned, but still, if not for Haven, she might have eventually captured Blythe's affections. Yet another bit of blame she laid at the scuffed boots of the Marquess of Haven.

"You didn't tell me, my lord, that you have a sister," Theo said before stumbling over a rock on the path.

Haven caught her deftly. "*Christ*, just wear your spectacles."

Theo gritted her teeth, deciding right then and there she

would continue to *not* wear them if only to irritate Haven. "Here's the wisteria." She stopped before the vines with their purple clusters of flowers. "Lovely, isn't it? Shall we return?"

"You never asked if I had a sister. Or anything else about me," he finally answered.

"I'll assume that since you only mentioned Jacinda over tea, there are no additional Collingwood siblings for me to contend with."

"The Collingwoods are not nearly as prolific as the Barringtons," he replied blandly. "There is only Jacinda. Not a bastard or a duke among the fold."

She pretended not to hear the slur against Leo. "And an uncle."

Haven had made no mention of bringing either his sister or uncle to London for their wedding. Maybe he thought, given the circumstances, their presence at the ceremony would be awkward. Though not as awkward as Lady Molsin's little party was bound to be. Theo felt ill just thinking about it. At least if she didn't wear her spectacles, she wouldn't see the looks of pity and derision directed her way.

"Jacinda and Phaedra are about the same age," Haven said. "She loves books. Reads constantly. The library at Greenbriar is fairly extensive, or at least it used to be."

Theo assumed he meant before the previous Marquess of Haven had bankrupted the estate and sold off everything of value, including the books. Cousin Winnie had given Mama the entire story. Theo had listened at the door, unseen by both women.

"Due to," he paused, "an *illness*, Jacinda resides at Greenbriar in the care of my housekeeper and cook, Mrs. Henderson."

So Haven possessed someone who cooked and maintained his crumbling estate, which Theo supposed was something. At least when she was to be dragged from London, there would be a decent meal waiting. Drawing a small hole in the gravel of the path with the toe of her shoe, she said, "So your uncle resides at Greenbriar as well?"

"He does. Erasmus returned to England just prior to my father's death. I was still traveling abroad."

Theo's brow wrinkled. She hadn't known Haven had lived abroad. "Where was your uncle? Traveling with you?"

Haven gave her a half-smile. "Erasmus? No. He's a sot. And a bit simple. Spent most of his life in a small village outside of Calais where my grandmother once owned property. He never married. I'd only met him once before I returned home."

Dear God. Things just kept getting worse when it came to Haven. A drunkard for an uncle and a sickly sister. "He never visited?"

He paused beside her, taking a deep sigh. "They were estranged. My father and uncle. And twins."

Theo tilted her chin to look at him, unable to stop her eyes from widening at this new bit of information. "Your father had a twin brother?" Surely if Cousin Winnie knew, she would have said so. "No one has ever mentioned him."

"I doubt anyone knows or remembers. Erasmus always had a nervous constitution which kept him from attending school with my father. He stayed at Greenbriar until my father married. I'm not sure he's ever been to London."

"Very unusual."

Haven just rolled his shoulders, the deep green of his eyes unfathomable. "It is. They were never close, their personalities very different. My father rarely spoke of Erasmus, and he only visited the one time. He's terrified of the ocean. Ships and such. So, once he left England, the journey back was terrifying for him. And as I said, he and my father didn't get along."

"What was the cause of their estrangement, if I can ask?

Aren't twins supposed to be each other's best friends? Always together?"

"Erasmus and my father both courted my mother, but she chose my father. He was a marquess, after all. Likewise, he wasn't afraid of his own shadow or spouting off nonsensical things like his brother. My uncle's heart was broken, I'm told, and he couldn't bear to be in England a moment longer. He was given the small estate in France, was instructed how to manage things, and was left alone. We never visited. I'm ashamed to admit I forgot all about Erasmus until I received my sister's letter."

Very curious. "You lived abroad, then. Anywhere in particular?"

"I wandered for a time." The low rasp of his voice scratched against her arms. "When I returned, Erasmus greeted me as I came up the drive, weeping with relief at the sight of me. He claimed the fairies told him I was dead."

"Fairies?"

"He speaks to them. Or they to him. I'm never really sure." Haven shot her an amused look. "Erasmus had braved the journey back to England, he said, to console my father over my death, though he didn't return when my mother died, and he'd loved her. I think he probably ran out of money, more likely, and had no other way of getting any. The estate was in poor shape by that time, but Erasmus had nothing to go back to, and he was adamant about not getting on a ship again. I'm glad he was there for Jacinda. He loves her dearly. Nearly as much as his brandy." Haven cast a sideways glance at her. "Though he will also drink gin, ale, scotch, or sherry." His face hardened a bit. "My father preferred scotch."

Theo digested the information, wondering at estranged twins who had both become sots. "You've done your uncle quite a kindness, I think."

"He's a sad creature. Lost. Harmless."

"Were they identical twins?" Theo thought that must be difficult for Haven, to have a drunken uncle wandering about who looked like his father, twins or not.

"Yes." Haven frowned, the small scar on his chin twitching. "But they aren't alike. The hair is different. The cadence of their voice. Erasmus is nervous, like a frightened rabbit. Incapable of doing anything but shuffling around. Always hunched over. Wanders about drunk, picking violets for Mrs. Henderson, stealing my sister's books. He reminds me little of my father, aside from the drinking. Of course, I never saw them together, save for the one time when I was a child."

What a fascinating, if not bizarre, tale. Like the plot of one of the books she so adored. Theo would never have guessed Haven to be so complicated beneath the threadbare coats and well-worn boots.

Drat.

Theo didn't want him to be interesting. Or fascinating. Or so beautiful in the afternoon light.

His fingers trailed over her wrist before wrapping around it. "Do you wish to know more?" Haven's thumb rubbed over Theo's pulse, already beating like a drum. Absently, his fingers caressed her wrist, pausing only briefly in his ministrations at a tiny speckle of paint on her skin.

"No, I think that is quite enough. I'm still considering fleeing England, possibly to Italy. I might yet be able to ruin my sister's wedding trip with the Frost Giant."

A small, amused sound left him. "Someone has been reading their Norse mythology. I've always thought if I could convince Granby to put on an eye patch, he'd make a decent Odin."

Theo decided not to tell him it was actually Phaedra who was up on her mythology. Theo's own interest in the subject was limited to the scenes depicted in paintings.

"Missed a spot." Haven's thumb paused to caress the small bit of paint on her wrist.

His words weren't especially erotic, yet they echoed down between her thighs.

Carefully, he pulled her wrist to his lips, pressing an open-mouthed kiss to the wild pulse beating there. "Probably couldn't see it," he murmured against her skin. "I shall have to remember to inspect you for paint."

Theo sucked in a breath, alarmed at how quickly the mood between them had shifted. One moment they were discussing his drunk uncle and unwanted social engagements and the next, his lips were trailing in a bold manner along her wrist.

"That isn't necessary." A tremor ran through her at the light touch. "To inspect me." A flood of sensation rippled over her, bringing to mind thoughts of bare skin and soft whispers. Of Haven pressing all his muscled warmth against her.

She tugged at her wrist, anxious to break contact. Destroy the sudden, unwelcome intimacy springing up between them.

Haven didn't release her. His eyes closed for a moment before the press of his tongue slid against her pulse, tasting her skin. It was an unexpectedly sensual gesture, one that felt even more wicked here, in the dappled sunlight of her brother's garden.

"Where is my miniature?" she whispered, determined to stop the slow spread of honey spilling down her wrist to encompass the rest of her body. Another image of what she'd seen at Elysium flashed through her mind.

"I'm keeping it." His teeth scraped against her skin. "I'd like to make some comparisons before giving it back to you. Size. Shape. Color."

Heat rushed up her cheeks. There was no way to mistake his meaning.

"I can inspect you for paint at the same time. There isn't any telling where some has landed. Possibly even under your skirts." He watched her from beneath his lashes, bits of emerald flashing across her skin.

Theo's heart fluttered. Not softly, but madly. Like the wings of a trapped butterfly. She had to turn away from the hunger flaring in his gaze. Haven meant to devour her as he had the tea tray. And she was much larger than a scone or a biscuit.

It is only envy of Blythe, she reminded herself, causing him to behave so seductively with her.

"There is no need to pretend affection, my lord." She snatched her wrist from his grasp. "Nor seduction. We are to be married whether we wish it or not."

"I deplore pretense, Theodosia. I don't have the patience for it and thus do not practice it." Haven's lips twisted into a smirk which made him more damnably attractive than he already was.

Drat.

"Good." She cleared her throat, trying to regain some control. "We should reach some sort of understanding, given our circumstances," she blurted, finding it increasingly difficult to breathe with Haven so close.

"Should we?"

Theo cleared her throat. "Politely, my lord, our marriage is one of convenience. An unhappy accident borne of society's rules. You and I both know nothing improper happened between us."

"*Do* I know that, though?" His voice had lowered to a dangerous purr. "You attacked me. My ribs are still bruised."

Theo pursed her lips, ignoring the subtle ache the sound of him stirred. "I only sought to retrieve the miniature, as well you know."

"You've yet to thank me for saving your reputation."

Those tiny lights, the ones that reminded Theo of fireflies in the summer grass, were dancing in his eyes.

"My reputation wouldn't have been damaged had you only returned the miniature to me. I would have left the study immediately. You arrogant wretch; how dare you behave as if you've done me a favor. All of London thinks I was lying in wait for Blythe."

"Well, weren't you?" He lifted his brows.

"You know I was not." Theo narrowed her eyes on him, ignoring the way the sunlight sparked along his jaw, turning the dark hair to copper. "My brother has an interesting theory. He thinks you compromised me on purpose. And Blythe helped." Tony hadn't said that . . . exactly, but she did enjoy the way Haven's smug look turned to ice.

He rubbed his fingers over the hair along his chin, drawing her attention to the tiny half-moon scar. There was a stiffness to his movements, as if he were struggling to rein in his temper.

She wondered again where the scar had come from. It resembled the bottom of a broken bottle. Or a glass. He probably got it in a bar fight.

"I fear the duke is incorrect." Haven's low rumble hung in the air. "It was actually Lady Blythe I conspired with. She's never liked you. Finds you far too bold. Inappropriate, I believe, is the word she used. Begged me to ensure you couldn't get your hooks into her precious son."

Theo glared at him. "You—"

"We practiced for several days before the party. I would pop out at her from various hidden nooks and stumble about, tripping over everything while pretending to be you. She would scream at the sight of me." His words dripped sarcasm. "How *fortunate* you decided to place yourself in Blythe's study at exactly the right time without my knowledge. Saved me the trouble of luring you there."

"You're impoverished, my lord," she said defensively. "It is a fair conclusion."

"That my father left me with nothing but a title? How incredibly astute you are, Theodosia. Perhaps you aren't the ninny everyone assumes you to be."

She fell back a step, surprised by the sharp cruelty of his attack. Theo had wanted to provoke Haven's temper, and she'd succeeded. His eyes no longer flickered with hunger for her but icy indifference. Drawing closer, Haven stopped a mere hair's breadth from her, looming over Theo until the tip of his nose nuzzled gently against her neck. A soft, soothing purr came from him.

Damn him.

A delicious prickling sensation cascaded downward, caressing every curve and hollow of her body. She arched ever so slightly toward Haven, unable to ignore the way his touch beckoned her to come closer. It made her forget almost everything, even the ugly words she'd forced from him.

Cruel words. Which she'd meant to return in kind.

"Doesn't it bother you?" she murmured in what she hoped was a silken tone. "Marrying a woman so obviously in love with another man?" Theo knew the mention of Blythe would infuriate Haven. Not because he gave a fig for her, but because he envied Blythe *everything*.

He raised his head from her neck, studying her with a cool, speculative look.

"Not at all, Theodosia. As you've so recently reminded me, our marriage is based on salvaging reputations and financial gain. Your affections," there was a note of mockery, "are free to fall on whomever you deem fit. Thank Her Grace for the tea. I'll see myself out."

She'd meant to anger him with the mention of Blythe. Ambrose knew that. But that didn't mean Theo's little ploy to spark his temper hadn't worked.

Pith, the duke's imperious butler, glared at Ambrose with dislike before shutting the door of the Averell mansion behind him with a slam. No one inside the duke's residence, including their priggish butler, cared for Ambrose's upcoming marriage to Theodosia. Granby had warned Ambrose about Pith. At his first dinner with the Barringtons, Pith had deliberately served Granby the poorest cut of roast. His soup had been cold. When he'd left the table for a moment, he'd returned to find his potatoes over salted.

Averell had merely regarded Granby over his goblet of wine with a tiny smile.

In addition to Pith hovering over all of them earlier in the drawing room like some overprotective rooster guarding his hens, the dowager duchess and Lady Richardson had viewed Ambrose with a sort of tired resignation. Neither appreciated his robust appetite.

Ambrose did not think his future treatment would improve. Not if Theodosia had anything to say about it. She wasn't indifferent to him, but considering most of what she felt was dislike, it didn't bode well for their future.

It doesn't matter. I'll have back what Leo Murphy took from my father.

Ambrose didn't require Theodosia's affection, though she seemed to wish to bestow it upon everyone but him. He only needed her dowry. That he desired her physically was merely a pleasant addendum to the entire affair. He hadn't put her in Blythe's study that night.

Furiously, Ambrose pushed against the guilt attempting to wiggle itself into his chest.

Yes, he wanted to bed Theodosia. *Christ*, what man

wouldn't? But Ambrose also truly liked her. Much more than he wished to at times.

Why does everything have to be so complicated?

It shouldn't be.

Ambrose blamed Leo Murphy and his pompous brother for beggaring a grief-stricken man who wasn't capable of coherent thought let alone the decision to sign away everything of value.

The fault wasn't entirely Murphy's, even Ambrose had to admit that, but a great deal of it was.

He paused, rubbing at his chest, the ache now there for an entirely different reason. The walk back to Blythe's home, though a bit of a distance, would be welcome. Now that Ambrose was about to be a wealthy man once again, he could have hired a hack. Or purchased his own carriage and horses. But thriftiness had become second nature. Poverty was something Ambrose was unlikely to recover from any time soon, if he ever did. Years spent scraping for every shilling, defiantly paying off the debts his father had amassed while struggling to ensure Jacinda and Greenbriar survived. He should have married immediately upon his return to England. Or at the very least, asked his friends for help.

But his pride was all he had left. He wouldn't take their charity.

And then he'd met Theodosia and her sister at Granby's house party. He'd fought against the solution before him, the one possessing a magnificent bosom and poor eyesight. A solution which would allow him to thumb his nose at Elysium and restore his pocketbook.

A surge of rightness, of validation, had coursed through him.

The duke was right to be suspicious of Ambrose's intentions, except, ironically, for the night at Blythe's. But then, if Averell had truly thought something nefarious had occurred, he wouldn't have handed over his sister, or her enormous, obscene dowry.

Ambrose had nearly fainted when he'd seen the amount.

There had been no flicker of recognition in Averell's face when Ambrose was formally introduced. No sign that Murphy had told his brother about the threats of the destitute heir to the Marquess of Haven. It had been wise to avoid the duke when Ambrose had called on Andromeda and then again at Granby's wedding.

'Someday I'll take back what was mine.'

Murphy had considered the words an idle threat. The ravings of an angry heir who now found himself destitute. And while he hadn't put events into motion that night in Blythe's study, the fact remained that Ambrose had always meant to ruin Theodosia Barrington.

He just hadn't expected her to help him do it.

10

Theodosia frowned and fluttered her fan. A ridiculous accessory she'd never found the use for. Certainly fans were pretty and could help cool you after a dance. Perhaps send a message to a gentleman if you wished. But none of those things was enticement enough for Theo to carry one. Which was surprising because she did adore mysterious secrets and clandestine conversations.

Tonight, however, she'd taken her mother's advice. If nothing else, the fan she carried served to hide the look of dislike on her face while watching Blythe dance with some dull blonde girl whose eyes bulged slightly, like that of a bullfrog. At least from what Theo could see.

The fan waved away such unkind thoughts. The atmosphere swirling about Lady Molsin's drawing room, combined with the presence of Haven, brought out the very worst in Theo. And squinting at everyone made her temples ache.

Lady Molsin, bless her, had assembled a guest list for this evening's event designed to demonstrate that the *Ruination of Theodosia Barrington* was nothing more than idle gossip on the part of Lady Blythe. To that end, Blythe and his mother, along with Lady Emerson and her daughter, were in attendance, a challenge of sorts from Lady Molsin, daring them to refute the declaration that Haven and Theo's impending nuptials had come about naturally.

Even without her spectacles, Theo could see Miss Emerson, shimmering like a desolate goddess, cast glances of longing in Haven's direction before turning to look down her nose at Theo.

Theo fluttered her fan in Miss Emerson's direction. She'd trade places with the girl in an instant if she could.

Haven, appearing far more elegant than Theo could have imagined in his evening wear, seemed oblivious to Miss Emerson mooning over him. The candlelight brought out the copper highlights lingering in the earthy loam of his poorly cut hair as he stood speaking to Estwood. The need for a proper shave and a decent haircut in no way diminished Haven's attractiveness. If anything, the slightly rumpled look gave him a rakish appeal. A wolf in sheep's clothing perhaps, a highwayman who dressed in finery merely so he could circulate among society. Before he robbed them all blind.

The tips of her fingers warmed.

She still wanted to paint him, more desperately now than she had that day in the park. Tonight, however, that urge was mixed with the unexpected desire to be close to him, inhaling the spicy scent she knew hovered about his broad shoulders.

Dammit.

Resisting such unwelcome thoughts, Theo turned away from her future husband, reminding herself that regardless of the ridiculous tale Cousin Winnie, Lady Molsin, and Theo's mother sprouted about the room, marriage to Haven was nothing more than a way to salvage her own reputation. The entire party was an exercise in futility.

Absolutely no one in attendance this evening believed the

match with Haven had come about after seeing each other again at Blythe's party, not when the memory of her pursuit of Blythe was fresh in everyone's mind. And Lady Blythe had *not* been silent. Her eyes, sunken into her plump features, alighted on Theo far more often than they should, each glance followed by a swat of her fan and a whisper to whoever stood near her. Which was usually Lady Foxwood and her daughter Beatrice.

Lord, why are they here?

The Foxwoods, Theo learned, had not been officially invited. They'd arrived with the Emersons, and Lady Molsin couldn't very well have them thrown out. Or at the very least, she was too polite to have done so. Maybe Lady Foxwood, still having not recovered from her daughter losing the Duke of Granby to Romy, was taking pointers from Lady Blythe on how to disparage a Barrington.

Miss Emerson, Lady Foxwood, and Beatrice were already clustered together, whispering and bemoaning the fact that yet another Barrington had stolen a young lady's anticipated bridegroom. Theo and the rest of her family should count themselves lucky that Miss Emerson and Beatrice hadn't yet joined forces to storm the Averell mansion with pitchforks. Lady Blythe would lead the charge, brandishing her fan instead of a saber.

Theo pressed a hand to her mouth. It wouldn't do to erupt in giggles for no apparent reason. Most everyone here already assumed her to be frivolous, and there was no reason to prove them right. She turned her attention back to Blythe, marveling at the way he danced with such agile, confident grace. He held the unappealing girl in his arms as if she were something rare and precious to him. Leaning in, he whispered, and the girl's cheeks pinked.

Blythe had looked at Miss Cummings in exactly the same way when he'd danced with her earlier. And Lady Meredith.

And me.

Ice cold water splashed over her. A bucket of it. Lest Theo should begin to believe, even for a moment, she'd been anyone special to Blythe. She hadn't been. The knowledge didn't make him any less attractive. He still shone like a golden beacon, only not quite as brightly as he once had.

"Now this," a dark rasp curled around her ear, "isn't nearly as terrible as I'd anticipated."

Theo's toes curled inside her slippers at the sound of him. She couldn't help it. There weren't many things to appreciate about Haven, but his voice was one of them. A low, raspy tenor which never failed to fall over her in a most delicious manner.

"No." Theo glanced over her shoulder, annoyed he'd interrupted her admiration of Blythe along with her unwelcome musings. "It is far worse."

"I thought Phaedra was the dramatic one in the family." His voice was deliciously rough.

Theo gave him a forced smile, her gaze floating over the tiny scar on his chin. "You've no idea how I feel, my lord. *You* aren't being looked at as if you are a rotten apple in an otherwise perfect bowl of fruit."

Haven's lips twitched as he clearly tried to contain the amusement he doubtless felt at her predicament. The motion drew her attention to his mouth.

"I doubt you can actually *see* any disapproval sent your way. And I think of you as more of a bruised peach."

A peach? Theo envisioned herself as something much hardier, with thicker skin. If not an apple, then a pear. "Your sarcasm, my lord, is duly noted. Now just leave." She waved her fingers to shoo him away. "Miss Emerson is staring at me as if she wishes to stab me with her fan. I hope Lady Molsin doesn't have a letter opener within easy reach."

"You won't be able to see her coming, in any case," he

murmured, his breath rustling softly over her shoulder. "That should be a comfort."

"Very amusing. Go away."

Haven made her light-headed. Muddled. In the way that glass of scotch she'd snuck from her brother's drawing room had made her feel.

"I came over," the low growl rolled over her skin, "to suggest you stop staring at Blythe as if he were a newly discovered color of paint."

She pressed her lips firmly together.

"It will go a long way toward ending the gossip swirling about your pretty skirts if you'd stop swooning over him."

"Be careful, Haven. Your envy is showing. Blythe draws the eye. He's a fine dancer, though his partner most definitely is not. Perhaps I'm only concerned she'll tread on his feet."

"You should dance with me."

"I don't care to dance." Haven from across the drawing room was attractively fuzzy; this close, he was all spice and blindingly handsome male. She preferred him on the other side of the room where he was reduced to only a mildly appealing blur.

Her spine warmed as he stepped closer, the heat of his larger body gently cupping her buttocks before wrapping around her mid-section.

"A shame. I'm quite a good dancer, as it happens."

"Yes, but as I've mentioned before," she said stiffly, "*you are not Blythe.*" Most definitely not. Blythe had never affected Theo in such a way.

Spinning on her heel, she turned her back, running away from him like a coward, cursing the traitorous nature of her body. She had no intention of losing herself in Haven or babbling like an idiot when he came near. There had been quite enough of such behavior with Blythe.

Storming away from the party, Theo wanted only a

moment to collect her thoughts, free of pitying looks and her future husband. Her skirts whipped around her ankles in agitation.

A hand gripped her elbow, halting her progress. "Theodosia."

"Let me go," she hissed back at him, noting the curious glances of two of Lady Molsin's servants who hovered nearby. "Go back. Everyone saw you come after me. There will be talk and there's plenty enough already. Perhaps you enjoy the attention, but I do not."

"I don't care," Haven snapped back. "Stop running away."

"If only I *could* run away. Far from those gossips flapping their fans at me. Far from *you*."

"Theo . . ." His tone gentled, his thumb rubbing softly over the hollow of her arm.

The sound of her nickname on his lips caused her insides to twist about pleasurably. She didn't want that. Didn't want him to make her feel such a thing. "Can you not allow me to mend my broken heart in peace, Haven? I am *despondent*."

The scar jumped a bit as his lips formed a grimace. "I don't care for female histrionics, Theodosia. Nor childish temper tantrums. I've not the patience for either."

"Histrionics?" Her voice raised an octave. How *dare* he. "Under the circumstances, I think I have every right to be miserable. You can hardly expect me to be cheerful as I face the unending bleakness of my future."

"Stop making it sound as if you are facing the guillotine." Haven gave her arm a tug, leading her further down the hall. Throwing open a door, he pulled her inside, ignoring her attempts to wrench her arm free. It was pitch black inside, not a lamp or fire lit.

"This is wonderful, Haven," she hissed. "The entire party will assume you've dragged me in here to take liberties with me. I suppose it doesn't matter. How much more can my reputation be tarnished?

"You need to calm yourself, Theo. Do not return to the drawing room in this state, one *you've* worked yourself into."

Theo huffed. "I had help."

"I have no desire," his voice roughened, "for you to become a spectacle for the London gossips to delight in. Do you wish for Lady Blythe to step up her efforts? Toss more conjecture and rumor at your feet?"

"Concerned my behavior may reflect badly on you? You need not worry. Your reputation is beyond salvaging," she shot back.

"No." Haven drew a ragged breath. "Because I can't bear to watch you be hurt any further."

The weight of his words pressed against her chest. "Stop pretending to care about me." Her voice caught. "And why must you smell like gingerbread? It's unsettling and—"

Haven's mouth brushed tenderly against hers, cutting off the rest of her useless tirade. Theo tasted apology on his lips. A hint of wine. And a great deal of wickedness. Her outrage, as justified as she felt it was, drifted away into nothingness at the press of his lips.

Oh, I remember this.

A blinding burst of pleasure jolting from where their mouths joined slid down her skin before wrapping tightly between her thighs. Her hands skimmed up his chest, fingertips attuned to the warmth and strength lying beneath his evening clothes.

"Do you like gingerbread, Theodosia?" he whispered against her mouth before his thumb roved over Theo's plump lower lip, grazing lightly over her teeth.

She nipped at the pad of his thumb, hearing the small, surprised hitch of his breath at her action.

"Yes."

Ambrose had to stop himself from tossing up Theodosia's skirts and taking her roughly against the wall of Lady Molsin's parlor. Which was certain to make the gossip surrounding them that much worse. But he *rarely* had a waking thought lately that *didn't* involve bedding her. His desire for Theodosia burned as fierce as the sun, blotting out everything *but* her, managing to shadow even his joy at finally taking his pound of flesh from Murphy. Even the thought that she'd probably already given herself to Blythe or possibly someone else didn't ease his hunger for her.

His thoughts flew to the miniature tucked safely in his pocket.

I would forgive her anything.

Ambrose broke away from her lips, jealousy and the tangle of complicated feelings he had for Theodosia spiraling out like a vine along his chest and limbs. He refused to admit to anything beyond liking her and plain lust.

Theodosia was a desirable means to a desired end.

But it was a lie, and Ambrose knew it. It became more obvious every day.

"Haven?"

"Ambrose," he said quietly, gently uncurling her fingers from his coat. "My Christian name. I would like you to use it." He struggled under the weight of his growing attachment to this lovely creature because she *meant* something to him, and she had from the second he'd seen her.

And then he'd set out to use her. It did not matter that he hadn't planned what happened at Blythe's; his heart had been filled with the intent.

"You should return." He gently pulled her fingers from his coat, afraid if they stayed here a moment longer, he would compromise her again, this time completely. Either that or he would confess everything.

"Yes," she choked, voice filled with embarrassment at what she likely perceived as his rejection.

It pained Ambrose to have her think such a thing, but still, he let Theodosia slide away from him. He needed to think—impossible with Theodosia so near.

"I'll join you shortly," he said, the words dismissive and far colder than he'd intended. He could practically hear the stiffening of her spine as he imagined her chin tilting mulishly in his direction. Theodosia and her sisters all possessed the same fire of defiance, the assertion that no one should dictate to them. Ambrose spared a tiny bit of pity for the Duke of Averell managing a household of such opinionated, forthright women.

"Ambrose."

His heart thumped hard. Must she say his name . . . with such promise?

"Go." Ambrose nudged her in the direction of the door.

He stayed silent until a sliver of light broke through the darkness of the parlor as she opened the door to the hall outside. The rustle of skirts met his ears before the door shut again and Theodosia was gone.

11

Theo stared out her studio window at the Averell residence, watching the stream of carriages roll through the park. Life moved on, oblivious to the one Barrington daughter whose future had been decided largely by those enjoying the day. The Duke of Averell and his family were once again mired in scandal while all of London stood by watching gleefully.

At least Theo's disgrace had provided everyone a decent amount of entertainment.

The evening at Lady Molsin's had been a trial for Theo. Polite congratulations had flowed her way, followed by the snap of a fan and small sounds of whispered amusement at her predicament. Cousin Winnie had spent most of the evening red-faced. Lady Molsin, deploying the chilliness of her nephew, had stood with Theo's mother, daring *anyone* to voice their opinions aloud. None dared, of course. Eccentric and slightly tarnished though the Barringtons were, Theo's brother was still a duke.

The only highlight of the evening—a soft flutter pressed across her chest— had been when Haven had dragged her into a dark room and proceeded to kiss her senseless. She'd never believed a woman could be kissed to the point that her mind became a tangled mess of nothing. Until now.

Theo drummed her fingers against her thigh in consternation.

Once Haven had dismissed Theo, forcing her return to Lady Molsin's drawing room, Theo had had the sense to stop before a mirror decorating one wall. Her eyes had been heavy-lidded. Her lips swollen. A light flush dusted her cheeks. Everyone at Lady Molsin's little party already assumed the worst about Theo. Their opinions would be cemented by her 'kissed senseless' appearance once she returned to the drawing room.

Theo had smiled back at her reflection in that mirror.

She was the daughter of the bloody Duke of Averell. A Barrington. Theo had *no* intention of allowing a bunch of old biddies, of which Lady Blythe was the worst offender, to make her feel less than who she was.

Let them talk.

She had returned to her mother's side, held her chin up at a defiant angle, and ignored the whispers about her. She would have avoided her future husband for the remainder of the evening, except Haven had never returned to the party, abandoning her to the wolves, so to speak. Theo had refused to glance in Blythe's direction again. It was time for her to consider the future.

She brushed the edge of her chin with the tip of her paintbrush.

The feelings Haven inspired in Theo were not welcome. Losing the upper hand at the critical beginning of their marriage would be a disaster. She couldn't afford to, not until they'd reached some sort of understanding. Yes, Haven might find her appealing. After all, he'd kissed her twice, but—there was no *real* affection between them.

But might there be?

Theo shook her head, not wishing to consider something more than a marriage of convenience only to be disappointed later. She wasn't a good judge of a man's intentions, given her experience with Blythe. She didn't trust the attraction between her and Haven. Or her own instincts. Far better to set down some rules with Haven to protect her future self. The discussion was long overdue.

She exhaled, watching as her breath fogged the glass of the window. Of course, it was impossible to have such a discussion before the wedding if Haven continued to ignore her. Since Lady Molsin's ill-fated gathering, Theo's future husband hadn't called. Not once. Which only added more fuel to her decision to reach an understanding with him. Society was littered with the deflated hearts of young ladies who'd found themselves in the same situation, mistaking that what their husbands desired most was them and not just their dowry. It would be easy to confuse physical attraction with affection, especially where Haven was concerned. Theo did not mean to be one of those young ladies. When Haven wandered off to his slew of mistresses, Theo promised herself she'd barely notice.

Theo frowned, the brush pausing beneath her nose. How many was a slew exactly?

Giving a sigh of exasperation, she lowered her hand. What difference would it make? Haven could have a slew, or a herd, or an entire *flock* of courtesans for all she cared. What *was* important was that Theo kept their marriage from becoming anything other than what it was: an unfortunate accident. Although, she supposed from Haven's perspective, the incident in Blythe's study had been fortuitous. He would no longer be impoverished, for one thing.

All because of the miniature.

Theodosia's Great Folly.

She lived in terror that Haven, desperate for coin before he received her dowry, might have sold the miniature. What if it ended up in the collection of a respected member of Parliament, for instance? During a party at this hallowed personage's home, Theo would admire her host's paintings and other objects d'art, only to come across the miniature of her half-naked breasts.

She butted her head against the glass, cringing at the mere thought. What if Freddie, her nephew, should come across the miniature when he was older, recognizing Auntie Theo? How absolutely horrifying.

"Careful, you'll break the glass."

The scratchy tenor pricked against her skin as Theo turned to face him. Annoyance filled her, mainly because she'd convinced herself he'd done something terrible with the miniature, but there was something else. A weakening of her knees. A soft flutter inside her chest.

The late afternoon sun set fire to the glints in his hair as Haven moved closer, giving him the sheen of copper. He was dressed in a lovely coat the color of freshly tilled soil and fawn riding breeches. The coat looked new, but the rest of his ensemble had seen better days.

Haven moved gracefully toward her, easily sidestepping the heaps of canvas, rags, paint, and other bits littering the floor of her studio. His agile movements added to the impression of him as a tomcat, as he deftly missed stepping on the small rosewood box which held her paints.

"*Christ*, what a mess." There was no real rebuke in his words. The very edges of his mouth were tipped up at the corners, showing the gleam of even, white teeth.

Oh, how I want to paint him.

"How do you ever find anything in this mess given you are half-blind?"

"An excellent reason for you to leave, my lord. I wouldn't

want you to trip," she shot back. Theo wasn't, by nature, very organized. The clutter surrounding her was the bane of her maid, Betts, who spent most of her day cleaning up after her. More importantly, Theo had no desire to pick things up just to please Haven.

His smile broadened, sending a burst of warmth in Theo's direction, eyes lingering over her face where her hated spectacles, in all their metal and glass glory, sat on her nose.

"I realize you aren't good at subtle hints to leave, my lord. So, allow me to be blunt." She pointed at the door with her paintbrush. Theo really wasn't in the mood for Haven's dubious charm, not after suffering through the evening at Lady Molsin's and the delightful small items printed about her in the gossip columns since then. She wondered if he'd seen them.

She returned her attention to the park.

This morning's paper had contained a simply delightful item about Theo and provided all the proof she needed that Lady Molsin's efforts had been in vain. Among the reports of gowns and balls, there had been a mention of the reckless nature of Theodosia Barrington. A girl who had gotten exactly what she deserved after her brazen pursuit of Lord Blythe. Accompanying this thinly veiled attack on Theo's character had been a satirical drawing depicting Theo popping out from behind a potted fern to surprise Blythe, only to find herself faced with Haven. Piles of gold coins were falling from beneath Theo's skirts as Haven salivated.

The artist hadn't even been very good.

Silly. Frivolous. Reckless. Brazen. All things Theodosia had never thought would ever be said about her. It was humiliating and made Theo wish to stow away on the first ship to America and beg sanctuary from Leo, who was still in New York.

"I'm surprised Pith let you into the house," she said as he

took a spot near the window. "Or showed you up to my studio." Theo turned to face him. "He doesn't like you. Nor does my brother. I'm sure we'll be adding to the list as time goes on."

The late afternoon sun sifted through the russet waves of Haven's hair as he came closer. The color was like maple leaves in autumn that had fallen to cover the ground, tickling your ankles when you rushed through them. The urge to paint him became stronger. Her fingers twitched against the brush.

"Your butler is a menace. Phaedra let me in."

Theo considered her younger sister nothing short of traitorous. Phaedra had formed an attachment to Haven, informing the family over dinner just the other night that he had promised to practice fencing with her once she'd taken proper lessons. Not one to be put off the slightest that the daughter of a duke shouldn't be fencing, Phaedra had requested that Tony find a fencing instructor for her as soon as possible. And she was giving up the violin. A collective sigh of relief had flooded the table. Phaedra's playing of the violin tortured the ears. She'd started out well enough, but instead of improvement, her mastery of the instrument had gone in the other direction.

Theo supposed the Barringtons all owed Haven some thanks for his intervention.

"If she runs off to become a pirate, we will all blame you." Her reply was sharp. She was still thinking of that blasted drawing in the papers. Had Haven seen it? Maybe that was what had finally made him come to see her. Mutual embarrassment.

"You're *incredibly* hostile this afternoon," Haven said quietly. "More so than usual." He was standing several feet away from her, facing the view of the park, and made no move to come closer. "I should have called sooner."

"It is of no consequence, my lord. I'm hopeful our marriage will continue in much the same vein. Avoidance. If only you had ignored my miniature that night in Blythe's study, we could continue to be nothing more than passing acquaintances. Think of how lovely that would have been."

"We've never been just passing acquaintances," he said. "Not when I kissed you at Granby's house party. Not in Blythe's study. Certainly not now."

"Compromised by a marquess of questionable reputation. Had I known during that stupid house party what my future would be, I might have avoided you altogether. At the very least, when we played bowls, I might have tossed one at your head."

"Bloodthirsty." He watched her closely. "I agree on the impoverishment, Theodosia. You behave as if it is some great secret. And my reputation may yet survive marriage to you."

Theo could *feel* her nostrils flare. That had never happened to her before. "You would have taken *any* chance to compromise a girl you came across *if* her dowry was rich enough. I fell into your lap like a ripe plum." She pushed the hated spectacles further up her nose, wanting to rip them from her face.

"But not a spoiled one." The sides of his mouth lifted. "Is there a point to this conversation?"

"Does my humiliation amuse you?"

"Dramatic *and* hostile today."

Theo jerked back, irritated beyond belief. He behaved as if her life were all some great joke. "And you wonder why I prefer Blythe."

"Actually, I don't." His jaw hardened at the mention of Blythe.

Theo traced the line of his torso, her gaze moving over the broad chest to the worn leather of his riding breeches. The corded bands of muscle in his thighs were visible, rippling beneath the surface of the leather, leaving little to the imagination. And Theo's imagination was already quite vivid in regards to Haven. She took in his boots. Old. Scuffed. Worn. Somehow that only enhanced his appeal.

Her stomach made a soft flip, muddling her insides. Exactly what she wished to avoid.

Focus on your anger, Theo.

"If you are done assessing me—"

"I was not. Assessing you, that is. I've seen you more than enough, my lord."

Haven cocked his head and turned to her, the moss green of his eyes contrasting dramatically with the coat and russet hair. There was a roughness to Haven, a sense of something dark and barely contained, waiting to burst forth. Theo could feel it coiling around her.

"You are put out, Theodosia, because I haven't called upon you since Lady Molsin's."

"No." She shook her head. "I'm only dismayed by your arrival today."

"You don't like to feel as if you've been overlooked. Or ignored." The rumble of his words ran over Theo, melting into her bones. "I will take better care in the future."

Theo gripped her brush tighter. Haven, in addition to all his other unpleasant, unwelcome qualities, was far too intuitive. She had felt overlooked most of her life, a dull wren hiding amongst the more vibrant, colorful Barringtons.

"Perish the thought, my lord. Ignore me as often as you like. Ours is not a relationship born of affection but based on other values. Financial gain being the primary one. My not being treated like a leper for the remainder of my life being the other. As it happens, now seems a good time to speak of our future. It is long overdue. We should discuss the rules."

"Rules?" A brow lifted.

"Yes. I'm sure you'll agree due to the circumstances of our

marriage, it would be best if we keep things somewhat distant—"

"No," he stated flatly.

"You have no idea what I'm going to say," she countered. Theo had spent many hours since Lady Molsin's considering how best to proceed. It made sense for both of them. Haven was merely being difficult.

"I have a general idea of your ridiculous proposal, Theodosia, and my answer is definitely no." Haven came closer, filling the air around her with spice and leather.

"It isn't ridiculous." Theo pushed the spectacles further up her nose. "And I don't understand why you would object. We aren't suited at all. We consistently argue—"

"It is because you are so hostile, as I stated earlier."

"Regardless, I am willing to come to an understanding, my lord. You are a marquess, after all, and will require an heir. And I do adore children," she assured him. "Therefore, I am willing to do my duty with the agreement that once completed, we will have a more distant—"

"No."

She blinked at him, surprised again at his quick response. "Why on earth would you object? I'm sure you'll prefer the company of your mistress."

"I don't have a mistress."

"Yes, but now you'll be able to afford one." She ignored the soft wince of her heart thinking of Haven and his slew of mistresses. It renewed her resolve to keep their marriage distant. "And I said I would do my duty. We both know I won't enjoy it."

"It?"

She waved her hands about. "The marital bed. Concourse."

"Concourse?" Haven's lips twitched. "I think you might mean congress."

Theo thought of what she'd seen at Elysium during her lone visit there. "Concourse. Congress." She twirled the brush in the air. "What difference does it make? You know my affections lie elsewhere."

A low growl of warning came from him. "So you keep saying."

This was not going as Theo had planned. She'd assumed he would welcome such an understanding and failed to see why he would object. Their entire marriage was bound for disaster. Surely he knew that.

"I shall lie in your bed," she said with determination, hoping her next words would deter him and force him to see the value of what she proposed, "and contemplate the color of the ceiling. Possibly the design of the canopy above the bed."

"I don't have a canopy over my bed," he snarled.

"Fine. I will think of Blythe, while you," she waved the brush around trying not to blush at the mere thought of being naked with Haven, "get me with child."

"What a generous proposal. I want to make sure I understand. You will submit to me, detesting every moment you spend in my bed, to provide me an heir?"

"Yes." She refused to back down. "I think it a fair trade. You'll have my dowry, after all. And an heir. I'm willing to do my duty."

"Hmm." Haven's brow wrinkled in consideration.

It appeared she'd convinced him. He looked . . . contemplative.

"All I must do is wave goodbye once your *distasteful* duty is discharged?" His voice dropped to a deep, silky rumble. "Then you traipse all over London, stumbling into people and flicking paint about? Perhaps create a few more self-portraits?"

"Yes." Haven made it all sound very unappealing.

His eyes narrowed as he moved swiftly to within inches of her face before jerking abruptly away from her. Muttering to himself, Haven marched angrily in the direction of the door.

Theo held her breath. He was leaving. She could celebrate her victory in peace. Plan her future. At least, she assumed she'd won. Haven appeared to agree. It was difficult to be sure. The conversation had gone so much better when she'd imagined it in her head.

The door shut. The click of the lock met her ears.

Oh, dear.

"Can anyone hear you scream from up here?"

"I—" Good Lord. She'd forgotten about his temper.

"I thought not," he hissed, circling her the way Theseus often did a mouse before he struck out with one large paw to end its existence.

Theo's finger ran over the wooden end of her paintbrush. Blunt. Nothing sharp about it. As a weapon, the brush was completely useless. She watched his reflection in the window as he approached her from behind, inhaling sharply as a wall of muscled heat pressed firmly into her back.

"What are you doing?" she stuttered, alarmed at the way her skin began to hum at the contact of his body. Just as it always did.

"Proving a point." Haven breathed her in, ruffling the hair at the nape of her neck. "Did you know I could find you in the dark, Theodosia? Most young ladies don't smell of paint and lemons." It sounded almost like an insult except he was still nuzzling against her ear. "Miss Emerson smells of rosewater."

"I hope my scent acts as a repellent," she shot back, not caring to be reminded again he had preferred Miss Emerson.

"You are not so fortunate," he said, his breath fanning over her cheek. "I find it alluring. More tempting a scent than anything else I could imagine." A finger trailed along the slope of her neck before pausing at her shoulder where he drew a circle. "Much like your spectacles. All that glass and gold perched on your nose is very enticing."

Theo's skin warmed. Stirred. "There is no need to flatter me, my lord," she said, trying to ignore the large hand which now splayed possessively across her stomach. None of the gentlemen of her acquaintance found spectacles to be the least attractive. Haven was only toying with her. "Our marriage is already assured."

"As I've mentioned before, I do not flatter." He breathed against the back of her neck, the tip of his tongue alighting along the lobe of her ear, nibbling gently. "I haven't the patience. I prefer a more direct approach. Honesty."

Theo's pulse beat wildly. A soft throb started beneath his hand, flooding down the lower half of her body. "Doesn't it bother you that I am in love with another man?" She didn't sound the least believable, not even to her own ears.

"Shall I show you how wrong you are?" The fingers stretched across her mid-section inched down to lay between her thighs.

Theo inhaled sharply at the intimate touch but didn't pull away.

"What you mistake for love," he pressed a kiss to her cheek, "is no more than girlish infatuation."

Her heart bounced violently against her ribcage. Unable to stop herself, Theo twisted her hips back against Haven, hearing him groan at the pressure. This was why their marriage must be kept distant. This terribly wonderful torrent of physical responses which led her breasts to throb and ache, the echo of which she felt between her legs. Blythe inspired none of this. She tried to focus on him, picturing Blythe's face as he flirted with her and failed miserably. There was only Haven.

He gently turned her chin, nipping seductively at her

bottom lip. A lush, sensual kiss fell on Theo's mouth, a plea to surrender herself to him.

A whimper erupted from her throat. Her mouth moved in tandem with his, lips opening with little protest as his tongue swept between them. Haven's fingers slid further between her thighs, cupping her mound atop the layers of muslin she wore, pulling her roughly back against the hardness pulsing so deliberately at the curve of her backside.

Theo dropped her head against his chest with a soft moan, unable and unwilling to move away. The throbbing between her thighs intensified, rippling out across her limbs. Her hand moved down to lay on top of his, feeling the strength of his fingers as he caressed her. All her worries of their marriage, of the horrible gossip circulating about her, and, most of all, her fear, ebbed away under such a blatantly erotic onslaught.

His fingers moved deftly over her sex, the layers of her skirts only heightening the sensitivity as his mouth slanted over hers.

Theo wasn't even sure if she was breathing any longer. Thoughts slowed. Sounds became muted.

"This is why," he whispered against the corner of her mouth, "you will not find my bed to be a duty. Nor will you be thinking of Blythe or any other man." He pushed her more fully against the thick hardness pressing into her backside. "*Christ*," he rasped against her cheek, "can you not understand I wanted you the instant you spilled ratafia on me? Are you really so blind?"

Theo's eyes snapped open in surprise to the view of the park before her. "I didn't realize you saw my ruining your coat as flirtation." There was much Theo had failed to comprehend about Haven. Their relationship was not to be as simple as she'd first surmised, but more tangled. Today was a perfect example.

"We will *not* live apart." His teeth sank gently into the lobe of her ear. "And I intend on sharing a bed with you. Should you feel the need to take a lover, I suggest you dispense with it. I'm far better with swords and a pistol than I am often given credit for. That is my rebuttal to your ridiculous proposal."

Haven was *possessive*. Of her. That was more shocking than having him admit he wanted her.

Her fingers bit into her palms, the paintbrush she held nearly snapping in half. She felt half-dazed. Intoxicated. "I don't like you. At all," she whispered, knowing it wasn't true, and he knew it.

"So you've said."

Theo took a shaky breath. This conversation had taken a rather unexpected, *carnal* turn, one she hadn't prepared for. "My affections," she stuttered, the words which had become rote coming out in her confusion.

Haven jerked back, releasing her, temper no longer in check.

"Are you attempting to convince me or yourself, Theodosia? I will tell you the truth. Had I not taken that bloody miniature, you would still be throwing yourself at Blythe in a shameless manner while all of London laughed behind your back. While you, so blinded by his glory and your lack of spectacles, failed to ascertain his disinterest."

Theo looked down at her feet, hating how she'd spoiled the beauty of the last few moments with him. Knowing that no matter how ugly, his words were true. It was difficult enough to admit to one's failings without having someone so harshly remind you. The drawing she'd seen in the paper this morning flashed before her.

"Your point is well taken, my lord. I realize what a goose I made of myself. There is no need to berate me further. I'm quite capable of doing that without your help." She bit her lip. "If I should forget, I can always have my brother remind me. Or Romy, but now that she's in Italy—" Her words fell short.

A deep breath came from behind her. "Theo." His voice was horribly tender as Haven reached for her, one arm circling her waist to pull her close once more. "I don't wish to argue." His nose slid across her neck. "I see you finished it, the one you painted in the park." Haven hugged her tightly to his chest.

Theo looked over at the canvas leaning carelessly against the wall, distracted by Haven's scent and the warmth of his arms. He'd remembered what she'd been painting that day. It was rare to have anyone comment on her paintings or sketches until they were finished, let alone recall what she'd been working on and when.

"You'll see that I did not forget the geese," she said.

A delicious rumble sounded against her back. "Is that what those little white puffs are? You will give me credit for the color at the edges of the water. Had I not been there to offer my assistance, it's doubtful you would have gotten the pond scum correct."

A smile tugged at her lips though she tried to stop it. "Untrue."

"There's a nook at Greenbriar requiring art of that exact size." Haven pressed a kiss to her temple, a very tender gesture which spoke of intimacy and affection. The action comforted her as Theo was sure he meant it to.

Her heart stretched in Haven's direction before she cautiously pulled back. Theo didn't trust herself. Nor him, when it came down to it.

He held her a long while, but they didn't speak again, both lost in their own thoughts. After a time, with a chaste kiss to her cheek, Haven slipped away from her, his footsteps sounding on the floor.

Once the door shut, Theo turned to stare at it, unmoving, missing the sense of security she'd found unexpectedly in the circle of his arms. Part of her wished him back, the other half willed him to never return.

Still clasping the brush, she once more stroked her chin with the bristles, her agitation rapidly turning into panic. Theo hadn't been prepared for this rush of affection in his direction. The ache of her body to be close to his. The circumstances she'd found herself in this morning had shifted dramatically. It had been one thing to contemplate a distant marriage of convenience with Haven, quite another to imagine—well, whatever this was.

12

"May I interrupt?"

Theo looked up from the book in her lap, blinking at a splendid Earl of Blythe dressed in a coat of indigo. His waistcoat, shot through with silver and gold thread, was dazzling, as was the rest of him, so blindingly attractive it hurt to look at him. But the desperate adoration Theo had once held for him failed to rouse itself. No flirtatious, mildly improper comment came to her lips, no hope that he would respond with a laugh. Most importantly, her heart made no leap up inside her chest at the sight of him. She had seen Blythe at Lady Molsin's, of course, but they hadn't spoken, not since the night of *Theodosia's Great Folly*.

"My lord, what an unexpected surprise."

"Hopefully a pleasant one." The sunlight turned his hair to pure gold.

'I've desired you since you spilled ratafia on me.'

The words growled against her skin as she took in the gentleman before her, repeating so loudly, Theo barely heard Blythe's charming response. How was she to know, Theo wished to rail at Haven, that all the teasing and innuendo he'd subjected her to at the house party had been meant to gain her attention? Haven had told Theo he didn't flirt, but he *did*, just not the same way a gentleman like Blythe might.

And I missed all of it.

"Of course, my lord." Theo glanced down at the book in her lap, shut it, and quickly pushed it beneath her skirts. Theo was reading *Lord Thurston's Revenge*, a novel best suited to twittering girls who wished to be kidnapped by pirates, and she'd no desire to have Blythe think her more of a nitwit than he already must. Besides, the enjoyment of the book had been dampened by the annoyance of an image of Haven invading her thoughts whenever Lord Thurston graced the page.

"I wished to call on you before the wedding. I understand it's tomorrow." Blythe nodded at the spot next to her on the bench. "May I sit?"

"Yes, my lord." Theo scooted over to make room for him. She'd come to the garden to read in peace and to escape Phaedra, who was running about the house with a stick clutched in one hand pretending to sword fight. And to contemplate her future.

She glanced at Blythe from beneath her lashes. A part of her wished she'd brought her spectacles into the garden, but Theo could read quite well without them. What would Blythe think to see Theo with her spectacles?

Haven didn't seem bothered in the least by them. He'd kissed Theo, possessively cupping her sex as they stood in the studio, all with the hated metal frames fixed firmly on her face. The entire episode, the feel of his fingers searching for her through the material of her skirts, left her unable to think clearly.

She pressed her thighs together. Now was not the time to

indulge herself with such thoughts. Not with Blythe looking at her strangely.

"You are well, Lady Theodosia?" There was concern in Blythe's eyes as he settled himself beside her. He turned his chin to take in the garden before facing her again, the close-cropped waves of his hair buffeting in the breeze.

"Yes, thank you." Theo *was* well. Or as well as she could be as London's latest scandal, being forced to marry a destitute marquess who had inadvertently ruined her. But aside from her impending marriage, Theo felt more like herself than she had in some time. There was also a huge sense of relief that Blythe had never seen the miniature.

Haven had saved her from that, at least.

"I've known Haven for some time, my lady."

"I'm aware, my lord."

"Well, then you must know we argue frequently, mostly because I cannot stop poking the bear." A dazzling smile crossed his features. "Haven is the bear."

Still not so much as a flicker of Theo's pulse. And she'd never had the urge to paint Blythe. "I gathered that."

"May I be blunt?"

"By all means."

"Haven is very sensitive about his . . . situation."

As well he should be. The late Marquess of Haven had not been well thought of before his death, according to gossip. Lots of gambling. Drinking. Women. "I'm aware, my lord."

"He feels responsible for what happened, though none of it was his fault. Nor what happened to his sister." Blythe looked at her for understanding. "Has he mentioned the uncle living with him at Greenbriar?"

"He's a drunk," Theo replied, wondering what accident had befallen Haven's sister. He'd only mentioned her being ill, nothing more.

Blythe nodded. "Haven is intensely private, even with those closest to him. Believe it or not, I didn't even know he had an uncle until recently. He rarely speaks of his sister. Never of the late marquess." A wrinkle creased his brow. "Won't ask for assistance. His pride won't allow it, I suspect." Blythe hesitated, probably assuming he'd said more than he should. "I wanted you to know, we spoke of Miss Emerson several times before your encounter with him in my study."

Was knowing Haven spoke to Blythe about the possibility of courting Miss Emerson meant to make Theo feel better? Because it did not. Her feelings for Haven were tangled enough without feeling second best to Viscount Emerson's perfect daughter.

Blythe gently took her hand. "You were doubtless in the study because of me. You were meaning to present the gift you'd brought for my birthday, weren't you?"

Entirely true. "Yes, my lord." Theo waited for Blythe to ask her about the gift, perhaps show some interest in what she'd planned to give him.

"It is my fault you were there," he said in a distressed tone. "I'm so—"

"You are not to blame, my lord." Theo interrupted the start of Blythe's speech. So, *this* was truly why Blythe was here. Not to reassure her that his friend wasn't an utter cad. Or to ask after her health. But to relieve his own guilt over the entire affair.

"I am sincere, my lord. I absolve you," she said, meaning the words.

Blythe nodded, relieved. "Haven is a good man. Once you get past all the anger. He is easy to rile, especially when insulted about his circumstances."

Or when taunted with Theo's affection for Blythe, which was steadily waning.

"My lord, may I ask you something?" Though she knew

what Blythe's response would be, and it would change nothing, Theo needed to hear the truth from him. If nothing else, it would help her move forward, as she needed to.

"We are friends, Theodosia. At least I hope we are." He smiled down at her.

How often had she dreamt of ways to get him to smile at her? Counted the number of times when he did? "We are friends, my lord."

"Then ask away."

Theo plucked at her skirts, choosing her words carefully. "If I were not compelled to marry Haven, if I hadn't been compromised, would you have asked to court me properly? Offered for me someday?"

Once the words left her mouth, Theo looked out into the gardens, focusing on a rosebush with its cluster of pink blooms. A child's laughter floated in the air, probably coming from the park. She thought about the day she'd spied Blythe from her studio flying a kite with his nephew. How she'd rushed down the stairs demanding Phaedra and Olivia immediately grab their shawls and follow her through the garden gate. What had she been doing before Blythe had distracted her?

I'd been looking at the sketch of my father and couldn't bear to do so a moment longer.

Theo hadn't seen Blythe for a year or so when he'd appeared in the park outside her studio windows. She'd thrown off her spectacles, determined to seek him out and capture his attention. The sketch of her father, one of many she'd done, had been placed back in a portfolio to be tucked away on a distant shelf in her studio.

The portfolio was still there, collecting dust across the top. She couldn't bear to look at it.

"Please do not spare my feelings." Theo turned back to

Blythe. "I value your honesty. As I said. We are friends, regardless. And always will be."

Blythe stayed silent a long time. *Too* long. He stood, taking her hand, and bowed. His lips brushed against Theo's knuckles.

Not so much as a tingle ran through her.

"I hold you in the highest esteem, Theodosia. I enjoy your company. But I would not have offered for you."

She waited for a rush of pain to follow his pronouncement, but all she felt was a slight shadow across her heart, the memory of a dream she'd once had.

"Thank you, my lord."

Blythe was so lovely with his golden perfection set against the palette of the garden, like one of her mother's Grecian statues come to life. But the sight no longer left her in awe. For the first time since meeting Blythe, Theo considered another, more imperfect face. One just as handsome, but also possessing flaws. Like a nose not perfectly straight. A terrible haircut. A tiny scar on the chin.

Blythe squeezed Theo's fingers before releasing her hand. "Good day, Lady Theodosia. I wish you every happiness."

"Good day, Lord Blythe."

How reckless she'd been to have thought to gift him a half-naked miniature of herself along with her heart. Blythe wouldn't have wanted either. Theo didn't pick her book back up as Blythe left the garden. Instead, she closed her eyes and listened to the wind stirring the flowers around her and the sounds coming from the park.

'I've wanted you since you spilled ratafia on me.'

Envy over Blythe had likely played a part in Haven taking the miniature, but Theo no longer thought that the sole reason he'd done so.

A bit of dandelion fluff floated past her eyes.

Theo still wasn't happy about her circumstances. The

future, her future with Haven, was a large gaping maw of uncertainty. She admitted to no one how frightened she was. Nor did she wish to give much weight to her developing feelings for Haven.

But for the first time since *Theodosia's Great Folly*, she was hopeful.

13

A wedding was meant to be a happy occasion. A smiling bride. Gracious family, thrilled to be united. Friends offering well wishes and congratulations. A carriage bedecked with ribbons and flowers to carry the couple as they waved to well-wishers.

At the very least, a wedding should not possess the atmosphere of a funeral.

Ambrose's wedding to Theodosia Barrington was very much the latter.

Averell and his duchess, a small, delicate woman who seemed far too intelligent to have married the duke, watched Ambrose warily, as if Ambrose were about to make off with the silver as well as Theodosia. Even the duke's son, Lord Welles, a plump child held in his mother's arms, let out a wail when he caught sight of Ambrose.

If Theodosia ever deigned to appear, she might well do the same.

The Dowager Duchess of Averell, looking like an enraged fairy queen in her pewter silk, tiny diamonds dangling from her ears, greeted Ambrose as politely as could be expected under the circumstances. Her acceptance of Ambrose had dimmed significantly since the evening at Lady Molsin's when he'd absconded, no matter how briefly, into a parlor with her daughter, then promptly disappeared.

Lady Richardson, thankfully, was not in attendance today. Theodosia's cousin, despite her outward show of support, didn't care for Ambrose. In Lady Richardson's defense, she hadn't liked him before he'd compromised Theodosia.

The Barringtons' ward, Miss Olivia Nelson, allowed him to take her limp hand in greeting, a delicate sniff her ladylike dismissal. Miss Nelson was the granddaughter of the Earl of Daring. Her status as the ward of the dowager duchess puzzled Ambrose. Daring was still very much alive. One would think he'd wish his granddaughter to live with him.

Ambrose supposed he'd learn why she didn't eventually.

Only Phaedra, Theo's audacious younger sister, seemed at all happy to see Ambrose. Plying him with questions on swords and dueling pistols the moment he arrived, Phaedra ignored the pointed look the duke sent her to cease. Either Phaedra was truly interested in weaponry, an odd habit for a young lady, or several members of Theodosia's family were planning on murdering him. Or possibly the duke's butler.

Ambrose shot a glance at the stoic Pith, hovering just outside the drawing room.

He'd worried over the last few days that Leo Murphy would somehow appear, rather dramatically, just as the vicar started the ceremony. But as the morning dragged on, the idea became more unlikely, even though Ambrose was sure the duke had written to Murphy of their sister's impending marriage. Perhaps Murphy was even now on his way back to London and simply wouldn't get here in time. More likely, he didn't remember beggaring the Marquess of Haven or even

Ambrose and his threats. The Collingwood family was a mere footnote in Murphy's life. Not worth recalling.

Insulted or relieved? Ambrose wasn't sure how he should feel.

'My father would never have signed away my sister's dowry for a game of dice and a whore.'

'And yet, he did.'

Once, he'd relished the thought of relaying the news to Murphy that he'd married Theodosia. Taken her and her dowry. Repayment for what Elysium had taken from the Marquess of Haven. *How does it feel*, Ambrose would sneer to Murphy, *to know she's been taken advantage of as my father was?*

Ambrose's heart, the organ least consulted in any of his machinations, squeezed tightly for an instant. Except, he hadn't been able to make himself ruin Theodosia. The night in Blythe's study *had* been an accident.

Somehow, Ambrose didn't think Theodosia would agree. Especially not if her brother remembered the threats Ambrose had hurled at him. She would recall how he'd taken the miniature instead of giving it back and assume he'd done so to keep her in the study. Remember how he'd nearly kissed her. Theodosia would assume the worst. And she would be right.

Christ.

Theodosia *mattered* to him. His mistake had been in thinking he could pretend she did not.

A sound rustled through the group of Barringtons, drawing Ambrose out of his thoughts.

Theodosia was making her way down the massive double staircase of the duke's home clothed in a spectacular gown of ice-blue silk. Brilliants and pearls peeked through the dark coils of her hair.

Ambrose frowned as he looked up at her. Theodosia's

complexion, usually a delightful peach color, because much like her sister she rarely used a parasol, was dreadfully pale. Almost sickly. Most alarmingly, there were no spectacles sitting atop her pert little nose.

Theodosia, at the sight of Ambrose, or at least the blurry outline of him, immediately tilted her chin at a mutinous angle, a clear signal she'd defiantly and intentionally decided *not* to wear her spectacles.

He should never have declared he found them appealing.

Ambrose spent the next few minutes in terror, holding his breath until Theodosia safely reached his side. He'd had visions of her tripping down the stairs because she couldn't see and breaking her beautiful neck. As she neared him, his eyes lingered over the slope of her shoulder, a fascinating expanse of skin he couldn't wait to touch again.

She took his arm, refusing to look directly at him. "Lead me to my doom, my lord."

Gorgeous, hostile little thing.

"As you wish, Theodosia," he answered solemnly.

Ambrose forced himself to focus on Theodosia's magnificent bosom and not the fact that his bride would eventually despise him one day, for his intent if not his actions.

As the vicar began to intone the words uniting him to Theodosia, the soft fragrance of lemons tinged with the aroma of paint met his nostrils. There was a tiny spot of blue right beneath her ear as if she'd been dabbing at a canvas in her studio before coming down. The freckles trailing up to her collarbone beckoned Ambrose to draw his tongue over them. He meant to nibble at each one.

Theodosia bit out her vows, making every word sound as if it was a piece of glass wedged in her mouth, antagonistic to the very end. He could hardly blame her, despite how their conversation in her studio had ended. Frustration had led him to lash out at her, his ego wounded that she still chose to voice her affection for Blythe. She had been surprised by his confession of wanting her nearly from the second he saw her—something that had little to do with Elysium and his relationship with Leo Murphy.

At the vicar's command, Ambrose brushed his lips against hers in a chaste kiss, sealing their vows. There was no clapping from the Barringtons or congratulations, only a collective sigh of resignation. His new wife didn't so much as glance in his direction as they made their way to the dining room, where an assortment of delicious aromas assaulted his nose. Ambrose had an immense appetite for many things. Food. Security.

Theodosia.

As he helped Theodosia to her seat, Ambrose had an epiphany, one so disturbing it threatened to ruin his enjoyment of the meal they were about to partake of. Perhaps he'd only buried it away inside him until now.

If the choice had come down to vengeance and money on one hand and Theodosia on the other, Ambrose wouldn't even deliberate.

He suspected he would have chosen Theodosia.

❧

"I WAS TERRIFIED YOU'D FALL TO YOUR DEATH ON THE stairs, Theodosia. Or worse, mistake the vicar for me and fondle him."

Theo regarded Haven over her shoulder as she settled in her chair. Not even their wedding day could remain free of his annoying comments. "There is not even a minor possibility of me ever mistaking you for someone else again, my lord. And I have never," she lowered her voice, "fondled you."

A light, humming sound came from him. "I would disagree."

Truth be told, Theo greatly preferred teasing Haven to the seductive gentleman who'd kissed her senseless in her studio. The day was already troubling enough with the wedding and the awkwardness of the meal they were about to share, she didn't need to consider the more physical aspect of their relationship over her meal.

Haven settled next to Theo, the thick waves of his hair falling in a shaggy mess around the rough planes of his face. He was in desperate need of a proper haircut, not one that looked to have been done with sheep shears. Not that she knew what sheep shears looked like. Or had even seen them in use. Phaedra probably did. It seemed like something her sister would know about.

Ill-cut hair, once broken nose aside, Haven's appeal was still apparent. He cut quite a figure in his wedding finery, the coat tailored perfectly to his lean, muscular proportions. Theo turned her attention back to her plate to avoid looking at his thighs and length of leg.

Big hands sliding across her stomach, possessively cupping her between her thighs.

She squeezed her legs together. It did little good to remind herself that hers was a marriage of convenience. That Haven was forced to wed her because she'd been compromised, and he was honorable.

Somewhat honorable.

He hadn't courted her. Not that Theo would have allowed him to, but that wasn't the point. Nor had there been a romantic proposal with flowers and Haven on bended knee before her. His sights had been set on another girl and her dowry.

The thought steadied her. Helped her put things in perspective. The last thing she wanted to do was become starry-eyed over her marriage. Or Haven. Yes, he'd admitted to desiring her—

Another throb between her thighs.

—but the fact remained, Theo was now married to a man she barely knew and was about to leave the protection of her family for the first time in her life. Whatever lustful feelings he'd inspired in her previously—and there were a great many —paled when compared to her mounting panic. Ridiculous, to be sure. Now would be an excellent time to display some bravery.

The dining room grew silent except for the sound of cutlery and the movement of the servants. No one seemed inclined to engage in conversation.

"Must you," she finally whispered at Haven who was waving over a footman to refill his plate for the second time, "enjoy your food so?"

"Yes. I must." The mossy eyes flitted to her. "I appreciate a delicious meal, which this is. You've no reason to be cross, Theodosia. It isn't my fault you can't see what you're eating."

Theo gripped her fork. Surely no one in her family would make the slightest objection if she stabbed Haven. She'd probably receive applause.

She took in her brother at the end of the table. Tony was watching Haven with bored dislike, his fingers drumming at the edge of his plate. The remainder of her family regarded Haven in mute horror as her husband demolished another mound of food on his plate.

Theo shot a discreet glance at Pith, the stone-faced butler who had been a fixture for the entirety of Theo's life. Desperately attempting to hide his utter revulsion at Haven, Pith kept glancing at Tony from the corner of his eye, silently pleading, Theo imagined, for the duke to issue a command to have Haven tossed from the Averell residence. For all Pith cared, Granby and Haven could both disappear, and they'd all be better for it.

"Those are mushrooms." Haven pointed discreetly with the knife in his hand. "And that is poached chicken."

Phaedra giggled on the other side of Theo, amused at Haven's teasing.

Haven winked at Phaedra before returning to his food.

Theo gave her sister a murderous look, toying with the small pile of mushrooms on her plate. She didn't care for mushrooms on principle, finding them slimy and unappetizing. That she'd accepted them to be put on her plate told Theo how distressed she was. "I can see my food perfectly well, my lord. I'm not blind."

"You aren't wearing your spectacles. I'm trying to be helpful."

Another snort from Phaedra. Theo kicked her under the table.

"Well, you aren't." Theo's show of bravery faltered as she pushed the mushroom around her plate. She longed for her father in that moment, wishing for his advice on how best to handle a marriage which had been forced upon her. One in which there was no affection between husband and wife, only a mild bit of attraction.

Oh, very well. There's a great deal of attraction.

But Papa was the only one who might understand. He hadn't loved his first wife, Tony's mother.

Yes, and remember how that turned out.

Papa's first marriage had ended in disaster, which had resulted in estrangement from both his sons. As a result of that experience, her father had decreed that none of his daughters, or Olivia, would ever marry against her will. They were not to be traded for titles and status, of which the Barringtons had plenty without having to wed more.

Theo tried to swallow a sip of tea, but the cup shook in

her hand, and she hastily pressed her napkin to her lips. Apparently, Papa hadn't made a provision for ruination. Or stupidity, as Tony had reminded her not so long ago.

Directly after this agonizing breakfast, Theo would change into her traveling clothes and be escorted out of the Averell mansion and into one of her brother's coaches, which he was generously lending to Haven, for the journey to Greenbriar, Haven's country estate. The contents of her studio, her paints and pencils, sketchbooks and the like, had been sent ahead yesterday, along with Theo's wardrobe and her maid, Betts.

Thank God I'll have Betts with me.

The journey, according to Haven, would take the remainder of the day. They wouldn't arrive at Greenbriar until well into the evening. But as Theo watched the sun rise ever higher in the sky while her husband managed another plate of food, she found it impossible they would reach Greenbriar today. They would be leaving London far later than originally anticipated because her new husband *refused* to stop eating. Which meant a wedding night at an inn somewhere.

Her fork wobbled in her hand.

She would be *alone* with Haven. Not even the company of Betts to calm her nerves.

Mama shot her a concerned look over her own barely touched plate.

Theo gave her a weak smile. "I'm not very hungry," she explained, trying not to burst into tears which would only add to her disgrace. She had meant to meet her fate with all the defiance and courage she possessed, as befitted the daughter of the Duke of Averell. But she was failing miserably.

Her fork finally slipped from her fingers and clattered against her plate.

Fingers, warm and strong, skimmed up the length of her thigh before taking her hand. Haven's gentle touch warmed her even though he was the cause of her distress. He laced their fingers together beneath the table, dispelling some of the chill from her hands. He didn't look up from his plate.

"At the top of your plate, there is a bit of pickled beet. Try a bite." His voice was soft. Cajoling. "I can't guarantee I won't eat everything in the basket I'm sure your overbearing butler will send with us. You could faint from starvation, and I'm in no mood to carry you out of the carriage. You look heavy."

"I've never fainted in my life," she snapped back as her fingers tightened over his, appreciating his attempt to calm her fears. He was good at that, she'd noticed. Anticipating her moods. Comforting her. It seemed completely at odds with what she knew of him, which admittedly wasn't very much. "We won't make it to Greenbriar tonight."

"No." He released her fingers, but his hand stayed, the palm flattening against her thigh. "I didn't think we would."

"You've done it on purpose," she said under her breath while smiling at her brother who was watching Haven as if he meant to leap across the table and strangle him.

"Done what?"

"Relished your meal for far longer than you should have, delaying our departure on purpose."

Haven turned to her, a patient, indulgent look on his face. "I was hungry." Placing his napkin on the table he said, "I didn't realize you were so eager to be alone with me. Not that I'm ungrateful, mind you."

Wretch.

"Perish the thought, my lord. I am only eager to get on with my imprisonment."

His hand trailed along the side of her leg before disappearing. "You won't get a lighter sentence no matter how well you behave."

Crushed gravel beneath my slippers. That's what Haven

sounds like. The slight innuendo in his words was difficult to miss. Theo's heart beat just a little faster.

"I'm not amused," she returned.

He stood and leaned over Theo's shoulder, meaning to help her out of her chair. "Nor are you well-behaved." His raspy whisper trailed seductively against her ear. "As it happens, Lady Haven, neither am I."

14

If Theo had assumed, after a series of tearful goodbyes with her family, a slightly threatening exchange between her brother and Haven, and her new husband's kind concern for her over their wedding breakfast, that their journey to Greenbriar would be a pleasant one, she would have been sorely disappointed.

The enormous woven basket, filled with what had to be the contents of half her brother's larder and carried aloft by Pith, was deposited by the scowling butler inside the coach. The basket took up a greater portion of one seat, leaving only a small space on the leather between it and the wall. Theo immediately claimed the area for herself.

At the very least, Theo anticipated a snide comment from Haven at her obvious preference to sit beside the basket and not him, but he barely seemed to notice. As he took his seat, Haven showed a marked interest in the basket, lifting the lid to peek at the contents before stretching out his legs. He made a great show of getting comfortable, wiggling about and flexing his arms and neck before stretching out a muscled length of leg. The toe of his boot slipped into her skirts.

Theo glared at him, not bothering to hide her irritation.

Finally, after all of his posturing, Haven clasped his arms across the expanse of his chest and closed his eyes. Not so much as a word was exchanged between them. He was snoring before the coach even reached the outskirts of London.

Theo told herself she was grateful Haven meant to leave her in peace. She opened her book, attempting to immerse herself in the exploits of Lord Thurston, only to be interrupted every so often when a loud, exaggerated snore met her ears.

After an hour or so, having read the same page at least three times, Theo snapped her book shut. The sound of Haven's snoring was deafening in the small confines of the coach. She kicked his foot.

A sliver of green regarded her as Haven managed to open one eye.

"You're snoring."

His lips twitched ever so slightly. "Am I?"

"Loudly."

"I don't snore, Theodosia. And there was no need for you to kick me half to death. A gentle nudge would have done the trick."

It had been one kick. One bloody kick.

"If you want my attention, my lady, you need only ask."

"I don't require your attention." She dearly wanted to knock the smirk from his lips, mainly because of his snoring but also because—"I need you to stop making the sounds of a wounded goose."

"You don't need to be insulting. Or did you kick me because you can't see me?" He sat up and wiggled his fingers. "Did you think someone else had crawled into the coach? A brigand? Or was it the vicar?"

"The vicar?"

"I saw the way you squinted at him, Theodosia."

"You're insufferable," she said, biting back a smile. Theo wasn't angry, not really. Her apprehension had calmed over the last several hours, and her emotions no longer threatened to burst out of her. Haven was right. She did want his attention.

"So I've been told by you, numerous times." He reached up and pushed back a wave of ill-cut hair, a wholly masculine gesture which did nothing but make him more roguishly attractive. "Tell me something true, Theodosia. About your family or yourself. Something more than I've already guessed at."

The question surprised her. "You guess at me?"

"All the time." The pools of moss green deepened. "I amuse myself by trying to decipher the riddle of Theodosia Louise Barrington."

Haven remembered her middle name. "Are you mocking me?"

"Not at all."

"Can you at least be honest with me for a little while?" Theo wasn't sure why she'd said it, only that she'd had enough uncertainty. "You are always teasing, and I never know when to take you at your word."

"Do you not?" The intensity of his gaze warmed down her mid-section. "I will always answer you truthfully, Theodosia. Will you vow to do the same? Share one thing that is true?"

"I do not like mushrooms," she blurted out. "I find them reminiscent of a garden slug, in both color and composition. My father didn't like them either, on the same principle." Theo's eyes caught his, and another bolt of sensation slid down her spine. "Mama loves them, however, as do Olivia and Phaedra."

"And Andromeda?"

"Mushrooms seem to be the only thing Romy doesn't have an opinion on."

The memory of Papa, sitting at the head of the table, insisting to Theo's mother that the mushrooms floating about in the gravy next to his piece of roast were wiggling about filled Theo's mind. And how, he'd said in an imperious tone, could she expect a duke to eat such a thing? Romy had laughed so hard, she'd snorted like a bull. Very unladylike.

Theo smiled at the happy memory, a time she hadn't appreciated then, but now, when viewed from afar, tugged at her heart.

"My father always made a great show at the dinner table if mushrooms were served. After a while, I suspected my mother made sure to include them on the menu just to see what he would do. He would turn to me and claim our mushrooms were racing across our plates, albeit very slowly."

The entire table would erupt in laughter. Craven, their butler at Cherry Hill, would have to turn around to hide his own amusement and keep from embarrassing himself. A small wince of pain crossed her chest, and without thinking, she pressed her palm to her heart.

"You miss him." Haven's hand stretched atop one muscular thigh reached just slightly in her direction before pulling back.

"Every day." Theo blinked to keep the moisture gathering behind her eyes at bay. She hadn't wept when her father died; instead, she'd crawled up to the spare room which served as her studio at Cherry Hill and painted with a violence which had frightened her. No miniatures. Just bold slashes of paint across every available surface, terrible abstract things in macabre colors. She had an entire book of sketches she'd done of her father but had been unable to paint a single miniature or small portrait of him. It simply hurt too much to do so.

"Papa said all his Barrington ladies sparkled like stars in the heavens. He was only a boring planet, not a heavenly body. Not celestial as he claimed we were."

"Yet you all revolved around him, did you not?"

Theo looked up, surprised at Haven's observation.

"I suppose we did. We still do, even though he is no longer with us."

Haven didn't pressure her for more; instead, he studied her from across the coach, large and slightly nefarious looking, the effect of the new suit he wore ruined by the scuffed boots and mop of russet hair. He regarded her with intense interest, as if Theo were the most fascinating creature he'd ever laid eyes on.

No one had ever looked at her in such a way before.

"Your truth now, Haven." Theo meant to ask him about his father, the architect of his misfortune, but didn't, unsure of where such a question might lead.

He leaned forward, the scent of spice filling the air. "I think about kissing you every moment of every day." He spoke without hesitation, the husky quality of his voice hovering over her limbs before sinking into her chest. "I've kissed you a total of four times, and I'm being generous in counting that chaste peck we shared in front of the vicar. I would have kissed you much sounder except I didn't want Pith to take my head off. If I'm not thinking of the way you taste, or the small sounds you make when I hold you, it is only because I'm asleep. But even then, I dream of you."

Haven said nothing more, instead relaxing against the seat, clasping his arms over his chest and closing his eyes.

"Haven." Theo stared at him. She kicked his foot.

A person couldn't make such an outlandish declaration and then just—

A snore met her ears.

Dammit.

Frustrated beyond belief, the space between her thighs still throbbing slightly from his words, Theo snapped her book back open with a vengeance. Casting a final glare in Haven's direction, she decided the only gentleman in this coach who deserved her attention was Lord Thurston.

After another futile attempt to progress past the second chapter, Theo gave up. She pulled herself into the corner, peering out the window to enjoy the passing countryside. There was nothing that merited her attention. A herd of cows. A wagon with several barrels lashed inside. All of it blurry. The rocking motion of the coach lulled her almost to sleep only to have her eyes pop open a moment later when the coach came to a stop.

Haven jumped out, taking her firmly by the hand to help her. He didn't seem the least bothered at having confessed such a deeply arousing truth to her earlier.

Insufferable didn't begin to describe Haven.

After seeing to her own needs, Theo took a walk about the small coaching inn's courtyard to stretch her legs. She returned to their vehicle in time to see Haven demolishing the contents of the basket Pith had prepared. Her stomach grumbled at the sight of a small apple and wedge of cheese he'd saved her.

"I adore the smell of paint," she said, settling inside and grabbing the apple with relish. "I sometimes go to Winsor & Newton without purchasing anything just so the scent will sink into my clothing. I'm such a frequent visitor that Mr. Newton has even named a color for me. 'Barrington Blue,' after my eyes." Theo looked at him and took a large bite of the apple.

"Indeed, I've heard of Winsor & Newton." Haven didn't even look up from the basket, but she could see a hint of a smile on his lips. "I'm always starving," he replied without a hint of apology. "My parents used to worry I'd grow as round as a barrel with the amount of food I consumed, but I never did. I think that must be why I put off so much heat when I'm asleep. At least," a hint of wickedness crept around his words, "so I've been told."

Theo bit into her apple again, crunching as loudly as she could. "I prefer a thick flannel nightgown buttoned all the way up to my chin to keep me warm."

He grinned at her. Had those delicious creases around his eyes always been there?

"Crunch softer, Theodosia." Reaching over, he placed the now empty basket on the seat next to her. With an exaggerated yawn, he once more closed his eyes.

So much for conversation. She bit into the piece of cheese, wishing it sounded half as loud as the apple. Resigning herself to being ignored for the duration of the journey, Theo opened her book and returned to Lord Thurston.

15

The coach came to an abrupt stop, jerking Theo awake. Lord Thurston lay open and discarded on the seat beside her. Blinking, she rubbed her eyes, peering through the window to the view outside. The sun had already dipped below the horizon, bathing everything with the misty softness of twilight.

Her head banged against the window as Haven jumped out, rocking the coach.

After being ignored for the better part of the day—and really, if there was one moment in a woman's life when she shouldn't be overlooked wouldn't it be her wedding day?— Theo was relieved to have reached their destination. Even if she didn't know exactly where she was. She assumed an inn. At this point, Theo didn't even care. At least she wouldn't have to hear Haven snore or have her bones jostled further.

"Are you coming?" Haven's rumble sounded from outside the coach.

Theo took a deep breath. She'd spent some of the time in the coach, when not considering how best to suffocate Haven, mulling over her behavior in regard to Blythe which, frankly, when viewed in hindsight, had been deplorable. It was time to take the reins, so to speak. Be the mistress of her own future.

Stop behaving like an idiot.

When *not* reliving the memories of how she'd made a cake of herself while listening to Haven snore, Theo also took the time to reflect on her new husband. Watching the rise and fall of his chest, Theo decided Haven was handsome, not pretty, as Blythe was, but carved and scraped like roughly hewn rock. He didn't disdain society, but neither did he embrace it. There was confidence in the way he moved, a natural athletic ability which would make him good at swords or fighting, she supposed. And Haven's skin fairly shimmered with resolve and ambition, much like Leo's did. A determination, an arrogance, which would not permit him to bow to the whim of anyone else. In fact, Theo looked forward to Haven meeting Leo. They were much alike.

But most importantly, Haven, Theo decided, *was* starving. Not just for food, although the amount he could consume was astounding. But to regain all the things he'd lost. Not just the wealth and material things, she thought, recalling the flicker of envy she'd sensed from him at the affectionate way the Barringtons dealt with each other. There was something else. She'd seen a darkness swirling in Haven when he looked at Tony. Smug defiance. As if he'd beat Tony in a game of cards.

That image stuck firmly in her mind, refusing to fade.

Haven reached for her hand, practically dragging her from the coach.

Theo shook her foot, which had fallen asleep, struggling to stand on the rutted dirt of the inn's courtyard. "Where are we?"

"At an inn." Haven peered down at her. "Can't you see it?"

He knew perfectly well she could see the inn. "I meant,"

she replied calmly, then shook her head. "Never mind. You snore like a wounded bear, by the way."

The side of his mouth lifted into an amused half-smile, making him more appealing than he had any right to be given her mood. He tugged her close to the warmth of his chest. "I don't snore. Not sure why you insist that I do. And how would you know what a wounded bear sounds like?"

A familiar ripple rolled up Theo's body as the heat of him bled into her skirts. Theo wanted nothing more than to lay her head on his chest and simply breathe in his scent. Did he feel the same pull in her direction? After his confession today, she thought he did.

"I'm starving." She tried to sound snippy, but instead, her words came out barely above a whisper, almost seductive in tone. Which given Haven's love of food, the seduction might well include a chicken leg dangling between her breasts. Or a bit of bread. Theo had to bite her lip to keep from giggling.

"What is so amusing, Lady Haven?"

"I was only thinking how you left me the smallest apple in the basket and there wasn't enough cheese to feed a mouse. Pith would be most distressed."

"Pith probably tried to poison me at breakfast. And I warned you, Theodosia. That was the first truth I told you." Small bits of light sparkled in the depths of his mossy eyes as they looked at each other, oblivious to the footmen standing just to the side, patiently waiting for instruction.

"So you did," she finally said, wanting to trace her fingernail over the scar on his chin.

"I get very hungry when I travel." His breath sifted through her hair as he spoke, sending a tingle over her shoulders. Haven's hold on Theo tightened just enough for her breasts to flatten against his coat.

"I don't see how that's possible," she murmured. His

closeness, the press of firm muscle against her softer form, was incredibly distracting. "You slept the entire time."

"Perhaps I was deep in contemplation."

"The book I've struggled to read through your snoring is *Lord Thurston's Revenge*." Theo was loath to abandon their game of truths. "It's lurid. Horribly romantic. Lots of swooning. Cackling pirates. Salty seadogs."

Haven took her hand, leading her into the inn. He paused before the door and grinned before whispering in her ear, "I've already read *Lord Thurston's Revenge*. You'll like the ending."

Disreputable, slightly nefarious Haven read the sort of romance which made young ladies fan themselves? "I don't see how that could possibly be true," she said.

He shrugged his broad shoulders. "My sister wanted to read Lord Thurston. I insisted she could not until I had read one of the books first to ensure her gentle mind would not be corrupted by such drivel." Haven's eyes glowed in the most amazing way as he looked down on her. "I found myself entirely engrossed. Now I've read them all."

"I'm not sure I believe you. But very well. And you really do smell of gingerbread."

He stopped, bits of russet falling over his forehead. "So you've said. That doesn't count as something new." Heat sprang up in his eyes, the sort which made Theo's insides twist pleasurably. She turned away and trotted inside the inn.

After a quick conversation with the owner, a round gentleman with an incredibly thick head of spikey ginger hair, Haven released her into the company of a thin girl who introduced herself as Mary as he went outside to confer with the driver and two footmen, all on loan from Theo's brother.

Apparently, Theo was to be ignored further. She followed the maid up the stairs and down the hall until Mary stopped before a door.

"Congratulations on your marriage, my lady," Mary said as she pulled a key from her pocket. "Our best room, as Lord Haven requested. I washed and changed the linens myself. You'll rest well tonight." A furious blush dusted her cheeks. "What I mean to say is—"

"Thank you, Mary." Theo saved the girl further embarrassment by answering. Her eyes fell on the large, comfortable-looking bed before taking in the rest of the room. There was a hint of beeswax in the air along with soap. Thankfully, everything smelled clean. A relief at an inn. A small bouquet of fresh wildflowers sat on the table next to the bed.

Theo supposed it was as good a place as any to lose her virtue.

Something coiled sharply inside her. Fear? Anticipation? Arousal? She was full of all those things and curious after what she'd seen at Elysium.

The lovers had been entwined on a bed in one of the private rooms. If they had sensed Theo opening the door, or her presence, they had given no indication. They certainly hadn't so much as paused in their enjoyment of each other. The man had his head between the woman's thighs, and she . . . had hers between his . . . her lips on the man's . . . *length*. Theo had been frozen, unable to look away, fascinated not only by the couple but by the way her own nipples had tightened and at the feathering sensation between her thighs. Moans and wet sucking sounds had filled the air. When the woman had cried out in pleasure, the man had abruptly shifted, positioned himself between her legs, and thrust—

Startled, body pulsing at the sight, Theo had silently backed out of the room, quietly closing the door behind her. She'd taken a deep breath before finding Romy, who had still been wandering about two doors down in a room empty except for a variety of feathers and long pieces of silk streaming from the posts of an enormous bed. Romy was holding the silk, muttering to herself in a dazed voice that the silk must be used to tie a person to the bed before engaging in—whatever they meant to do.

Theo, flustered and with a dull ache between her legs, had said not a word to Romy about what she'd witnessed.

As luck would have it, Theo had had the pleasure of being introduced to Lady St. Martin at the first ball she'd attended upon her family's return to London. She'd nearly choked on her punch when she recognized the countess as the woman she'd seen at Elysium.

The room grew warm, though Mary had only just started the fire. Theo wanted Haven to do those things to *her*. Imagined him touching her in such a way. No wonder all of London considered her to be brazen. Because if Theo were any sort of proper young lady, she would be weeping quietly at the horror of what awaited her in the marital bed.

Not thinking of Haven's hand possessively palming her sex as he sought to make his point.

Theo fell back on the quilt covering the bed, staring at the ceiling above her.

How in the world had she found herself here? Married to the Marquess of Haven, of all the eligible gentlemen in London?

"Stupidity," she finally said aloud. Aided and abetted by a glass of spilled ratafia and an exquisitely painted half-naked miniature of her breasts. Which she didn't think Haven meant to ever return to her.

"My lady?"

Theo looked up. Mary had finished unpacking her valise and now stood at the door, a question on her thin face. Behind her was a big, buxom girl and a copper tub.

Theo had been so lost in her scandalous, arousing thoughts, she'd never heard Mary even leave the room. The maid must think her a terrible snob, one of those titled women who never acknowledged servants unless something was required. Mama would have her head for behaving in such a manner. It was a rule all the Barringtons lived by; treat everyone, no matter how lowly their station, with the same respect you might give the queen.

"I'm so sorry, Mary. I never heard you leave."

Mary nodded shyly at the apology. "A bath, my lady. Lord Haven said you might wish it. But if you do not, we can take the tub away."

"No, I do." Thoughtful of Haven, considering he'd abandoned her not moments after their arrival.

The tub was soon filled, a haze of steam hovering about the copper edges. Mary had set a bar of soap and towels on a nearby chair. Theo picked up the bar and took a whiff, her nose wrinkling at the harsh scent. She went to her valise and retrieved the soap smelling of honey and lemons Betts had carefully and thoughtfully packed for her. Carrying it to the tub, she turned to the young girl who was placing out Theo's hairbrush and tooth kit.

"If you don't mind, Mary?" She turned so the girl could undo the line of buttons trailing up her spine. Once she stood in her chemise, Theo sat on the bed as the maid helped take off her small half-boots and stockings.

"I've brushed out your dress, my lady." The girl came forward. "Should I assist you with your bath?"

"That won't be necessary." Theo wanted a moment alone, which she now had since Haven hadn't appeared. Shouldn't he have at least come up to see her settled? Theo glanced over to a battered valise she hadn't noticed previously sitting next to hers. At least Haven planned to appear at some point. "Do you know the whereabouts of Lord Haven, Mary?"

"No, my lady. But he's asked me to bring up a tray." She bobbed politely.

Very well. Haven would likely join her for dinner.

Theo sighed and tossed off her chemise, watching as it fluttered to the floor. This wasn't exactly how the evening was supposed to proceed. Shouldn't he be stalking her about the room, maybe leering at her? Spouting more somewhat lustful declarations about wanting to kiss her? Possibly offering her comfort for what was about to transpire? Wasn't that what a husband should do? For all Haven knew, Theo was drowning herself in the tub out of despair.

Sinking into the water, Theo closed her eyes. And just when she'd gotten used to the idea of . . . she and Haven . . . well, *somewhat*. That is to say, she expected—

She grabbed the soap and furiously began scrubbing her arm.

Theo freely admitted that she was a terrible judge of a man's intentions toward her. There was no reason to revisit her pursuit of Blythe, but Haven had stated his desire for her. Bluntly. He'd said as much on at least two occasions. But possibly he might not *exclusively* desire her. She hadn't really considered that.

Most gentlemen, outside of her father and Tony, had mistresses. And Granby. Theo didn't think for one second her sister would tolerate a mistress.

Hard enough to imagine *Romy* wanting Granby's company, let alone any other woman.

Theo shook her head in frustration. The fact remained that many gentlemen took mistresses during their marriage. Especially if the gentleman didn't love his wife. Which Haven did not. Love her, that is.

Mary, the inn's maid, for example, could be a mistress. Theo's brow wrinkled as she scrubbed her shoulder.

Very well. Not Mary.

But Haven could be downstairs right now cozied up to some luscious widow while Theo sat in her bath. Possibly he was whispering tiny bits of desirable truths into her ear as well.

A few minutes later, once Theo had scrubbed her arms raw, a soft knock came at the door. Mary had returned with a tray of roasted chicken, peas, and several slices of warm bread with butter. Thankfully, there was also a bottle of wine. But only one glass.

Theo stared at the tray and that single glass.

The soap dropped into the water. Suddenly her wild imaginings seemed far more possible than they had earlier. She was in a strange inn, on her wedding night, after having been dragged halfway across England—

All right, a possible exaggeration.

—and deserted by her husband for the delights of a widow in the common room. A luscious, golden-haired widow with perfect eyesight.

Her mood was not softened by the warmth of the water, nor the chicken which she proceeded to eat in the bath. Mary, with a sympathetic look, had been kind enough to put the tray within easy reach. The wine, ruby-colored with a mellow taste, helped somewhat, giving a slightly euphoric edge to her mounting anger.

By the time the sound of heavy, male footsteps stopped just outside the door, Theo was in a bloody horrible frame of mind and the bathwater was starting to cool.

The door opened quietly and then shut as leather, spice, and the scent of scotch floated in the air above her head. The wretch had been drinking downstairs while she sat up here eating chicken in the bath by herself.

"Get out," she said over her shoulder. "Go sleep with your widow. Or take another room. I find I don't care."

"Widow? You do realize it's me, don't you? Not another gentleman come to stare at you in your bath. I knew the wine was a mistake." Haven stalked past the tub, loosening his cravat before taking a seat on the bed. He stretched out his legs and proceeded to tug off his boots, tossing them with a thud into the corner.

Theo lifted her glass of wine and tilted it toward the door. "I'm enjoying the wine. Go sleep downstairs. And take your lustful nature with you." Her feelings were terribly hurt. Which only made her madder.

Haven placed his cravat over the other chair in the room, discarding his coat and waistcoat. "Why would I do such a thing? There's a perfectly good bed here. Can't you see it? Where are your spectacles? Are they in your valise? Should I fetch them for you?"

Theo pulled her lips tight, pleasantly annoyed to the very tips of her toes. Her heart skipped. "Of course I can see the bed. I keep telling you my eyesight isn't nearly as bad as you make it out to be."

"I know." A slow, devastating smile crossed his lips. "And there was no widow downstairs to tempt me, though I do find it interesting you assumed a widow. I do find them attractive," he said in a faraway voice.

Theo tossed a pea at him.

"But most ladies would have suggested a tavern maid." He smiled again.

"I'm not trying to amuse you." That smile did things to Theo. Lovely things.

"Banish such thoughts. There was only a merchant, as it happens. Mr. Barnaby. I would have asked him for a kiss, but he has a huge wart above his lip." Haven gave a mock shudder. "He's from Warwick, which is close to Greenbriar. Married with ten children. Very prolific is Mr. Barnaby. In spite of the wart. I suppose his wife doesn't mind."

Haven was utterly breathtaking when he looked at her as he was doing now, heat banked in the depths of green, the light playing over the tiny bump in his nose. There was no practiced flirtation with him, no overly charming manner or platitudes. Nothing but his potent maleness to recommend him. She wondered how many women had taken one look at his rough attractiveness, listened to his wicked, gravelly voice, and fallen into bed with him.

Scores. Theo was certain she was going to be one of them.

Waves of russet hair danced against his broad shoulders as he peered at the tub. "You're very tempting, Theodosia," he whispered, the words sliding into the bath water with her. "Despite being wrinkled like a wizened apple. Must be my lustful nature which makes you seem so."

She settled down further in the tub, realizing her nipples were visible above the sparse bubbles and that he was staring at them with the same look he'd given his plate at breakfast this morning.

Anticipation slowly curled down her naked body.

Haven sauntered toward her, his bare feet making no sound on the wood floor. "Shall we be truthful again, Theo?"

She snuck a look at his feet, wishing there were more bubbles left floating on the surface of the water. Of all the things Theo had considered about Haven, she hadn't once thought of his feet. And they were rather nice. She shut her eyes against the sight. What was wrong with her if she could be undone by the very sight of a man's toes?

"Theo?"

"You've lovely feet," she whispered, opening her eyes.

Haven burst into laughter. "Good Lord. I really should take the wine from you. I'm missing part of my little toe on one foot."

Peering over the edge of the tub, she took in his feet and toes. They looked perfectly normal to her. But things were fuzzy. She blamed the lighting in the room and her lack of spectacles.

A small growl came from him.

Theo had forgotten how exposed she was in this stupid little tub. Haven was watching her with a heavy-lidded look, all smoldering heat and intent. He started unbuttoning his shirt, eyes never leaving hers.

Did he mean to join her? The tub was barely large enough for her.

The fabric of his shirt opened, displaying a wide swath of muscles rippling beneath supple skin. Hair a shade darker than his head spread across the upper part of his torso, across clearly defined lines of sinew. The hair trailed down around his navel before disappearing into the edge of his trousers. She stared at his navel, wondering how in the world he didn't carry any extra padding there, considering his appetite. But his trousers hung low against the harsh cut of his hipbone, creating a lovely line of shadow.

"It's me, you know. Haven." He wiggled his fingers in front of her eyes.

It was becoming difficult for her to breathe with Haven and all his near-naked magnificence. Yes, she found Haven handsome. Appealing. But now, looking at the way the firelight played over the hard ridges of his body, Theo felt as if she was heating slowly from the inside out, her skin sensitive to the brush of every bubble in her bath.

Haven kneeled at the tub, drawing his face so close to her, their noses nearly touched. "Did you think of me while soaking in your bath, Theodosia?"

"Of course not," she whispered, wishing he didn't smell so delicious. "I thought of Blythe." Theo didn't know why she'd said such a thing except she was feeling somewhat abandoned by Haven and part of her wanted to hurt him. The truth was, Blythe hadn't once entered her thoughts today.

"I wasn't ignoring you, Theo." There was a brief flash of anger in his moss-green eyes before his finger traced lazily along her arm. "Nor overlooking you. I thought you might want to relax in a bath without me here. Have a meal because you must be starving. But I suppose we should just get on with the consummation." He nosed into the nape of her shoulder, sending a ripple down her spine. His voice was chilly when he spoke again. "If only so your prick of a brother doesn't try to take your dowry back."

And she'd been just about to apologize for mentioning Blythe. "My brother isn't a prick, you bloody—"

"You've such a mouth on you, Theodosia. I always suspected it. Ever since I heard the vile curses spilling from you when you couldn't find the miniature in Blythe's study. No *innocent* young miss for my wife."

There was an edge to his words, as if he were questioning her character. Theo opened her mouth to defend herself but instead said, "Fortune hunter. Gambling marquess from an impoverished family. Prone to fighting like a common mongrel in the streets. Which, by the way, is how you approach a plate of food."

"I always find it interesting," Haven replied casually, pools of green threatening to drown her. "Miss Emerson *never* had so many complaints about me. She was quite heartbroken I was *forced* to marry you."

Theo's fingers gripped the side of the tub. "Poor thing. She might be stunning and can walk across a room without tripping, but Miss Emerson exhibits poor taste."

Haven pushed a soap bubble away from one breast. There was a smile tugging at his lips.

"Very well, do your worst, Haven. Get it over with," she said, but there was no bite to her words. Theo didn't want to argue with him. Honestly, she didn't. Not after he confessed that he thought about kissing her all the time. And she really didn't think he'd been downstairs seducing a buxom widow. Theo opened one eye. "It isn't required that I have to watch, is it?"

"No." A tiny smirk wavered on his lips, the tension between them softening. "You don't have your spectacles on anyway. I've no desire to see you squinting at me the entire time."

"Very well." She sighed. "Just get on with it." Theo lay back in the tub, not bothering to cover herself. The wine had made her very brave indeed.

One long finger slid up the soapy slope of her breast, barely touching the skin. The tip glanced lightly against her nipple, rubbing softly against the small peak. It was delicious torture. The best kind.

She bit her lip to keep from moaning with pleasure. "I'm not going to enjoy this."

"Probably not," he said, pinching the taut peak. "I've never had the least complaint before, but I suppose there's a first time for everything."

"I'll imagine Blythe the entire time," she said half-heartedly, hating the jealousy at the very thought of all those unnamed seductive ladies who had bedded Haven. It was bad enough feeling second best to Violet Emerson.

"Even though he doesn't want you?" Haven said quietly, teeth grazing the slope of her neck. "And I do?"

"Haven—" Her breath caught on his name. His hand floated over Theo's stomach, fingers lightly stroking her skin. When his mouth fell to hers in a slow, deliberate kiss, Haven left no doubt of his intentions. His fingers tangled in the hair of her mound before moving gently across her slit.

The featherlight caress was exquisite. Theo's legs widened in slow inches, her hips brushing up against his fingertips, begging him silently for more. "I feel nothing," she whimpered.

"Oh, my dear wife. Now who isn't being honest?" Haven placed his free hand possessively around her neck, squeezing gently, warning her not to move. "I fear there is no escape from the horrible, fortune-hunting marquess you were forced to marry." His fingers moved leisurely against her in the water in light, teasing waves.

"No, I don't suppose there is." Her hips rotated against his hand, wanting more of the bliss radiating from the spot between her thighs. The tips of her breasts breached the water of the tub, the tiny buds taut and sensitive.

A low purr lingered over her neck. "The miniature, while a work of art, did not do your bosom justice. But I'm not sure you got the color of your nipples correct."

A tremble went through her as one of his fingers sunk deep and slow, curling gently inside her, before retreating to glide around the delicate nub, aching for his touch. Pausing, he pinched the sensitive flesh between his fingers, oh so gently, before resuming his teasing path to her core.

Theo gave into everything, the decadent pleasure coiling within her, Haven's scent filling her nostrils, the feel of his teeth grazing her neck.

"Who are you thinking of now, Theodosia?" he growled. "Don't you dare lie."

"You." The word broke across her lips. Haven's fingers drew out the most exquisite sensations. She was close to begging, wanting desperately to reach the summit he dangled before her. Something Theo knew would be marvelous.

He pressed a kiss to her lips before speaking again, his voice thick. "I told you I wanted you from the moment you spilled ratafia on my coat. I adore your spectacles. I often imagine you wearing them and little else. Your talent with a brush leaves me awestruck."

"And my dowry," she whispered.

A wrinkle marred his brow. "I will be honest and admit it. But my want of you, Theodosia," he paused to press a kiss to the tip of one breast, "which is bloody considerable, has absolutely nothing to do with your dowry. One does not preclude the other. I liken it to finding out that the ripe berries I've been eyeing—"

A tremor rippled over Theo's skin, sinking deep into her bones.

"—come with a large helping of fresh cream."

A hoarse whimper came from her. "Please, Haven."

"I have never," wickedness imbued his words, "wanted anything so much as you, Theodosia Barrington." The heat of an open-mouthed kiss pressed against her throat. "Never question it. Anything but that. Promise me."

Theo would have agreed to anything if Haven allowed the pleasure curling tightly between her legs to uncoil. "I promise."

His mouth fell on hers, hard and possessive, taking what little breath was left in her body as his thumb pressed against her, releasing a wave of sensation.

The water splashed out of the tub, covering the floor as she arched, eyes closing as her hips pushed upward. His mouth trapped her cry of pleasure, his fingers never once halting in their torture, pulling every bit of sensation out of her body and leaving her gasping for breath.

With a predatory growl, Haven dragged her from the tub, hefting her to his side like a large, dripping wet bag of grain. He pressed her down on the bed, his hands running possessively over the freckles spraying up toward her collarbone, then between her breasts to her stomach, his fingers tangling in the soft hair of her mound.

"*Jesus,* you're beautiful." The words were filled with reverence.

"So are you," she answered.

"You can't see at all, can you?" One side of his mouth lifted. He didn't look away from her as he shrugged out of his shirt, tossing it to the chair. His thumbs hooked into his trousers and pulled them off, watching her carefully.

Theo's pulse beat faster as she inspected him beneath her lashes. Haven was so big and male and . . . *naked*. Her gaze traveled over the sculpted pectoral muscles, the brief outline of his ribs, the curvature of all that lovely sinew lurking just beneath supple skin. The sharp indentation of his hipbones drew her eye which led to—

Theo bit her lip. The man at Elysium, Lady St. Martin's lover, hadn't been nearly so well endowed. But she didn't look away. Lifting her eyes to his, Theo allowed a small smile to grace her lips, one she hoped would convey that she wouldn't collapse into a fit of tears or something equally unwelcome. She stifled the urge to cover herself, reasoning she'd been naked for some time. First the bath and now the bed. It seemed pointless to pretend modesty.

A small, barely noticeable frown tugged at his lips as he looked down at her, but it was gone in an instant, replaced by a predatory look which was mildly frightening. Haven appeared as if he were about to devour her.

Theo gripped the quilt atop the bed.

His hand slid down his stomach until his fingers wrapped around the hardness jutting from between his thighs. "Can you see anything?" The low growl lit against her skin. "Or is my cock indistinct as well?"

"No, I see perfectly fine when the object is closer." She'd heard the word from her brothers, not directly, mind you, and it failed to shock her. But now that she was looking at Haven's *cock* a bit of nervousness settled in her stomach. Her tongue flicked out to wet her lips while she considered something clever to say.

Haven cursed under his breath.

He came to the edge of the bed, stroking himself, eyes never leaving her. For only a moment, the sense that she had earlier, that he was not angry exactly but disappointed in her, returned, but it vanished in an instant.

Was she supposed to do something? This was the part missing in her education. She'd seen the act, of course, and her mother had explained how everything fit together, so to speak, but there was a vagueness to what Theo's role should be in the process.

Lady St. Martin had had her mouth on—well, her lover's *cock*. Was that what Haven expected?

Theo came up to her hands and knees and approached him, feeling the gentle sway of her breasts as she came forward.

Haven's eyes narrowed to slits, the rise and fall of his chest quicker than it had been a moment ago.

Placing a tentative palm against his stomach, Theo stretched out her hand, entranced by the way his muscles jumped beneath her touch. Next, she trailed her fingers along his ribcage and down across his hip, lightly brushing against his thighs.

Haven's free hand threaded through her hair, pulling gently at the pins until the strands fell down her shoulders.

Theo placed her hand around the length of him, carefully pushing his fingers aside. He was smooth and warm against her palm like the finest silk poured over muscle. Clasping him firmly in her grasp, Theo stroked back and forth, mimicking what she'd seen him do.

A hiss escaped him.

Encouraged, Theo pumped slowly; each stroke had him swelling beneath her palm, leaving her to wonder *how* this would ever fit inside her. Pushing the thought aside, Theo focused instead on watching Haven's beautiful features contort in pleasure at her touch. Bending, she brushed her lips across the top, then pressed a kiss. He smelled warm. Musky. A hint of spice surrounded even this part of his person. She licked up the side, the taste of salt filling her mouth, before placing Haven fully in her mouth.

"Christ." Haven jerked forward, his fingers tangling in her hair. "Theo." His hips thrust forward.

Theo opened her jaw wider, listening to the sounds he made. Haven liked this. Boldly, she swirled her tongue around the top. It was smooth. Bulbous. She licked around the edge before sucking gently, pulling him deeper into her mouth.

His hand cupped one of her breasts, rolling the nipple between his thumb and forefinger, brushing the tip.

A soft hum started inside Theo, throbbing delicately between her thighs, her earlier pleasure returning. Every soft groan from Haven's lips echoed inside her own body.

"Theodosia," he murmured. "I want to bury myself in you." There was a hitch in the words. "Now."

A small plop sounded from her mouth as he pulled free. They stared at each other, a haze of desire winding over them both. Haven wrapped the curling strands of her hair around his wrist and pulled her close.

"Are you going to ravish me?" Theo whispered.

"God, yes." His lips fell on hers, urgent and hot before pushing her down on the bed, mouth sucking and licking at hers. He lifted his head. "I have such hunger for you, Theodosia."

"I'm not a biscuit, Haven."

A soft chuckle left him as he bent to explore the curves and hollows of her body, lingering over every inch with soft, fluttering touches. Each breath against her skin was agonizing, exquisite torture. Every part of Theo was claimed, either by his mouth or his fingers, her pleasure building with each caress. Lips moved along the underside of one breast, toying with her nipple until the warmth of his mouth sucked in the taut peak, grazing his teeth across the tip.

"I want to paint you, Haven," she panted, rubbing her legs along his.

The nipple in his mouth vibrated as he chuckled. "If it will please you."

Oh, it would please Theo greatly. "You're so lovely," she whispered, running her fingers through his hair. "Hint of *Rose Madder* in *Umber*."

"What?" He looked up at her, eyes heavy-lidded and sensual. Wickedness personified. She wished she could sketch him right at this moment, but there were other things which required her attention, namely the way his fingers were moving against her.

"The colors I shall use for your hair," she breathed.

Haven explored every inch of her body for what felt like forever, bringing her close to the release she sought again but never allowing her to reach it. Wet and aching, she pushed her hips up against him, begging Haven as her fingers sifted through the thick strands of his hair.

This was so breathtaking. So wonderful. So much more *right* than Theo had ever imagined. Her heart firmly reached for his, tethering itself to Haven. A tear slipped unbidden down her cheek, and she wished she could put the feeling into words. "Ambrose," she whispered, "I wish—"

Haven cupped her cheek, wiping away the small bit of moisture with the tip of his finger. "It doesn't matter, Theo," he said roughly before kissing her deeply. "I promise."

Theo was too far gone to make sense of his words. He'd drawn her pleasure into a sharp point, a precipice, one she wanted to fall from.

When he finally settled between her thighs, Theo welcomed him. She knew what to expect, or at least the basics. The same bliss she'd experienced in the tub awaited her. But a small pinch first, according to her mother. Nothing more.

Haven grasped her hips and thrust firmly, seating himself deep inside her.

All pleasure fled Theo's body as pain speared up inside her. She struggled against the invasion, the awful rending tear. A whimper came from her lips before she bit down, trying to keep from sobbing.

A bit more than a bloody pinch.

Theo would have compared it to something inside her being torn. Ravaged. He was wedged inside her and it—*hurt*. She sucked in her breath.

"Jesus." A stricken look came over Haven's face, his eyes wide with regret. "Theo. Sweetheart. I'm sorry." He didn't move, not an inch. He stayed perfectly still, allowing time for her body to accommodate his. He kissed away the salt of her tears, the low rumble of his voice purring against her neck until she relaxed.

"This is terribly uncomfortable," she said, looking up at him.

"Gorgeous creature." Haven bent, lips running up the side of her neck. "Is it getting better?"

"Yes." She nodded. The pain was starting to ebb, the sting not so terrible. The sense of fullness was odd. Knowing Haven was inside her body was strange but also wonderful.

He brushed her lips tenderly with his. Taking her hand, he laced his larger fingers with hers before thrusting gently inside her, watching her face for any signs of distress.

Theo felt herself soften more, her hips tilting as he rocked into her.

Haven pressed his forehead to hers. "My hunger for you is infinite, Theodosia. Never to be assuaged. I kept my distance today," he sucked gently at her bottom lip, "because I was afraid if I touched you, I wouldn't be able to stop myself, and I'd ravish you in your brother's coach." He slowed further, his fingers moving between their bodies, sparking an echo of her earlier pleasure. Their mouths met, tongues mingling as they rocked together.

Her pleasure peaked softly, slowly stretching across her lower body, growing stronger each time he moved against her. One big hand reached beneath her, pulling her tighter against him.

She found the rhythm easily, wrapping her legs around his waist, matching every thrust. Her pleasure was different this time, tied to Haven in a way she hadn't expected. When her release thundered through her, the bliss was so sweet, so unexpected, Theo sank her teeth into Haven's shoulder, the exquisite shattering with him inside her blocking out everything else.

"Theo," he groaned, slamming into her so hard, she thought she might break. Her inner muscles tightened around the length of him, and she felt him pulse along with a burst of warmth. His head fell to the curve of her shoulder as he stilled, the rasp of his breath ruffling her hair.

His lips moved, smiling against her skin before rolling to the side, taking her with him.

She curled against him, listening to the thump of his heart keeping time with hers. The rightness of the moment struck her again. The absolute completeness.

She was far happier than she'd ever imagined.

16

"Wake up, Theodosia." Lips traveled up the line of her back, nibbling along her spine before disappearing.

Blinking, Theo opened her eyes, the dream fading as consciousness returned along with a view of the small room where she'd spent her wedding night. She'd been painting Haven. And she was naked wearing only her spectacles. They were outside in a field, butterflies floating around her head as Haven stood before her, his eyes the exact color of the summer grass. The sun was glinting in his hair as he raised a hand, palm up, in her direction.

"Haven?"

"Of course, it's me." He appeared before her, partially dressed. "I know you can't see, so if you'd like to be sure," the bed shifted as he leaned over her, "feel free to grope me."

Theo snorted, laughing into her pillow. "You're horrible. And my spectacles are in my valise."

"I am. But I'm also hopeful. There's a difference." A lone finger trailed against her ribs and along the side of one breast. "Are you well, Lady Haven?" He pressed a soft kiss to her lips.

"Yes." Theo pulled herself up, deliberately allowing the sheet to slip, exposing one breast.

"Tease." His gaze raked her before taking hold of the sheet, pulling it lower until the edge brushed her navel. He leaned forward and pressed an open-mouthed kiss to her stomach before licking against one of her nipples. "On second thought, I do think you got the color correct."

"But not the color of the pond?"

"I want only to be helpful." His fingers were gliding over her skin, warming her with his touch. "I know nothing about art—"

"Shocking," Theo interrupted sarcastically, sucking in her breath when his mouth fell to her hip. "I'm certain you have other talents."

"Mmm. Possibly. But what you need to know is that I am appreciative of your talent and creativity. I want you to paint. Create. Or anything else you wish to do. I will be a supportive husband."

Her heart constricted gently. "But not a distant one?" After last night, the very thought of her and Haven living apart bothered her greatly.

Haven nipped the skin of her upper thigh. "No. No distance. That is not up for debate. I fear I will be prone to give you whatever you wish, Theodosia, except for that." He raised his head, taking her hand to press a kiss in the center of her palm. "I am sorry about last night. I assumed—" A slight frown brushed across his lips. "Had I known, I would have gone slower. Taken greater care. Forgive me."

Haven was terribly apologetic, as if he'd done her a much more grievous injury than deflowering her. Surely, he hadn't presumed—but how could he possibly think that she—

The absolute wonder of the previous evening dimmed somewhat. "What is it exactly, my lord, that you ask forgiveness for?" she said quietly, pulling up the sheet. It took her far longer than it should have to comprehend his meaning.

"I was careless." Haven had the grace to look embarrassed. "I was only taken aback."

He hadn't been overly careful because—"You thought I wasn't a virgin." Her mind raced over every interaction they'd had up until this morning. Why would he think such a thing? "Is that why you kissed me the first time? Not because you were jealous of Blythe but because you thought I'd welcome you taking liberties? No wonder you claimed to want me the minute I spilled ratafia on you. You thought I was a *harlot*." Theo took a deep breath. "A wanton duke's daughter with poor eyesight."

"No," he snapped back at her. "That *isn't* what I thought. Nor why I kissed you. And as seductive as spilling ratafia on me was, I didn't think you wanton. But—" He paused as if assessing how best to frame his next words. "Try to look at it from my perspective. You painted a half-naked miniature of yourself to give to Blythe. What sort of gently reared virgin does such a thing? It was an honest conclusion. Obviously, I know now that is not the case." He nodded to the bed.

Theo looked down to see a bit of blood on the sheets and on her inner thigh.

"And whatever else you've allowed—"

Whatever else I've allowed? Haven should really learn when to stop talking. Now would be an excellent time. "Yes, now you know I was a virgin. But despite that fact, you still assume," she cleared her throat, "that I may have encouraged other liberties?"

"A virgin doesn't take a man's cock in her mouth on her wedding night." He stood and walked to the other side of the room, looking away from her. The fingers of one hand drummed against his thigh.

"You think I've put another man's *cock* in my mouth?

When would I have done such a thing? At a ball?" Theo was incredulous. She'd performed such an act on Haven because she'd wanted to please him and because . . . it was *him*.

"If—we all have a past, Theodosia." He took a step in her direction and halted.

"So, because I *desired* you, because I had some *limited* knowledge of what transpires in the marital bed, but most of all, because I wanted to *please* you and didn't fall into a sobbing fit when you discarded your clothing, you thought I was—" Theo closed her eyes for a moment. Even Haven thought the worst of her, it seemed.

"It doesn't matter to me. I promise."

"Obviously, it does, my lord." Theo was angrier than she had ever been in her life. "I wonder, how do you suppose I engaged in these other activities? Brazen Theodosia Barrington. She'll do anything to garner a gentleman's interest." Her voice grew hard. "All it requires is a dance. Perhaps some poetry."

Haven stared at her, stone-faced. "Have you? Answer me."

She merely smiled back at him, satisfied to see how his fingers curled into fists at his sides. That, at least, gave her a modicum of satisfaction. Let him wallow in his own uncertainty. He'd no idea how much he'd wounded her. Just when she'd thought their marriage could be more than that of a silly girl being compromised by a desperate marquess. "Hand me my chemise. Now."

"Theodosia." He ran a hand through the tangle of his hair. "We'll discuss this later when you are less overwrought."

"No, we won't. Your destruction of my character may leave me *overwrought* for quite some time, my lord. My chemise, if you please."

He ignored her, his jaw hardening.

Maybe her outrage over the whole situation was foolish. Most gentlemen would want to know if their wife had had a previous lover. She could see his point about the miniature and possibly other things. But since the day in her studio, Theo had grown used to Haven knowing *her*. And realizing that he didn't was rather painful.

"Fine." Theo threw aside the covers. After last night, she'd little shame over her body and certainly not with Haven. Bravely, she stood and walked with excruciating slowness across the room. Her hair fell around her shoulders, brushing against her waist as she moved. Deliberately, she paused to seductively brush a curl off her breasts.

A noise came from Haven, much like that of a wild animal. Or a feral tomcat.

She bent, picking up her discarded chemise, taking overly long to shake it out.

"Never fear, my lord. The enthusiasm I displayed for you which led to such unwelcome assumptions about me," she flung the chemise over her head, "will not be repeated."

17

For the first time in her life, Theo wished she knew how to faint properly and ask for smelling salts.

At her first glimpse of Greenbriar, the estate which was to become her home at least for a time, fainting would be merited. Had she not known better, she would have assumed the estate to have been abandoned and left to rot.

Along with Haven's heart.

The house itself wasn't overly large, resembling more of a country cottage than a grand estate, at least in comparison to the ducal seat, Cherry Hill. The oriel windows looking down at her and peaked roofs with multiple chimneys told her the house must have been built around the time of Elizabeth I and probably had not been renovated since. The remnants of once-magnificent gardens surrounded Greenbriar, but the beds now lay either barren or full of weeds with only a spot or two of color.

Neglect hung in the air like a thick mist.

Haven had been careful not to mention the state of Greenbriar to her and, now she could see, with good reason.

Had Theo known, she might not have agreed to come here. At least the house had good lines.

Theo declined Haven's hand as she leapt out of the coach, just as she had refused every attempt at conversation since their heated discussion this morning. Theo admitted to herself that most gentlemen might have come to the same conclusions given the miniature and her behavior over Blythe.

But she hadn't expected Haven to be *most gentlemen*.

Maybe she was ascribing an excess of emotion to the act. Perhaps being bedded was always magnificent and earthshaking, though if that were the case, she didn't understand why so many women didn't look forward to their marital duties. During the silent coach ride to Greenbriar, Theo had mulled over all these possibilities and come up with the same conclusion each time. She was *insulted* he'd thought her so free with her person, whether his assumptions were justified or not. She wasn't ready to forgive him. Not today, but possibly later and only if he groveled a bit.

She tried to imagine Haven groveling and couldn't.

I can always return to London.

Haven came toward her, and she took a step in the opposite direction, enjoying the sharp blaze of irritation in his eyes.

"Not as splendid as Cherry Hill, I suppose," he said, the words like the rumble of stones in the road. "Don't judge. You can't even see it properly, I'm sure."

Theo didn't bother to look in his direction. Instead, she pulled her spectacles from the pocket of her skirts and placed them on her nose. "There's very little improvement even with them on. You failed to mention the extent of the repairs Greenbriar might require. Looks quite decrepit. Might not even be livable. A challenge of epic proportions."

He shot her a hard look. "You refused to speak to me in

the coach. And it isn't as bad as you make it out to be. I would have told you everything had you asked."

Theo snorted. "As I would have, had *you* asked. Like you, I find it far better to make unfounded assumptions."

A low growl came from him. "Theodosia— "

"It was much more pleasant *not* speaking to you." She turned her head. "I don't care to engage you further in conversation." She pushed her spectacles up her nose and started toward the large doors, ignoring the glowering male behind her. He looked as if he wished to strangle her with her bonnet strings.

It would serve Haven right if she simply climbed back in the Averell coach. Fled him and Greenbriar, never to return.

'I have never wanted anything so much as you, Theodosia Barrington. Never question it. Anything but that. Promise me.'

Those words, whispered against her skin, were the only reason Theo was standing here in the courtyard of Greenbriar instead of running for the coach.

She believed Haven.

Theo wasn't overly surprised to find no servants bustling out of the house to greet them. She'd hoped for at least a butler in addition to the previously mentioned Mrs. Henderson. But servants required payment for their services, which Haven, until recently, had lacked the ability to provide. She made a mental note that a butler must be hired immediately. Someone who reminded her of Pith.

Greenbriar grew larger at her approach, making Theo wish she'd never put on her bloody spectacles. Better to be blind in this instance. She supposed it would keep her busy, restoring Greenbriar to the best of her abilities. Give her time to sort out what was between her and Haven.

She looked to the coach her brother had lent them along with a driver and two strapping Averell footmen. All were devoutly loyal to the duke. Tony had probably instructed the three men that Theo was to be taken back to London whenever she wished it.

"Do not walk away from me." Haven's frustrated snarl came from behind her.

Theo continued in the direction of the front door without another glance in his direction, pausing only to say over her shoulder, "I just did."

※

He should just pick her up and drag her off somewhere. Possibly the barn. Press Theodosia into the hay and pleasure her until she couldn't form a coherent thought. When he apologized again, possibly she'd listen.

Instead, Ambrose turned back to the coach and instructed the Averell footmen to take their things into the house. The duke had graciously allowed Ambrose to borrow two of the lads in his employ along with a coach and driver until staff could be hired for Greenbriar. Ambrose didn't mistake his new brother-in-law's concession as kindness. Averell only wanted to make sure his sister had the means to return should she need it.

The driver, a bulky man named Stitch with an outrageous mustache, was polite to Ambrose, but little else. He suspected Stitch would be reporting back to the duke on a regular basis. Averell, pompous prick that he was, had obviously decided the pointed threat he'd made before Ambrose took Theodosia from London wasn't sufficient.

'Your future existence is tied to my sister. Pray, keep that in mind.'

The duke deemed Ambrose unworthy of Theodosia. It was virtually the only thing he and Averell would ever agree on. He had seen the suspicion in the duke's eyes, so like Theodosia's, stabbing him with accusation down the length of the dining room table while Ambrose tried to enjoy his meal. The same way Theodosia had looked at Ambrose after he'd blundered so badly with her this morning.

She had been *glorious*, striding across the room this morning, stark naked and without a shred of modesty. Her breasts were bloody magnificent, every luscious inch of them. He'd been hard-pressed not to take her back to bed, but Ambrose didn't have a death wish. Anger at him had emanated with every step she took, deliberately flaunting herself before Ambrose as part of his punishment.

He'd been half afraid she'd trip over something and spoil the moment, but she hadn't.

At Theodosia's approach, the front door of Greenbriar, covered in chipped paint and squeaking on rusty hinges, opened to reveal Ambrose's sister.

Jacinda, a shy smile of welcome on her face for Theodosia, hobbled out, her cane sending small puffs of dust up around the patched hem of her skirts.

Mrs. Henderson trailed behind her, apron flapping about her broad hips as she wiped her hands.

No sign of Erasmus the sot, thankfully. Probably out picking half-dead flowers so he could bestow a bouquet on Theodosia when she arrived. She might well take one look at his uncle's alcohol-soaked form and head right back into the Averell coach.

Ambrose stalked behind Theodosia, hating how, in hearing him, she moved quickly out of the way so that not even her skirts would touch him.

His teeth ground so hard, he thought his jaw would break, but Ambrose said nothing. Sometimes retreat was the better part of valor, especially when it came to Theodosia. The awkward, agonizing coach ride to Greenbriar from the inn advised him to leave her be for now. At least she was wearing her spectacles.

Jacinda was practically dancing at their arrival—or as

much as one could dance with a lame leg. A thick braid of deep auburn hair flew back and forth over her shoulder as she came to greet them.

Ambrose stepped forward, pulling his younger sister into a tight embrace, feeling the fragile bones of her shoulder blades beneath his palms. She seemed thinner and much more delicate than she had only a few weeks ago when he'd come to tell her he was to be married. She'd beamed at the news, happy and excited, the relief on her face so profound, Ambrose had nearly wept.

He would do anything to save Jacinda.

None of the circumstances which had befallen her were of her own making. Jacinda hadn't forced their father to become a sot. Or to gamble away every bit of the Collingwood wealth, including her dowry. Nor was she to blame for the tragic accident which had cost her full use of her leg.

A wave of guilt broke over Ambrose, one which threatened to engulf him at the very sight of Jacinda and Greenbriar. He should have been here. Instead, he'd been roaming the Continent in a fit of rage at his father, drinking excessively, fighting, and bedding lovely women. Many of them widows, as it happened. If Mrs. Henderson hadn't heard the bone crack as she made her way to the library, or if Erasmus hadn't been here, there wasn't any telling how long Jacinda would have lain on the floor. His father had been passed out drunk in a corner, but his uncle, who'd arrived at Greenbriar a few weeks earlier, had been sober enough to summon a physician.

He owed Erasmus for caring for Jacinda as best he could.

"Where is our uncle?" Ambrose whispered into Jacinda's ear.

"The village tavern. Mr. Owens stopped earlier and asked him to take a pint. I thought it best if he weren't here when you arrived with your wife," she quietly replied so Theodosia couldn't hear.

Owens was the village drunkard, whereas Erasmus was the titled drunkard. The pair were most often found passed out together on the floor of a local tavern. Sometimes his uncle even slept there amongst the spilled ale and sawdust.

"I didn't give him any coin," Jacinda said in a tight voice. "I hid what you left me under a loose floorboard in my room. He did try to sell a couple of books. But don't worry," she assured him. "They weren't any of my favorites. Nor yours."

"Good." Ambrose nodded. Ambrose's father had already decimated the collection of tomes, some of which had been the property of the Collingwood family for more than a century, by the time Ambrose had returned to Greenbriar. The remaining books would only fetch a coin or two, but enough for Erasmus to buy a bottle.

Releasing Jacinda from his embrace, Ambrose waved over Mrs. Henderson, anxious for them both to be introduced to Theodosia.

Edmund Collingwood, as impossible as it was to believe, had been directly responsible for Jacinda's accident. Drunk and stumbling, he'd knocked the ladder out from under her as she'd reached for a book, then passed out. Mrs. Henderson had related to Ambrose the depth of his father's despair when, upon waking from his stupor, he'd realized what he'd done.

Jacinda even claimed their father had refused to leave her bedside as she'd healed and had stayed relatively sober, vowing never to drink again.

All of it was a lie because at some point during her recovery, Edmund had gone back to London, started drinking again, and signed away the only thing left, the sum set aside for Jacinda's dowry, so he could dice at Elysium. He died a short time later. Ambrose never told his sister what their father had done, or where. All he'd said was that their fortune and estates were gone, save Greenbriar. Better to remember the loving father who wouldn't leave her than the weak sot easily manipulated by the owner of Elysium.

Ambrose had to shut his eyes against the absolute fury rising within him, opening them only when he extended an arm in Theodosia's direction.

She ignored his hand. Not unexpected. She did give Jacinda a brilliant smile.

"Theodosia, this is my sister, Lady Jacinda Collingwood."

Jacinda bobbed politely, or as best she could with a cane. "Lady Theodosia, I'm so pleased to meet you." Her eyes took in Theodosia's obviously expensive traveling dress and matching bonnet, lingering over the gloves and leather half-boots with a small flash of envy.

Jacinda barely remembered what it had been like to have such luxuries before their father had gambled everything away. She'd never been to London or seen the house, long since gone, the Marquess of Haven had once owned. No, his sister had been stuck in the country, first watching their father's decline and then waiting for Ambrose as he bled what little was left of their estate to support them. When that was gone, Ambrose played cards, lived with Blythe or Granby, and sent every purse he won to Jacinda. He did everything he could, and it still wasn't enough.

"Lady Jacinda, I assure you I've felt the same," Theodosia replied. "And you must call me Theo. My sisters all do."

Jacinda might melt into a puddle of joy at his feet. He could feel her trembling with happiness. She'd been so lonely at Greenbriar with only Erasmus and Mrs. Henderson for company. His hand fell to his sister's head out of habit, gently stroking her hair. The first thing he meant to do was to ensure Jacinda had something new to wear. He couldn't bear to see her in dresses which should have been tossed in the rag bin years ago.

"Ambrose." Jacinda wiggled away from him with an embarrassed smile in Theodosia's direction. "Cease. I am no longer a child."

"He likes to make assumptions, doesn't he?" Theodosia raised her eyes to his, daring him to snarl back at her in front of his sister. "But not to worry, Jacinda. I do not."

Jacinda fairly bloomed under Theodosia's regard. Ambrose hadn't seen his sister so happy in years, at least not since before he and his father had quarreled so terribly. Upon his return from the Continent, Ambrose had been told his father was dead and the estate bankrupt, and Jacinda was lying in bed with a shattered leg that would never heal properly. He'd been taken aback by the sight of Erasmus, not because he thought Erasmus was his dead father—the two didn't even really look alike—but because Ambrose, like everyone else, had forgotten about the existence of Erasmus.

Poor Erasmus.

"Mrs. Henderson, our housekeeper and cook." Ambrose introduced the woman who had tended to his sister for years. She and her husband both lived at Greenbriar.

Theodosia turned and greeted Mrs. Henderson with more warmth than most ladies of her station would. But the Barringtons were known to treat their servants far better than many of their peers. It was another thing Ambrose liked about his wife, her complete lack of pretension.

"Jacinda, will you show me inside? I'm sure Lord Haven has much to attend to since he's been gone for some time," Theodosia said smoothly, dismissing Ambrose without actually speaking to him.

A clever trick.

"Of course." His sister blushed prettily, thrilled to have Theodosia's attention.

"I'll need your assistance." Theodosia leaned in and took his sister's arm, careful to match her steps to Jacinda's. "With Greenbriar, I mean. There's much to be done." She turned slightly, glaring at Ambrose. "And I fear Lord Haven won't be much help."

Dismissed again. But at least Theodosia had claimed Greenbriar.

It had taken Ambrose the better part of the journey from the inn to admit how poorly he'd handled what had been meant to be a heartfelt apology and how he'd wounded Theodosia. His temper had flared this morning. Jealousy caused him to say things he shouldn't have.

Ambrose was no rake, not in the same way Blythe was, but he had also never lacked female companionship. Taking a woman to bed was an enjoyable, physical release. But he'd never desired any of those previous lovers in quite the same way he did Theodosia. Their joining had been shattering. Intense. It had been more than consummating a marriage, more than a physical release. Ambrose knew the difference.

Theodosia hadn't thought last night meant anything to him and couldn't see what it meant to her. That's why she was angry.

Ambrose took one last look at his sister and Theodosia before he set out in the opposite direction, heading toward the village. The weather was fine, and he needed to walk off some of the tension pulling at his muscles. Being here did that to him. Made him remember.

Besides, the only horses at Greenbriar were the ones still hitched to the Duke of Averell's coach.

18

"**Good** Lord," Theo said under her breath, not wanting to upset Jacinda clinging to her arm as they swept into the main hall of Greenbriar. The tile beneath her feet needed a good scrubbing but otherwise seemed intact. Daring a peek into the drawing room, Theo saw the room was bare except for two chairs, a small table, and a moth-eaten rug which looked as old as the house.

Jacinda cleared her throat. "The drawing room." Her eyes glistened with a mixture of shame and pride at the state of her home.

"A very nice space," Theo told her, not daring to comment further.

Pale green paint peeled from around the windows. No artwork adorned the walls, though there were plenty of obvious spots where paintings had once hung. An enormous crack split the ceiling just above one of the windows with a battered pot beneath it. The fireplace appeared to still be in working condition and intact, but from the amount of black soot staining it, Theo surmised a good cleaning was in order.

Theo could feel herself deflate as the enormity of the situation looked back at her. She'd been expecting a pared down estate, not . . . this. "It's quite a lot to take in at first glance."

"I know it doesn't look like much," Jacinda said. "But when there is a fire roaring in the hearth and a good book in your hand, I promise you'll be very comfortable." She looked askance at one of the chairs where a spring had broken through the upholstery. "We've a marvelous library. Quite spectacular. I mean it was before—" Her voice faltered.

Theo squeezed her hand. "I adore books. And this will be a lovely room."

No wonder Haven simmered with such desperation. Not only for his family home but for Jacinda. Theo would be devastated to see Cherry Hill in such a state, her sisters reduced to wearing a dress patched so frequently it resembled a quilt more than a garment. Why hadn't his friends helped him?

Because he hadn't told them.

She would venture to guess that Granby and Blythe knew of Haven's poverty, but not the extent of it. And his friends only knew the destruction Haven's father had caused from gossip. Blythe was generous to a fault. He would have gladly offered assistance had he been asked, especially for Jacinda's sake.

Jacinda tugged on her sleeve, next showing Theo a large dining room with dusty wainscotting, absent the large table which must have once graced it. A smaller table, dwarfed inside the room, sat surrounded by six mismatched chairs.

Next, the once magnificent ballroom at the back of the house, stripped of chandeliers, the fine marble gouged and dirty beneath her feet. Several sections showed pits and cracks, as if someone had tried to pry out the marble in pieces.

Probably to sell it.

The sight of all this beauty left to rot or stripped bare

made Theo physically ill. Greenbriar was a mere shell of what it must once have been. If she were to make something of her marriage, and Theo still thought she would despite Haven being an idiot, restoring Greenbriar would be her responsibility.

Her knees buckled just a bit.

Theo had never imagined having to renovate an entire estate, or even manage one. Yes, she was a duke's daughter, but one woefully ill-equipped for this endeavor. Theo painted miniatures. Small landscapes. That was the extent of her talents and abilities. Mama had allowed her to thrive on her own, so to speak. Nurture her creativity. Theo's education was lacking in several key respects. She couldn't even plan a dinner menu properly.

The one time in her life she would have welcomed Romy's opinions, and her sister was off with her duke. Romy, blazing warrior that she was, wouldn't think twice at having such a task as the restoration of a crumbling estate set before her. She would have already hired an army of servants, all of whom would have been waiting for her before she even set foot in Greenbriar.

Jacinda touched her hand before leading Theo down the hall to a set of large double doors. "This is my favorite room in the entire house," she said, opening one door with a flourish.

Oh, my.

Theo took a deep breath, inhaled the dust floating about, and promptly started coughing. After the unnecessary and enthusiastic thumping of her back by Jacinda, she straightened and took in Greenbriar's library.

Absolutely stunning, despite its current condition.

Floor-to-ceiling windows faced the parkland surrounding Greenbriar, which would be a lovely view once the grounds were restored. The heavy velvet curtains hanging from the windows—all of which needed a good cleaning—were restrained by frayed, gold cording. Mildew showed in gray patches amidst the velvet, making it difficult to discern what color the curtains had originally been. Evergreen, she thought. The room was two stories, the second-floor landing and more bookcases clearly visible. A small spiral staircase so rickety Theo wouldn't dare to stand on it twisted up above her to the landing. Dozens of half-empty bookcases met her eyes as the aroma of old leather and rot filled the air.

A ladder stood against a set of shelves.

Jacinda's fingers ran down the scarred wood of the ladder, features pinching up.

Theo looked down at Jacinda's leg. She'd fallen from that ladder, ruining her leg. Theo was certain of it.

"What do you think?" Jacinda's smile was weak, searching. Begging Theo to love this space as much as she did. "I'm slowly cataloging the books we have left."

She must spend hours in here every day. Theo could picture her on the ladder, reaching up for a book, only to wobble and fall to the floor. It must have happened when Haven was living abroad.

"I think, Jacinda, this is the most amazing library I've ever seen. Far grander than I could have possibly imagined. I don't think I've ever seen one finer, and that's saying something."

Jacinda beamed back at her, bouncing on her feet at Theo's praise.

How old was Jacinda, exactly? Theo took in her delicate bone structure and petite form. Haven said his sister was about the same age as Phaedra, but her eyes belied the hardship she'd endured, making her seem far older than she was. Her heart ached for her new sister-in-law, stuck in the country with only her daft uncle and Mrs. Henderson.

"The windows need to be cleaned from top to bottom," Theo stated. She knew that much at least. "The floors scrubbed until they shine." An image took shape in her mind. Rather like one of her miniatures. Only larger. "What would you think of a reading nook, just there by the window? Comfortable chairs. Lots of cushions. Several small tables."

Nodding eagerly in agreement, Jacinda said, "Perhaps a small settee?"

"Of course, if you wish it."

Jacinda's excitement faded as she looked down at her feet. "Won't you need to ask my brother first? It all sounds lovely but rather expensive. He may not approve, and I've no wish to upset him."

"Haven has made it clear I'm to take over the care of Greenbriar, or at least the portion we'll live in." She'd no intention of cozying up to Haven in the drawing room and studying fabric samples with him. "And I'm obscenely wealthy." Theo winked at her. "Expense is the least of your worries."

The smile returned. "Ambrose told me you are an artist. You paint and sketch. He said your work consists mainly of miniatures and is some of the finest he's ever seen." Her cheeks pinked. "The miniature you painted for him as a betrothal gift is exquisite, at least from what Ambrose tells me. A self-portrait." A wistful look crossed her face. "How romantic of you, Theo."

"Yes, terribly romantic of me." It was obvious Haven hadn't shared the *exact* nature of the miniature, nor the circumstances of his marriage to Theo, with his sister. A good thing, because Theo would be hard-pressed to look Jacinda in the eye. How like Haven to have turned his thievery into a romantic gesture.

Wretch.

A smile tugged at Theo's lips. "My finest and final miniature," she declared. "I'm moving on to painting on a larger canvas."

"You are?" Jacinda said hopefully. "Perhaps you would paint something for the library."

"It would be my honor." Theo pulled her rambling thoughts away from Haven. She was still nursing the wounds he'd inflicted earlier today.

"Shall we go upstairs? Unless you wish to see my brother's study?"

"No. I believe I'll save that for later." Theo didn't want to run the risk of bumping into Haven yet, though she wasn't sure he was even in the house. Since coming inside with Jacinda, Theo had seen nothing of her husband. Perhaps he'd abandoned her again. Or he was giving her temper time to cool.

Jacinda led her up the stairs, pointing out where not to place her feet as at least two of the steps sported small, cracked boards. How the poor girl managed to make her way to her room without injuring herself on a daily basis shocked Theo. The library would not be the first thing repaired. These stairs would.

And the bannister, Theo thought ruefully as the beautifully carved wood tilted dangerously beneath her fingers. The entire house was battered and bruised, begging for someone to care for it.

Once they reached the landing, Jacinda pointed to a hallway to her left. "Guest rooms for guests we no longer receive. I'm not sure what we'll find in them, Theo. They've been shut for some time. This is the family wing," she said, starting down the hall leading to the right. There wasn't so much as a small table on which to set a lamp, and the walls, much like those below, were devoid of any art or personal effects. "These are your rooms." Jacinda stopped before a door, a look of trepidation on her pretty face. "When your maid arrived, Mrs. Henderson showed her up. I believe she's been unpacking your things."

"Betts." Oh, dear. Poor Betts. Theo hadn't spared her a thought. Between the argument with Haven this morning and their arrival at Greenbriar, Theo had forgotten all about her maid. Ashamed, she stepped ahead of Jacinda, her only thought to greet the stalwart, faithful Betts and seeing a familiar face. A small, unwelcome sound burst from between her lips as she opened the door.

Betts stood at the far end of a very large, spartan room next to a dresser, muttering to herself. Theo's valise stood next to her feet. Behind Betts rose a small mountain of Theo's trunks, most of which had not been unpacked.

Because there was nowhere to put Theo's clothing.

The armoire, the only other piece of furniture in the room besides the enormous bed sitting atop a raised dais, wasn't overly large. She could see the sleeves of one of her dresses poking from behind the doors of the armoire. There didn't appear to be room for anything else. Haven's clothing must be in the dresser.

Oh, dear.

"My lady." Betts came forward with a forced smile. She was a plump, no-nonsense girl, cousin to Romy's maid, Daisy, and as loyal as they came. A sideways glance from Betts told Theo everything she needed to know about the situation at Greenbriar.

At least the room was large, though without proper furniture, the area seemed especially cavernous. The windows, as filthy as those in the library, overlooked the mangled remains of a garden and part of the drive circling the front of the house.

"I cleaned as best I could, my lady," Betts whispered out of the corner of her mouth, sparing a glance at Jacinda. "She's a sweet one, is Lady Jacinda. And I didn't wish to upset her."

Theo looked toward the door leading to an adjoining room.

"There is an adjoining room, Lady Theodosia, but no bed," Betts murmured. "No armoire. No furniture of any kind. The room looks as if it were stripped. Nothing left."

Theo's stomach sank. No wonder Haven said there would be no distance in their marriage. It was physically impossible unless she wanted to sleep elsewhere.

"I see." Theo didn't bother looking around for a valet. She had the impression Haven no longer had one.

"I know it all needs," Jacinda hesitated, "work." She shifted back and forth on her feet, leaning on the cane and looking utterly devastated. "I am sorry for the poor welcome."

Shadows of Haven appeared in the mulish tilt of Jacinda's jaw.

"My welcome has been anything but poor, Jacinda. There is nothing here that soap and hard work can't fix." This house must be put to rights, if for no one else but Jacinda. "I'll admit, I'm not known to be especially good at tidying up and such—"

Betts gave a quiet snort.

"But I promise you, Jacinda, we'll have everything put to rights. And you must be patient." She squeezed her arm. "Haven told me what to expect. All the things that must be done," she lied. "I'm not the least surprised. I assumed it would be much worse."

Jacinda nodded, looking relieved.

Theodosia's Enormous Endeavor.

She tried to view the room as the artist she was, envisioning it as a blank canvas upon which she must create. It made things simpler, looking at each room and Greenbriar as nothing more than the barest outline of a sketch. The stroke of the brush, the hues and shading. All must come later.

"I do wish my sister were here. She's clever with fabrics and how things must go together." Theo might not share

Romy's creativity at designs, but she *was* good at color. Light. Shadows.

This is nothing but a very large painting.

"Granby's duchess," Jacinda said. "Ambrose told me."

"Yes," Theo said, surprised Haven had told Jacinda about her sister. "Romy has quite an eye for fabrics and such. But we'll muddle through without her."

Jacinda's room, the last on Theo's tour, was closer to the front of the house. It was the only compliment Theo could give the spot where Haven's sister slept. The wallpaper covering the walls was so ancient it had yellowed, the pattern unrecognizable. A stack of books served as the missing leg of what was once a finely carved table. Another armoire, this one in fairly decent shape, sat open against one wall, allowing her to see the near emptiness inside. The bed at least looked comfortable, unlike the one residing in the room Theo had just left. This mattress appeared free of lumps, but the faded blue coverlet was torn. Books were stacked everywhere, most in worse shape than the room.

The first place Theo meant to take Jacinda, after the dressmakers, was a bookstore.

Propped against the mantel of the fireplace was a portrait of a woman with hair the same color as Jacinda's. It was the only painting Theo had seen in the entire house. She guessed, by the resemblance to Jacinda and Haven, the woman was their mother.

"She's lovely," Theo said, admiring the portrait.

Jacinda's cane thumped softly behind her. "My mother," she replied. "Matilda. Ambrose says I favor her. I wasn't very old when she died. Childbirth. A fever took her and the babe."

And then Haven's father had slowly fallen into despair. Drink. Gambling. Taking his family with him. Theo regarded the painting of the auburn-haired woman with soft hazel eyes, seeing Haven's rough attractiveness in her feminine features.

"I'm so sorry, Jacinda."

"It was some time ago." She gave a shrug. "I wish I remembered more about her. That's what bothers me the most." A stricken look entered her delicate features as she tapped the cane on the floor. "Ambrose is older, so he tells me stories, but it isn't the same. Father never recovered from her death. His heart was broken. Ambrose and I weren't enough for him." Stark sadness bled through her words. "Then he died too." Despite his leaving her impoverished, Jacinda had loved her father. Theo could hear it in her voice.

"I lost my own father," she said, taking Jacinda's hand. "I miss him very much."

"The Duke of Averell. Uncle Erasmus told me about him when Ambrose said you were marrying. He said your brother looks remarkably like him, considering."

Theo's brow wrinkled at the odd comment. "Considering what?"

Jacinda shrugged again. "I've no idea. My uncle doesn't often make sense. Besides the drink, he's slightly addled. Something he and Mr. Henderson have in common." She gave a small laugh. "You'll see when you make his acquaintance."

"Erasmus lived in France, didn't he?" She wondered how Erasmus had seen the late Duke of Averell and either of his sons. Maybe the first time he returned to Greenbriar? When Haven was a child?

"He did. But he ran out of money, which Ambrose says he was bound to do because he hasn't a mind for such things."

"What sort of things?"

"Running an estate. Managing servants. Ledger books. Tenants. All the things a lord must do. At least according to my brother. Ambrose likens him to an oversized infant that one must care for." She giggled. "Albeit one who smells of spirits."

Yes, that sounded like something Haven would say.

"I was shocked when my uncle appeared. I didn't even know I had an uncle, let alone one who looked like my father. But I was glad he came to Greenbriar. He'd heard Ambrose was dead and came to console my father. He was trembling something terrible from his journey. My father and Erasmus argued. Drank a lot. I'm grateful he was here when my father died, though my uncle is a bit of a handful at times. It's the drink and his nervous condition."

"Haven wasn't here, was he?" The story fascinated Theo because it sounded like one of her novels. She shook her head. Twin brothers consumed by their love of spirits wasn't exactly something anyone would wish to read about.

"No, Ambrose was in Italy, living in a villa. That's where he met Granby. During a swordfight outside of Venice."

"A duel?" Given Haven's temper, she could imagine him brandishing a sword as someone mistakenly insulted him.

"Oh, no." Jacinda shook her head. "He *saved* Granby who *was* in a swordfight." Jacinda rubbed her finger over the bridge of her nose. "That's why Ambrose has the bump there. Granby was swinging at someone during the fight, and my brother was trying to help him. Granby elbowed Ambrose in the nose. My brother often says had he only let that Italian count skewer Granby, he'd still have a perfect nose." Jacinda gave a soft laugh. "Or if Blythe knew how to wield a weapon properly. But Ambrose saved him anyway."

Haven had come to the aid of Granby and Blythe during a swordfight. How noble of him. Something stirred inside her as she imagined Haven with a sword, jumping into the fray to come to the rescue of his friends. A very dashing thing to do.

Even so, my anger has not yet cooled.

"What was your brother even doing in Italy?" Haven

hadn't been very forthcoming about his adventures. "He's already told me he knows nothing of art, and that's why most people go there, besides the weather." Theo hated to admit that a part of her wondered if he'd gone for a woman.

"Ambrose hasn't a clue about paintings and such. Which is why I find it ironic he's married an artist. I was far more upset when my father and uncle stripped the walls than he was."

It pained Theo to know Jacinda had witnessed such a thing.

"It was the argument with my father which made him leave. About the drinking and—" Jacinda plucked at her skirts. "All the gambling. My father was so in his cups he didn't even remember Ambrose being here that day or what they fought about. He was terribly upset Ambrose was gone. Uncle Erasmus says if he had been here at the time, he would have tried to stop them from parting in anger." She looked up at Theo, anguish shadowing her eyes. "Ancient history. We should go down. I think it must be time for tea."

19

Theo sat back, trying to get comfortable in one of the two chairs in the drawing room, nearly impossible since both lacked a decent cushion. She took the one with the spring sticking out to spare Jacinda.

The conversation with Jacinda still echoed in her thoughts. Why couldn't Haven have just stayed in his role of the disreputable, sarcastic marquess who liked to spout insults about her eyesight? Why must he be so bloody interesting?

Haven deserved some sympathy. It didn't even seem fair for her to continue to call him a fortune hunter. Jacinda was lame. She had no hope of finding a husband without a dowry. That alone made Theo's heart break. He'd been forced to care for Erasmus, and even though Haven kept saying his uncle didn't really look like the late marquess, it still couldn't be pleasant to see him every day. The estate, the only property he had left, was in bits and pieces. And Haven had never made peace with his father before his death.

Theo knew a thing or two about estranged fathers and sons.

All of which muddled her feelings even further. She didn't want to consider Haven and his suffering. At least not today.

"Tea, Lady Haven?" Mrs. Henderson, robust and comforting, interrupted her thoughts, standing before her holding a tray loaded with biscuits and a chipped teapot, steam rolling out of the spout.

"You are a treasure, Mrs. Henderson." Theo nodded in appreciation. "Lord Haven has told me so on many occasions." A small lie, one she thought the housekeeper might like to hear.

Mrs. Henderson's plump cheeks pinked at the compliment. "Will you wish to inspect the kitchens?"

Bollocks. Theo had no idea what to even look for. "Perhaps tomorrow, Mrs. Henderson. These biscuits," Theo said as the housekeeper set the tray on the table, "look divine."

"I do hope you like them, my lady. My own twist on an old recipe. A favorite of his lordship since he was a lad."

"Well, then I hope you've baked dozens." Theo bit into the biscuit. "Given my husband's appetite."

A small chuckle came from the housekeeper. "Several dozen, my lady."

Jacinda munched on a biscuit. "Ambrose will eat them all."

"Have you seen Lord Haven, Mrs. Henderson? Is he wandering about your kitchen?" It was mildly embarrassing, not knowing where her husband was, even if she wasn't supposed to care. The kitchens seemed a likely spot for him to be. Haven was always hungry.

Mrs. Henderson's face shuttered almost immediately, the polite smile faltering. "No, my lady. I saw him walking to the village earlier. I can check with Mr. Henderson if you like—"

"I'm sure he's gone to fetch my uncle," Jacinda interrupted through a mouth full of biscuit.

"Poor soul," Mrs. Henderson stated. "He'll find him, I've no doubt."

"I'm certain of it." Theo took up the pencil and paper Jacinda had found for her. There was much to consider. Work to be done. No time to be worrying about the sot of an uncle or Haven.

Theodosia's Enormous Endeavor.

She began to make notes. A great many of them. Though she'd no idea, really, of what she was doing. When Mrs. Henderson tried to leave, Theo stopped her. "Would it be all right, Mrs. Henderson, if Jacinda and I eat in here before the fire?"

Jacinda nodded as she sipped her tea.

"Of course, my lady. I've made stew."

"Perfect. And I want a list of everything you think the kitchen requires, including additional servants. The larder must be restocked. I trust you to determine what is needed."

Mrs. Henderson's eyes bulged at the request. "Yes, my lady. But might I make a suggestion, Lady Haven?"

Theo stopped scratching away and looked up at her. If Mrs. Henderson decided to retire from her post, she might be forced to beg the older woman not to leave.

"Greenbriar needs a proper cook."

Theo had assumed Mrs. Henderson *was* the cook as well as the housekeeper. "I see," she replied carefully.

"I was the housekeeper before," she waved a plump hand, "but took over other duties as was needed. Not that I minded," she hastened to add. "While I am a passable cook, my lady, I'm not what you need to run a proper kitchen. My skills are biscuits, pies, stew and the like. A marquess needs a skilled cook."

Theo adored stew, but she could see Mrs. Henderson's point. "I appreciate your honesty, Mrs. Henderson. And in the same spirit, I feel I should inform you I'm terrible at running a household." She tapped the pencil against her chin. "I realize I should know such things, but I was far too busy painting. Ordering people about is really my elder sister's forte." She smiled up at Mrs. Henderson. "I desperately need your help. Will you stay on as housekeeper?"

Mrs. Henderson beamed. "Of course. I've no wish to leave Lady Jacinda or Greenbriar."

"I've no wish to have you leave me either, Mrs. Henderson." Jacinda smiled up at the housekeeper.

"I will not let you down, my lady," the housekeeper said to Theo, looking as if she were about to lead a military charge. "I know how things are to be done at Greenbriar. If I may be so bold, Lady Haven, I've someone in mind for a cook and you'll be needing a butler, will you not?"

"I will. Someone fierce, Mrs. Henderson." The butler would need to be made of iron to stand up to Haven.

"I've just the gentleman in mind. A cousin of my sister's husband. Recently left his position with the Duke of Haverly."

"Wonderful. Bring him tomorrow." Maids and footmen needed to be hired immediately, along with a team of women to come and clean the house from top to bottom.

"Mr. Henderson knows everyone in the village," Mrs. Henderson added. "My husband can find you cleaning women and put the word out that Greenbriar is looking for staff."

"Tradesmen must be found as well." Theo tapped her finger against her lips. "Carpenters. We need new paint. Rugs. Wallpaper. Furnishings." She snagged the last biscuit from the tray. "Please sit down, Mrs. Henderson. We have quite a lot to do." Theo had only just arrived, but she already felt the urgency pulling at her to fix Greenbriar, whether for herself or Haven and his sister, she wasn't sure.

"A moment, my lady." Mrs. Henderson fled to the kitchen for more biscuits and another chair, summoning her husband. Mr. Henderson arrived a short time later, his angular features obviously confused by the summons, his long white hair flowing over his shoulders. After introductions were made, the housekeeper sent Mr. Henderson to the village, advising him not to return until he'd hired enough women to clean the house from top to bottom.

Theo hoped he could remember his way there and back. Mr. Henderson seemed a bit forgetful.

"War injury," Jacinda whispered to her. "A blow to the head."

Feeling much better, Theo ate another biscuit, ideas flowing to the pencil in her hand. Several hours passed swiftly as she and Jacinda made plans. Theo scratched out instructions. Bits of paper piled around her. Every so often, she would close her eyes and pretend to walk through Cherry Hill. She knew each room by heart. Every painting, table, bit of china, and rug. Her eyes would snap open, mind churning with inspiration.

Mrs. Henderson arrived after a time with the aforementioned stew, the smell of which made Theo's mouth water. She'd been too upset to do more than have a cup of tea and a nibble of toast before leaving the inn. Had it only been this morning? The remainder of the day and evening had passed swiftly and, Theo thought, productively. Night was falling. Theo had no idea what time it was. In addition to everything else it lacked, Greenbriar didn't have a clock.

She made another note.

The stew was excellent and accompanied by fresh baked bread. Theo finished every bit. Still, there was no sign of Haven. Or his uncle.

Jacinda, eyelids drooping, finally bid Theo goodnight. "It has been a most exciting day, Theo. Like a whirlwind." A tired smile crossed her lips. "Very diverting." There was a touch of Haven's sarcasm in her words.

Theo adored her all the more for it.

Finally, her own eyes burning with exhaustion, Theo

decided Haven would appear when he wished it, whether she waited up for him or not. It wasn't as if she planned on engaging him in conversation. She stretched, hearing the creak of her neck, and made her way up the stairs, carefully avoiding each of the broken steps Jacinda had pointed out earlier. She arrived at her room to see the ever-efficient Betts waiting for her.

"Have you eaten, Betts? I keep forgetting you're here, and I don't mean to. It's just—well there was quite a bit to occupy me."

"You've been inspired, my lady. You behave much the same way when you've found something you must paint. And very much like Her Grace, your mother, when she's found a project."

"You think so, Betts?" Romy was most often compared to their mother, not Theo.

"I do indeed." The maid raised one brow. "It's a shambles, isn't it, my lady? Greenbriar, that is. I can't imagine if something like this were to happen to Cherry Hill."

"I hadn't thought it would be so bad." Theo took her maid's arm and led her to the bed so they could both sit down. "Haven didn't exactly prepare me. Not well, at least. I can't believe he allowed Greenbriar to fall to shambles. And before you try to find a discreet, maidly way to ask me, yes. I had a wedding night. It was fine."

Betts raised her brow. "I wasn't going to ask."

Theo narrowed her eyes. "You were. And don't ask anything else. Tell me what you think of Greenbriar. I value your observations."

Her maid puffed up a bit at that. "Mrs. Henderson's a lovely woman. Clucks over Lady Jacinda like a mother hen. She's the glue holding this place together, especially with his lordship gone so much. Husband's a good sort too, though he's a bit daft, much like the uncle."

"I had the pleasure of meeting Mr. Henderson earlier. He's gone to the village to find some women to clean this place from top to bottom. And I've a man coming to interview for the position of butler tomorrow. And a cook."

"A good start, my lady." Betts smoothed her skirts. "I explored a bit when I arrived, as I assumed you'd wish me to. Discreetly, of course. The larder is nearly bare, though the kitchen itself is in decent shape. Mrs. Henderson isn't creative in her cooking, but the food is satisfying."

"She said as much."

"The kitchen garden has been run over by rabbits with only a few greens worth salvaging. While you were with Lady Jacinda, I put the two Averell footmen along with the driver in the head groom's quarters, which were empty since there isn't a head groom or any grooms at all. But those rooms are in much better condition than the servants' quarters upstairs." Her eyes rolled to the ceiling. "The lads are fine. Well fed."

"And Stitch?" Betts had a flirtatious relationship with the driver.

Betts turned pink. "He enjoyed the stew."

Theo's fingers thumped the mattress. Now that she was sitting and not in motion, or arguing with Haven, the enormity of the situation was starting to form itself into a large ball of dread in her stomach. "I should have just fled to America. Better to be a pariah than to have to deal with Greenbriar. We could be eating oysters and drinking champagne with Leo."

Betts snorted. "You don't care for either. And I've never known you to run from anything, my lady."

Theo laughed. "I believe you're thinking of my sisters. I am in no way suited for this. I paint miniatures, Betts. I barely have the courage to branch out onto a larger canvas let alone make repairs to a country estate. You know as well as I do, I'm merely the flighty, artistic Barrington. The strange one who hides on the third floor and paints. I wear hideous spectacles." She gestured to her face. "I threw myself at the first man who paid me the least amount of attention." Theo sucked in her breath as the words came out in a rush. "Which resulted in me being compromised by *accident*. By a destitute marquess who brought me to," her voice raised an octave, "this."

Betts gave her a patient look.

"I'm not Romy who can take charge of everything and have it come out perfectly, or Olivia who would know exactly what to do. God forbid, I'm not even Phaedra who would just blaze in here and demand attention, I'm—"

"Lady Haven," Betts said firmly. "*You* are Lady Haven. And mess or not, *prepared* or not, this is now your home. At least until you decide to take His Grace's coach back to London. If you do not think you can do a thing, you must prove yourself wrong. Not once, my lady, have you fainted, fallen to the floor weeping, or otherwise become morose over your circumstances. Don't forget it was you who assisted your mother when she made the renovations to Cherry Hill. Not Lady Andromeda."

"Yes, but I was barely Phaedra's age. All I did was pick some colors. You helped me."

"I recall a young lady who, in finding out the painters your mother hired had taken advantage of her good nature, demanded a better price."

She had done that. Papa had endured his first of many declines, and her mother had been sick with worry, preoccupied with caring for him.

"It was you who chose the color for the guestrooms. The proper light to display those statues and paintings Her Grace so loves. And your painting is glorious."

"Useless talents, I'm afraid. I never paid much attention to running a household."

"You've Mrs. Henderson for that. And me. Your 'useless' talents, as you call them, are in dire need here, my lady." Her arms swept out in what Theo imagined was meant to encompass all of Greenbriar.

Theo steadied herself. What would she do without Betts? "I'm done with my tirade of self-pity." She took her maid's hand. "Thank you."

"Very good, my lady. I find such things as exhausting as cleaning your paintbrushes." Her maid winked.

Betts had cleaned exactly one paintbrush in all the time she'd been Theo's maid. "It was *one* brush, but I take your point."

The maid stood, nodding at the bed. "A new mattress should be at the top of your list, my lady. I'll pop downstairs and heat some water so you can wash and be back in a moment. I've a small packet of herbs for the water. You can soak a wet cloth." She looked pointedly at Theo. "To ease any pain."

"Thank you, Betts." Theo hadn't paid much attention to anything but Greenbriar today. There was a tiny bit of soreness from last night, but she wasn't in any pain. "I don't think I require any special attention."

Betts just raised a brow at her before bustling out the door. Once she was gone, Theo flopped back on the bed, mind whirling with the list of things required to bring Greenbriar back to life. Possibly, she shouldn't even care. She could just ignore the crumbling estate for a few weeks and return to London. The idea had merit.

And where was Haven?

Theo had anticipated a *bit* of groveling from him after their argument this morning. Maybe some teasing. At the very least, he could have joined her for dinner. Instead, he'd taken off without a word for the remainder of the day, allowing her to be shown around by Jacinda.

I dismissed him.

True, but she hadn't thought Haven could be dismissed.

She rolled her head over and sat up, looking out the window at a lone rose bush struggling to survive among the weeds along the side of the house. "I suppose I need a bloody gardener too." This might be the only time in recent memory she actually missed Granby. He'd have the withering plants outside blooming again in no time.

Betts bustled into the room again with warm water, soap, and a towel. "You must add linens to the list, my lady. Most of what I could find are," she held up the towel which Theo could see through, "not in the finest shape."

"Nothing at all is in fine shape here, Betts. Whatever would I do without you? I'm so grateful you are here, as well as Ronald and Coates." She named the two Averell footmen.

"And Stitch," Betts reminded her.

"Of course. And Stitch."

Betts held up the towel for Theo, casting a glance out the window as she did so. "Lord Haven has just returned with his uncle, my lady. The terrible sot."

"Is he really so bad?"

"I should be asking you that, my lady."

"I meant Erasmus, Betts."

Her maid bit back a smile. "I had a cousin. Trembled something terrible. Couldn't even attend a dance due to his nervous condition. Always counted all his steps, no matter where he walked. The only way for him to get through the day was his gin. Lord Erasmus reminds me of my cousin. The worst thing he'd done, according to Mrs. Henderson, was steal some of Lady Jacinda's books to buy drink. Which she forgave him for, though Lord Haven did not. Yelled at his uncle for it. Lord Erasmus is tetched in the head, I warrant. Much like Mr. Henderson."

"A war injury," Theo said absently. "Mr. Henderson, that is."

"He's harmless but bothersome. Gave me a half-dead rose just this morning. You'll form your own opinion, I'm sure. Stays drunk a great deal of the time, always mumbling. Sometimes in another language—"

"French, most likely. Erasmus lived there for many years until, well, until he couldn't."

"Whatever it is, it hurts these poor English ears to hear it. Trembles something terrible due to the drink. When I arrived, I found him passed out in the drawing room. Nearly tripped over him. Screamed as if I'd stabbed him. It was so dark without the lamps lit, I thought he was a rolled-up rug."

"Until you realized there are no rugs left at Greenbriar."

Betts shot her a grin. "Nor proper chairs or beds. According to Mrs. Henderson," Betts lowered her voice, "the uncle was the one who suggested the late marquess sell everything that wasn't nailed down. Encouraged it. Probably because the marquess was so deeply in debt."

"I'm sure," Theo answered.

"There's not a portrait, vase or knickknack left." Betts clucked her tongue as she helped ready Theo for bed.

"Betts, you must think me terrible. I completely forgot. Where will you sleep if there aren't any beds in the servant's quarters?"

"You're not to worry, my lady. I've found a spot downstairs in a small parlor Mrs. Henderson said once belonged to Lord Haven's mother. A veritable paradise. There are two sofas. They've seen better days, mind you, fabric torn and such, but they aren't uncomfortable. Probably why they weren't sold along with everything else. Made myself a cozy little nook. Had the things from your studio all put inside so

I can keep an eye on them. As well as your extra trunks. I keep the room locked up. Mrs. Henderson assures me I've got the only key."

"Is it really necessary to lock things up?" she said before recalling what had happened to Jacinda's books. "Never mind. I assume because of Haven's uncle."

"Things do tend to walk off, according to Mrs. Henderson, especially if Lord Erasmus is out of drink. Don't want him trying to sell one of your gowns or a miniature you've done. Like any true sot, he has bottles of spirits stashed all over the house. And in the tree at the edge of the drive. But don't worry, he won't dare come up here. He's terrified of Lord Haven. And before you ask, I'm not sure where he sleeps." She shrugged.

"I'm sure he has a room somewhere." Haven had still not made an appearance despite the statement from Betts that she'd seen him come up the drive with Erasmus in tow. She'd have expected he would at least check on her.

Stifling a yawn, Theo waved Betts goodnight before sinking beneath the sheets. At least they were clean and smelled of soap and sunshine. Probably the doing of her maid. Betts deserved something special for tolerating such poor working conditions. Perhaps Theo would have Romy design a dress for Betts. One she could wear on her day off or if she chose to let Stitch court her.

She rolled over on her side, trying to get comfortable on the mattress—impossible because it sagged dreadfully in the middle. The soreness made itself known when she moved. Theo could still feel Haven's mouth on her breasts, the featherlight touch across her skin. Annoyance tightened her lips. She shouldn't have had to navigate today without him regardless of whether she'd dismissed him or not.

A moment later, the door opened. Finally. Theo didn't bother to roll over or greet him.

"I doubt you're asleep." Exhaustion colored the low timbre of Haven's voice.

He circled the bed, lamp in hand, until he faced her, dripping water all over the floor and across the bed. The corner of his shirt was torn and covered in dirt. His mop of hair stuck out sharply, drops of water dripping from the ends. One of his cheeks had a cut, and his knuckles were scraped and raw looking.

Dear God. He is Theseus the tomcat.

It was obvious he'd been in a fight. And just as apparent he'd bathed somewhere. A pond or a stream would be her guess. There was a thin strand of grass stuck in his hair. He sat on the bed and took off one boot, flinging mud across the room.

"What are you doing?" Theo sat up. Surely, he didn't think they were sharing this room tonight after what he'd said to her this morning. Because they weren't.

"Taking my boots off." He craned his neck to take her in. "What does it look like."

Not so much as an apology for leaving her adrift in this bloody heap the entire day. Not a hint of groveling for his false assumptions. "It looks like, my lord, that you are planning to disrobe, which I insist you do in another room."

"You sound very prim this evening, Theodosia. Quite a departure from last night. And I feel as if we've already had this conversation."

"Sleep with your uncle. I assume you've found him."

Haven tossed his other boot across the room, stood, and stripped off his shirt as he walked, completely disregarding her request that he disrobe elsewhere. The muscles of his back flexed, bunching beneath his skin as he tossed the shirt to the floor.

Despite her anger at him, Theo couldn't look away. Her fingers stretched at the remembered feel of all that sinew beneath her fingers. A soft throb at the apex of her thighs had her clutching the sheets.

Dammit.

It was very hard to make her point and stand her ground when her own body betrayed her so blatantly.

"I'm very tired, Theodosia," he growled. "I promise, I've no desire for anything but sleep. You are safe from my attentions."

"You left me here to flounder—"

"I sincerely doubt you've ever floundered in your life, Theodosia. Of all the things I admire about the Barrington women, I find your ability to let nothing deter you to be one of your finest qualities."

Why must he compliment her? "That's a nice way of saying we're stubborn."

He shrugged and started to pull off his trousers. "If you will recall, you dismissed me and set off with Jacinda. Declared, not in so many words, that you would take charge of this house."

God help her, she could not look away. The rise of muscular buttocks and thighs appeared. He had a scar along one shoulder blade as if someone had swiped at him with a sword from behind. Or a knife. Such beautiful lines. Haven would have made such a lovely pirate.

An ache, like the slow drip of honey, slid lower, making her thighs tremble.

"I'm still angry." The declaration was more for herself than for him.

"And I've apologized. It isn't my fault you don't want to accept it." Haven flipped back the covers, meaning to get into bed with her.

She reached over and flipped them back.

"I told you. There isn't another decent bed," he said. "In case you haven't noticed, because you can't see most of the time, there is also a shortage of furniture at Greenbriar in general."

Only a blind person, of which he just accused her of being, wouldn't have noticed. The sarcasm in his reply did little to hide the shame lingering in his words. A rush of pity filled her, something Haven would detest if he glimpsed it.

"Miss Emerson would never have survived this," Theo said in a casual tone. "She would have run screaming back to her carriage, wedding bouquet still clutched in her hand."

"As I said, you are made of much sterner stuff, Theodosia. Though you claim to be a frivolous, odd Barrington with little to recommend you but scandalous self-portraits."

"At least," she pretended to be offended by his nakedness, "put something on."

"Why? You've already seen everything. Or at least the blurry outline," Haven shot back. "I don't often wear anything to bed, and I don't expect to start tonight. Go to sleep."

"Don't you dare touch me," she felt the need to say even though he'd made no attempt to do so. Taking two pillows, she neatly divided the bed in half.

"Don't *you* dare touch *me*, Theodosia," he said before blowing out the lamp. And with that, Haven collapsed on the bed.

༺✦༻

AMBROSE FLOPPED BACK ON THE MATTRESS, THUMPING hard to smooth out a tiny rise poking him in the side. Theodosia's mood wasn't nearly as bad as he'd thought it would be, though he didn't care overmuch for the pillows in the middle of the bed. She had every right to toss him out of the room and kick him down the stairs after leaving her alone today, especially after their heated discussion at the inn.

Greenbriar and the events which had led to its current state often left Ambrose in turmoil, and today was no exception. How often had he arrived here from London, exhausted by his efforts to continuously plug the holes in a sinking ship, to be greeted with the neglect of both his family and the home he loved? Had he been a different sort of man, Ambrose might have avoided Greenbriar and its inhabitants altogether. He could have provided for his sister from London, but being here was a very specific sort of torture for him, and so he always returned. Today, Theodosia had needed distance, which he had been happy to give her. Not just for her sake, but his own. He didn't think he could bear to see her face as she looked at Greenbriar. Cowardly of him, but true.

Genteel poverty was not a state Ambrose had ever thought he and Jacinda would be subjected to. He had been woefully unprepared for the responsibility. The disbelief over his father's flagrant disregard for anything other than his own pleasure, along with the sadness, would sink into him the moment Greenbriar came into view, bringing back every word of the ugly argument between them. His father had been roaring drunk, snarling at Ambrose for daring to approach Leo Murphy to cut off his credit at Elysium.

The guilt slowly ate away at Ambrose, taking pieces of him as the years went by. Because he'd lost his temper and left England, not even bothering to tell Jacinda goodbye. He hadn't been here to stop Leo Murphy, selfish prick, as he proceeded to take advantage of a grief-stricken man. Ambrose had been unable to halt the bleeding of Greenbriar and his family fortune. Nor present to save his beloved sister from the accident that lamed her. At least Erasmus had been here to care for her, no matter his reason for returning to Greenbriar.

Ambrose pinched his nose, feeling the small bump,

longing for the time in his life when he hadn't felt such overwhelming regret over the choices he'd made. Now the yawning abyss of guilt which always threatened to swallow him had stretched to include Theodosia. If Ambrose didn't succeed in driving her away out of sheer stupidity, she was still bound to leave him if Leo Murphy saw fit to inform her of Ambrose's threats. How the heir to the Marquess of Haven blamed Elysium and Murphy for beggaring his father. The threats Ambrose had made to take back the Collingwood fortune under any means necessary. Murphy would explain to Theodosia that she'd only been a pawn in Ambrose's bid to avenge his family's nonexistent honor.

Pain lanced across his chest.

He'd taken his time looking for Erasmus because he hadn't really wanted to find his uncle, nor did he want to face Greenbriar and his own guilt, trapped neatly within the confines of its walls. Instead, Ambrose had stopped to check on the tenants he'd been successful in either luring back or convincing to stay. There was a pig farmer, Jasper, who he had high hopes for. A portion of the fence around Jasper's pigs was in disrepair, so Ambrose had gotten in the muck with the farmer and helped him fix it.

Feeling somewhat lighter after the physical labor but still unwilling to see Theodosia's reaction to Greenbriar, Ambrose had made two more stops, greeting his few tenants and asking what he could do to help them. His father had taught him the importance of listening before he became a walking tragedy.

It would take several years or more for Greenbriar to be profitable again, or at least be self-sufficient, but even so, Ambrose wasn't about to pin his financial hopes on the estate. Poverty had been a bitter pill to swallow, and one he vowed never to taste again. After the marriage contracts had been signed, Ambrose had paid a visit to Estwood. His friend had already invested a portion of Theodosia's dowry. There was more than enough left over for Greenbriar.

Eventually, he'd found Erasmus, so drunk he could barely speak. The punch he'd thrown at his nephew, because he thought Ambrose to be a 'frightening monster' as he put it, missed. It did not miss the tankard of ale sitting on the bar, which splashed all over another one of the patrons. After a small fistfight which Ambrose had enjoyed more than he should have, he'd pulled his uncle up from the tavern floor where he'd fallen asleep once again. He probably should have just left Erasmus there with bits of dirt and sawdust stuck to his face, but he didn't. Uncle Erasmus, for better or worse, was all Ambrose had left of his father. He considered Erasmus a sort of penance for leaving Greenbriar. A punishment for never mending things with his father before he died, something Erasmus reminded him of often.

Looking up, Ambrose remembered Theodosia's ridiculous declaration that she would rather admire the ceiling than dare to enjoy being bedded by him. His chest still ached at knowing he'd hurt her. He was bound to do so again. The sound of her breathing, deep and even, met his ears over the mound of pillows and the scent of lemons caught in his nose. Placing a hand on one of the pillows, he pushed it down until he caught sight of Theodosia's back.

"I'm hiring servants. An army of them," Theodosia said clearly.

She hadn't fallen asleep after all. Little faker. "I would expect you to. I'm only shocked the house isn't crawling with them already."

"Miss Emerson might know how to plan a menu, but I doubt she knows how to pick out the appropriate hue for a drawing room."

Ambrose had no idea what Theodosia was talking about, nor did he care. What mattered was that she was speaking to him again. "Fortunate I compromised you and not Miss Emerson then, isn't it?"

A small, feminine grunt was his only response.

His chest constricted as Ambrose's feelings for his wife took on a more brilliant sheen, one he didn't even try to push away. He wanted so badly to touch her and tell her again how sorry he was for hurting her.

Gorgeous, half-blind creature, I adore you.

20

The next several days passed in a flurry of activity. Theo arose early, Betts at her side, and faced the challenge of Greenbriar with all the confidence she could muster. When her bravado flagged, she reminded herself there was no one else but her to put the estate to rights.

The line of pillows stayed in the middle of the bed she shared with Haven because Theo refused to remove the barrier while she was still hurt. She was asleep when Haven finally came to their room at night, barely stirring at the sound of him taking off his boots, and he was gone when she awoke. She was certain his avoidance was on purpose to allow her anger towards him to fade. And it was working.

On the morning of her third day at Greenbriar, as she and Jacinda were enjoying a pot of tea and a small tray of freshly baked scones before tackling the frightening task of opening some of the guestrooms, Theo finally made the acquaintance of Uncle Erasmus.

Erasmus shuffled into the drawing room reeking of brandy and disappointment, thin strands of dark hair clinging to his pale scalp. Watery but kind eyes took in Jacinda before he approached Theo, stopping just a few feet away.

"Lady Haven." The words trembled between his thin lips. "My apologies for not greeting you properly when you arrived at Greenbriar." His face took on a worried look. "I quite forgot—that is to say—I was indisposed. Please forgive me."

Erasmus must once have been handsome, but his love of drink was now etched across his features. His fingers trembled against his thighs as he approached, his gaze running over Theo with more focus than she'd expected before he shook his head and began swatting at a non-existent bug.

No wonder Haven pities him.

"There is no apology necessary," Theo replied with a broad smile. "I am happy to make your acquaintance, Lord Erasmus."

"Uncle Erasmus." He lifted a finger, grinning wide and showing yellowed teeth. "I've a new niece, have I not?"

"You do, Uncle," Jacinda said crisply from beside Theo.

"I was hoping," he looked nervously at Jacinda, "you might spare some coin?"

Jacinda held out her hand to Erasmus who came forward like a dog looking for a treat. "Now, Uncle," she chastised, "remember what I told you. It will last much longer if you buy something other than brandy."

He snatched the coins from her palm. "But brandy," he said in a quivering voice, "is my favorite."

Jacinda only nodded and returned to her book, dismissing her uncle without another glance. She didn't see the way her uncle's trembling lips pulled apart into what resembled a sneer.

But Theo did.

She looked to Jacinda, who seemed oblivious to her uncle's continued presence in the drawing room, and when Theo looked back at Erasmus, he was waving at her, the smile back on his features, his eyes dreamy as he looked down at his hand clutching the coins.

"Good day, nieces," he said with a shaky bow before closing the door behind him.

Theo opened her mouth, meaning to question Jacinda about Erasmus, then shut it. Jacinda was very much like her brother. She held things tightly to her chest, rarely revealing her thoughts unless she wished to. The day of Theo's arrival, Jacinda had confessed quite a bit, probably more than she'd meant to, and since then, Haven's sister had kept to topics relating to the decorating of Greenbriar. Resolving to not say a word, Theo went back to her list.

"So now you've met Erasmus," Jacinda said, startling Theo from her thoughts. "You must be firm in your dealings with him, Theo. He's very much like a child. Loving but prone to tantrums when he doesn't get his way."

Erasmus was a sot. One with trembling lips which could be mistaken for a sneer. She was being foolish.

"I'll take care." Theo nodded.

21

Theo sidestepped around a pair of strapping young women carrying a bucket of water, soap, rags, and a mop, headed in the direction of Haven's study. The pair bobbed politely in unison before hurrying down the hall.

She smiled back. *Thank God for Rolfe.*

Theo adored the imposing man, who'd once been the Duke of Haverly's butler, on sight, hiring him after only a brief conversation. He had a certain bit of Pith about him, something Theo appreciated. While his explanation for leaving the duke's employ was a bit vague, she surmised, after some careful questioning, that it had had something to do with Haverly's housekeeper marrying the duke's valet.

Rolfe, bless him, had immediately taken charge and set about hiring the remainder of the staff required to run Greenbriar properly. Mr. Henderson would stay on to help when needed, but since Theo guessed him to be seventy if he was a day, his main job would consist of offering his opinion when required, keeping track of where Erasmus had fallen asleep, and napping.

The cook, Mrs. Dottie, arrived with an apple-cheeked smile, marshaling the kitchen into order even before her staff had been hired. The roast she'd prepared for dinner on her first night nearly made Theo burst into tears, it was so delicious.

Haven had yet to dine with her, often arriving home well after she'd gone to bed. Theo made sure Mrs. Dottie kept a plate warm for him.

Now that she had secured Rolfe and Mrs. Dottie and the running of the household seemed to be in hands far more capable than her own, Theo felt far less overwhelmed. She could take a deep breath and feel the satisfaction of the enormous progress she'd made in such a short time.

Greenbriar was being scrubbed from top to bottom. The floors gleamed and smelled of beeswax. One could now see through most of the downstairs windows. Yesterday, Theo had left a stone-faced Rolfe in charge, requested the Averell coach, and taken an ecstatic Jacinda to Warwick.

She hadn't bothered to ask Haven if he'd like to join them, mainly because she'd had no idea where her husband was and was too embarrassed to ask.

Now today, beds arrived. Mattresses. Rugs. Linens. A decent dining room table. Cutlery. Plates, cups, and saucers. She sent to London for swathes of velvet for the windows. And most importantly, Theo had written to Olivia, who liked to read as much as Jacinda did. The order from Thrumbadge's, London's finest bookseller, would arrive next week. She couldn't wait to see Jacinda's face when all those leather-bound tomes fell out of a crate.

Not once did Theo visit her trunks, locked way with Betts in the parlor; she was far too busy creating upon a much larger palette. Still, she found herself scribbling on bits of paper at odd times because it was a compulsive habit, the need to draw. Paint. While she made notes on the color scheme she envisioned for the drawing room, Theo looked down to see she'd drawn the outline of Haven. He'd still been in bed when she awoke this morning, snoring softly on the other side of *Theodosia's Line of Demarcation.*

At least, that's how Haven referred to the line of pillows dividing their bed, which he'd made no attempt to remove. Theo had started to make a great effort to stay awake until he came up to their room, if only so she could inform him of her plans for Greenbriar, almost daring him to disagree. He never did.

Nor did he kiss her or touch her.

He'd been beautiful lying on his stomach as he slept this morning, one foot sticking out from the sheets. Had she not been afraid of waking him, Theo would have examined the extended foot to check for the damaged toe. Instead, her gaze had lingered over the curve of one muscular buttock disappearing beneath the sheets, the magnificent expanse of his back with the scar above the shoulder. Haven's entire upper body and face had darkened to a light amber, proof he was spending his days out in the sun. Shirtless.

The mere thought of Haven, scandalously strolling about without a shirt, his glorious form on display for anyone to see, such as a widow possessing good eyesight, was incredibly unwelcome. Theo didn't care for the idea of other women casting their lures at Haven. Or that he might wish to be caught.

Annoyed at both herself and Haven, Theo tore up the paper and threw it into the fire.

Except for being shirtless, Theo had no idea where Haven was all day, and she refused to ask. She assumed Mrs. Dottie and her delicious cooking were keeping Haven's appetite satisfied, but what about his other appetites? Haven had a lustful nature.

A small growl left her. Haven, whether out of kindness or

out of the need to just annoy her, was allowing Theo's anger towards him to thaw slowly.

Far too slowly.

22

"Oh, there you are, new niece." A trembling voice addressed her. "I wondered where you'd gotten off to."

Theo looked up from the notes she'd been making, disturbed to find yet another sketch of Haven instead of the recommendations Mrs. Dottie had asked for on next week's menu.

Erasmus.

Instantly, Theo forced a welcoming smile to her lips, not wanting Haven's uncle, whom everyone regarded as a burden, to receive the same treatment from her. Erasmus had taken to popping in on her when she was alone. He'd shuffle about. Stutter. Bring her a wilted spray of flowers. But the conversations all ended the same way, with a quivering request for a bit of coin.

Which Theo *always* gave him.

Jacinda treated her uncle with absent affection. She was kind to him but rarely displayed any patience for his riddles which made no sense, his habit of bursting into song, or when he explained how brandy was made. Haven, on the one occasion Theo had seen them interact, dismissed his uncle with a patronizing smile and a wave of his hand. Neither Haven nor his sister seemed to think Erasmus of any consequence.

Which, in turn, caused Theo to be far kinder to Erasmus than she should.

The scent of gin filled the drawing room. Not unusual. Erasmus liked gin. Any sort of spirit, really. But brandy, by far, was his favorite. He spent most of his time beneath one of the trees outside, drinking whatever his coin could afford. She still had no idea where he slept or took his meals. No one paid the least attention to him. He could have disappeared for days, and neither Jacinda nor Haven would have likely noticed.

"Good morning, Uncle."

Erasmus was a soft-looking man. A wobbly mass of pale, sunken skin and bloodshot eyes, like most sots. He smiled at her, extending his fingers. "You look lovely today, Niece. I know where the forget-me-nots grow. I'll gather some for you."

"How lovely, Uncle." First, he smiled. Second, the mention of flowers. Sometimes he might sing or hum a tune. Last, he always asked for coin.

"I find I've a terrible thirst, Theodosia."

She'd noticed the greedy, desperate edge to his words, knew why he'd come to her. Erasmus twitched and trembled, barely able to hold himself upright. His dedication to drink was obvious to anyone who saw him.

Sometimes far too obvious. Almost practiced.

"Of course, Uncle." She pushed her spectacles up further on her nose. Her imagination, always erring on the side of being wild, ascribed deviousness to Erasmus he simply didn't possess. Haven's uncle was harmless. Genuinely kind. He was such a pathetic soul, it was difficult not to feel some pity for him. Reaching into the pocket hidden in her skirts, Theo took out several coins and laid them on the table.

Erasmus, fingers quivering, scooped them up, but he didn't leave. "I was hoping we could discuss a matter of great importance, Theodosia."

"What is it, Uncle? I'll try to help in whatever way I can." As pathetic a sot as he was, Haven's uncle was also manipulative. Today was a perfect example. Theo expected most drunkards were, in their devotion to drink.

"So dear, aren't you?" He placed a hand to his chest. "You brighten up Greenbriar with only your presence, Theodosia." Erasmus circled about aimlessly for a moment. "I wish to discuss Ambrose. I have great affection for him."

There was the slightest trace of dislike in his quavering words, wasn't there?

Stop it, Theo. She was being ridiculous.

"Of course, you do, Uncle. I know how much you love Ambrose and Jacinda."

"Which is why I've come to you." Erasmus trembled and shook, reeking of spirits and pomade. His face contorted as if he would weep. "I would have a small allowance. Ambrose refuses me, with good reason, I suppose. But I hate coming to you so often. Pleading."

Theo could understand that. And it would save her having him pop out of nowhere and ask her for coin, which was rather unsettling. "I'll speak to Lord Haven about providing you a weekly amount for your comfort. Would that suit, Uncle?"

"I was hoping we could keep this between us." Erasmus smiled slightly, showing his yellowed teeth. It didn't reach his blurry eyes, now focused on her.

Stop it, Theo.

She looked down at her hands. The problem wasn't Erasmus, it was her. Since she'd tossed the sketch of Haven into the fire a short time ago, Theo had come to the conclusion that the distance between her and Haven needed to come to an end. Neither of them seemed willing to make the first move. Erasmus, or rather the topic of his allowance, provided a perfect excuse for her to speak to Haven directly. She was ready to have him beg for her forgiveness or kiss her senseless. Either would do.

Theo looked up to reply, startled to see Erasmus right in front of her, watery gaze flicking over her bosom.

Unsettling.

"You've the Barrington eyes." His head cocked slightly before smiling broadly at her. "The same as your brother. Always surprised me a bit." Then he turned and started to hum. Theo was sure she heard him say *"the bastard"* under his breath.

"You mean my brother, the Duke of Averell?" Theo raised a brow, her tone sharp. "Jacinda said you knew of him and my father."

"*Duke?*" Erasmus shuffled a bit, regarding her with horror. "No, I—" He pulled out a handkerchief and dabbed at his lips. "I would never cast such a slur on a duke." He looked as if he would fall to the floor at her feet and weep. "Ambrose calls him that. I'm afraid he doesn't speak highly of him. Your brother."

Well, that was certainly true. Though Haven had used other, more colorful words when describing Tony.

"Don't be cross, dear niece. Sometimes, Theodosia, I speak without thinking. Thoughts ramble in my head with no meaning. It's been that way for as long as I can remember." Erasmus gave her a sad shrug. "Brandy helps, you see, quiets it, but not all the time."

Theo nodded in sympathy, recalling what Betts had said

about her cousin. It seemed Erasmus was also afflicted. She immediately regretted her earlier, unkind thoughts.

"My parents didn't know what to do with me. Nor my brother. I fear I embarrassed them all." His voice grew thick. "Just as I do Ambrose and Jacinda."

"No, Uncle. I'm sure that isn't the case." Her eyes drifted to the hall, willing anyone, Rolfe, Jacinda, Mrs. Henderson, even one of the carpenters, to please interrupt this dreadful conversation. She hadn't meant to set Erasmus off and felt terrible for doing so.

"Oh, it is." He shook his head sadly. "And well I know it. It got worse, and when Edmund married, he told me I must leave Greenbriar, and I agreed, under the circumstances. He said I was fragile, and I suppose I am."

Theo gave his hand a gentle pat. "I'm sure that isn't at all true."

"I've been forgotten for so long, all because of *one minute*." The trembling left his voice.

"A minute?" Theo looked again at the doorway. It seemed she was doomed to hear more of Erasmus's nonsensical ramblings.

"Edmund was only a minute older than I." The bloodshot eyes filled with moisture as if he would start sobbing at any moment. "But for a *minute*, I would have been the marquess and my brother the twin everyone forgot. Do you know, Theodosia, what it is to feel forgotten? That's the real reason I came back to Greenbriar, though it nearly killed me to cross that horrid stretch of ocean again. Ambrose thinks I came back for money, but it wasn't that. I swear I was told my nephew had perished. The fairies told me." His eyes pleaded with Theo for understanding. "And I wanted to console my brother and repair our estrangement." He dabbed at his eyes. "But mostly, I didn't want to die one day and have no one to mourn me. Forgotten. You understand, don't you?"

"I do, Uncle Erasmus." Her heart filled with pity for him because she did know what it was like to feel overlooked. Different. To be less dazzling than your siblings. What would it matter if she gave Erasmus an allowance? Haven probably wouldn't care. And Erasmus deserved some kindness.

"You must come to me at the start of the week," she said softly, taking his hand, "and I will provide you with an allowance for your comforts, Uncle. But in return, you must promise not to sell anything else in this house. Or there will be nothing. No allowance. No coin for drink. Do you understand?" What a sad creature he was. "Do not touch Jacinda's books."

"I promise. Thank you, Theodosia. I knew from the moment we met that you and I would get on. My dear niece."

"Good day, Uncle." Relief at his leaving filled her, and she instantly reprimanded herself for being so cruel.

He bowed and shuffled out the door, muttering under his breath. Or singing. Theo wasn't sure.

When Rolfe came to check on her barely a quarter-hour later, Theo requested tea and some of Mrs. Dottie's currant scones, a new favorite of hers.

Anything to ease her suddenly unsettled stomach.

23

Two cups of tea later, Theo brushed a crumb from her lips and decided to visit Jacinda in the library. She had the sudden urge to ensure her gentle sister-in-law was well and surrounded by her beloved books.

And not on the ladder.

While many of the more rare and expensive books had been sold long ago, there was still an extensive collection in the library, sitting in heaps around the half-empty shelves as if Haven's father or Erasmus had gone through, book by book, and taken only what would fetch a price. Jacinda had taken it upon herself to catalogue the poor tomes left, an impossible task with no one to help her but Mr. Henderson. But now, Coates, one of the Averell footmen, had been enlisted to help her cause. Despite her limitations with the cane, Jacinda spent hours roaming about the large, two-story library, Coates following behind her.

Theo had grown very fond of Jacinda in the short time she'd been at Greenbriar. She was intelligent and well-read, unsurprising given her love of books. But she was also possessed of a dry wit, much like her brother. Just yesterday, when Theo had realized she'd left her spectacles upstairs, Jacinda had offered Theo her cane telling her to 'swing it about' to avoid running into anything.

Trying to keep the laughter out of her voice, Theo had reminded Jacinda she was *not* blind.

Jacinda deserved a proper education, perhaps a governess who could also be a lady's companion. She needed to learn to dance decently, even with a limp. Yes, Jacinda was lame, but that didn't mean she had to resign herself to a life spent sitting at balls instead of enjoying herself. A seamstress had already been summoned from Warwick to attend to Jacinda's immediate clothing needs, but once Romy returned from Italy, Theo meant to ask her sister to design a completely new wardrobe for Haven's sister.

Theo entered the library, relieved to see Coates on the ladder and not Jacinda.

"How are things going, Coates?" she asked.

The footman, a big lad whose brother worked the door at Elysium, turned and smiled. "Good afternoon, my lady. Lady Jacinda is just making her way through the books on animals and their husbands."

"Animal husbandry, Coates," Theo corrected him. Coates had grown up in London and likely thought roasts and plump chickens magically appeared at the butcher shop.

Jacinda came around the corner, cane thumping against the wooden floors. Theo had already ordered rugs for the library, but they wouldn't arrive until next week. At least the floors were now scrubbed. "Hello, Theo. I was just about to come fetch you."

"Busy in the library, I see. You know there are spiders and other despicable creatures about, don't you? I wish you would wait until I can have it all properly scrubbed." The army of cleaning women, armed with their rags and soap, hadn't yet made it to the bookshelves, which first needed to be clear of books, something Jacinda refused to allow until she'd cataloged nearly everything.

Greenbriar's new butler, Rolfe, appeared, a stack of dusty tomes in his arms. There was dirt on his coat and gloves. He bowed as much as was possible with his burden. "Lady Haven."

"Rolfe would terrify any spider who had the audacity to bite me, wouldn't you, Rolfe?" Jacinda smiled at the dour butler.

"Undoubtedly." The deep baritone filled the room.

Very Pith-like. It was no wonder Theo had hired him on the spot. "I see you've been recruited to library duty as well, Rolfe."

"Not to worry, Lady Haven. I've already checked on dinner. Mrs. Dottie has been instructed to remove the mushrooms planned with the meal and further instructed that no mushrooms of any kind should be included in anything she prepares."

Theo was taken aback by the comment. "Oh."

"I was instructed to do so by Lord Haven," Rolfe added.

"Ambrose says you don't like them." Jacinda took her arm. "Mushrooms. I quite agree. I've never liked them myself."

"Indeed, I do not," Theo confirmed, unsurprised that Haven had remembered. He was very good at that. Making Theo feel seen. Even when he drew incorrect assumptions. Just now, she missed him fiercely. All the more reason to speak to him as soon as possible.

"And we're having gingerbread for dessert tonight aren't we, Rolfe?" Jacinda made a noise of delight.

"Yes, Lady Jacinda."

"I *adore* gingerbread. Do you like it, Theo?"

Theo clasped her arms, warmth spreading across her chest. "I love gingerbread. Who does not?"

"And there is a surprise for you, Theo." Jacinda gently batted Theo's ankle with her cane.

"A surprise?" Theo looked at Rolfe. The stone lions manning the front door of Greenbriar possessed more expression than her butler. "More delicacies from the kitchen?"

"No. Rolfe isn't involved." Jacinda dragged her over to the spiral stairs at the edge of the library. "You must go up."

Theo gave the steps a doubtful look. The entire staircase appeared to have been newly repaired. Had she sent the carpenters in this direction? Honestly, the entire house was buzzing with tradesmen, there wasn't any telling. But at least the stairs no longer looked as if they'd fall to pieces if she climbed them.

"Are you *sure* it's safe?" Theo asked. She *was* wearing her spectacles so she could see if she fell to her death.

"I took the staircase not a moment ago myself, Lady Haven. 'Tis safe," Rolfe assured her.

Theo looked at Rolfe's large, bulky form. If it could hold Rolfe, it would certainly hold her.

"Safe, Theodosia." Jacinda looked about to burst. It was all she could do to contain herself. "Ambrose says it will remind you of home. Your surprise."

Ah. So, the surprise had to do with Haven. Much like the lack of mushrooms and the baking of gingerbread. It seemed her husband had decided she'd thawed long enough.

Theo quite agreed. She had relived her wedding night repeatedly as Haven snored next to her, hidden by the row of pillows. Sheer torture.

Cautiously, Theo made her way up the spiral stairs, sparing a look at Rolfe, Jacinda, and Coates below. "Rolfe," she said over her shoulder. "If I should fall, could you please set down that stack of books and catch me?"

"Without a doubt, Lady Haven," came the rumbling reply.

"Very good," she muttered. Moving upward, she paused every step or so to glance down at Rolfe and Jacinda whose faces were both turned in her direction, watching her as she climbed. When her foot met the solid wood of the second floor, Theo breathed a sigh of relief. She hadn't ventured up here before, as the stairs had been in a state of disrepair. An empty space, meant to be a sitting area with lamps, was before her, identical to the floor below. What a perfect place this would be to spend a day lost in a book, hidden from the rest of the house. There were more shelves here, all filled with tattered books and bits of paper. The entire area smelled slightly of mildew and neglect.

In her mind, Theo immediately saw a lush Persian rug, possibly in rich gold and crimson, two or three overstuffed chairs in complementary colors, and a small table to hold a lamp. The windows were bare of any coverings, and Theo thought she would keep it that way, for the view outside was stunning. She could see clear into the woodland surrounding the estate. An old stone fence meandered well out of eyesight, crumbling and covered with bramble in places. The leftover remains of what looked to be a wagon sat nearby, now covered with flowering vines. She tried to imagine Haven as a child, running into the field, perhaps along the stone wall.

Turning from the window, Theo spied a narrow hallway partially hidden by a row of bookshelves. Atop a stack of moldering books on one shelf was a rock. Someone had taken red paint and drawn an arrow pointing forward.

Theo tapped her chin. How curious.

The scent of fresh paint assailed her nostrils as she strolled further and found another rock. This arrow pointed up to a narrow set of stairs. A door, painted the same brilliant red as the arrows, stood at the top.

Vermillion, her mind automatically whispered.

The door stood ajar, a silent invitation for her to come inside.

Very mysterious. Exactly the sort of thing Theo adored.

She climbed the stairs, gasping softly in surprise as she reached the top.

Bright light cascaded across freshly swept and scrubbed floors. A block of tall windows, the same as what could be found below in the library, stretched floor to ceiling, providing an even more impressive look at the glorious vista surrounding Greenbriar. Her studio in London had such a sweeping panoramic view, but those windows overlooked the park.

Shelves held an assortment of her miniatures, a half-finished canvas along with several sketches. There was a sofa sitting in one corner, a bit worn and tattered but perfect for Theo to rest on while needing inspiration. Her gut told her the sofa had once sat in the parlor Betts had been staying in, a sitting room Haven's mother had used, for the fabric and lines were feminine. There was a table with a stool, her small easel sitting on top. A larger easel, one she hadn't purchased, stood just to the side.

Oh. A tear slipped unbidden down Theo's cheek.

Rows of paint tubes were laid out neatly according to color, all brand new, meaning Haven must have ordered them in London before their wedding. Her brushes were all clean and placed in a cup. A stack of fresh canvasses, all of differing sizes, sat in the corner. Her portfolio and sketch pad sat on another shelf, along with pencils and charcoal.

There was much more here than what had been packed in her trunks. Much more than she'd had in her studio in London. He'd done this for her. No one had ever gone to so much trouble for her before. She sniffed, trying not to burst into tears.

"It wasn't meant to make you cry. Do you like it?"

Haven was standing in the shadows at the far reaches of the room, hands clasped behind him. As usual, she found it difficult to decipher his mood.

"It's wonderful," she assured him. Her heart fluttered softly within the confines of her chest, desperate to be free and reach his. This studio, more than anything else Haven had ever done or said to her, told Theo the truth of his feelings for her.

'I wanted you from the moment you spilled ratafia on me.'

Haven leaned down slightly, peering at her in concern. He was dressed in a plain linen shirt and worn leather breeches, scuffed boots firmly on his feet.

I should buy him new boots. Her chest constricted again.

Strands of russet hair were blown about his head as if Haven had just come in from riding through a field. Perhaps he had. She wasn't sure how he spent most of his day. She'd never asked.

When they had spoken lately, in passing, Theo would take a deep breath and relay all that she was intent on doing without ever asking after him or allowing him to speak. She wasn't even sure she'd told Haven she'd gone to Warwick. She talked *at* him, but not to him, and he'd allowed it. Not once had he objected to anything she planned. Or undermined her authority with the tradesmen flooding Greenbriar. He never questioned how much money she was spending or told her to stop.

And Theo should have told him, in addition to asking how he spent his time, that she understood—even if she didn't like—the conclusions he'd made about her. Because his assumptions had made their wedding night seem less special. That *she* was less special.

I no longer think that's true.

"I'm glad you like it." Haven pushed away from the wall, glancing at her from beneath his lashes, uncertain of his welcome. "I want you to have a studio. A space of your own which belongs to only you." The sun dappled across the broad expanse of his shoulders. His sleeves were rolled up to show muscular forearms, with their light dusting of hair. The scent of the outdoors mixed with spice met Theo's nose as he came near, tinged with something else that belonged to Haven alone.

"Tucked up under the eaves. My sisters used to tease me. I only wanted to be bent over one of my tiny paintings and never cared to have tea or watch Romy make clothes for her army of dolls."

"Who would? All those fripperies. And I detest tea. I only pretend to like it."

"You haven't fooled anyone." Theo thought of the way he frowned whenever a cup was placed before him. "I'm sure you only appear for the scones and sandwiches."

The left side of his mouth tugged up. "It isn't a crime to enjoy a tiny sandwich. But I don't care for cucumber."

"Duly noted." Theo wandered over to the shelf displaying her miniatures, wondering where he kept the one she'd painted for Blythe. "I preferred to hide from the world in my studio on the third floor. If I was really immersed in something, I didn't even leave. Pith would come up the stairs bearing a tray of food. Or Craven, if we were at Cherry Hill. They're related, as it happens. Craven and Pith." She gave him a smile. "My family worried over me, wondering why I wanted to be left alone while Romy was determined to save the world, Olivia focused on being the most proper young lady in London and Phaedra . . . well, I think we all know Phaedra is bound to be a disaster at some point."

"Her newly formed interest in swords has me concerned."

Theo nodded. "It seemed easier to stay in my studio. The strangely reclusive Barrington, painting her ridiculous tiny portraits which no one would ever see. Not dazzling or sparkly like the others."

"You are not odd." Haven's voice was gravelly and low as if he'd just woken up from a long nap. The sound floated over Theo, pricking deliciously at her skin.

"I was, Haven. I still am. I am the daughter of a duke who doesn't care for society. I have no real friends outside my sisters and Cousin Rosalind. And Betts, my maid. Ask yourself, how many other young ladies of your acquaintance paint miniatures?"

"Of their breasts? None that I know, save you."

"Not both my breasts. Only the curve of my left, enough to draw the viewer's eye—

"To your delectable pink nipple." He was smiling at her, his arm stretched out. "I do not wish to argue with you."

"How unusual." Theo took his hand, a tingle moving through her as his fingers laced with hers.

Haven's brow wrinkled as if contemplating his next words, and he gently released her hand. "This room," he made a sweeping gesture, "was once mine, as it happens. Not where I slept, mind you, though there were times when I did spend the night up here. This was more a playroom. A space my father gave me," he hesitated, "for me to look at the stars and record my observations."

There was so much pain at the mention of his father. Theo could see it in the lines bracketing his mouth, the tightness around his eyes. She remembered what Jacinda had told her, that Haven had left for the Continent, not returning until after his father was dead. It was obvious from the flash of anguish he wasn't quick enough to hide that Haven's relationship with his father was far from resolved. Much like Tony and Leo's with her own father. "The stars?"

"I was an amateur astronomer. Or at least I thought I was. My father would take me out to the lawn." He pointed to a slight rise in the grass. "We would lie on our backs in the grass, and he would name the constellations, tracing them in the air for me."

Out of all the things Haven could have told her about himself, that was the one she'd least expected. "I thought you spent your days getting into trouble. You don't seem the sort to quietly sit and gaze up at the heavens."

"Oh, I found plenty of trouble, Lady Haven. Or it found me. I've a short fuse. Quick to anger, as I'm sure you know."

She did, though it showed itself rarely as of late. Haven seemed much more peaceful now than when he'd been in London. Theo liked to think perhaps she had something to do with that. "Is that how you got this?" She reached out without thinking and touched the tip of her finger to the scar on his chin.

"Tavern brawl." He wiggled his brows. "It was glorious, Theo."

Theo exhaled softly. She did love it when he used the shortened version of her name. The sound, in Haven's gravelly rasp, never failed to disarm her. "Glorious. A brawl? Are you joking?"

He shot her a mischievous grin. "Most glorious."

"Did you have a telescope?"

"I did. As well as star charts and stacks of books on navigation. At one time, I was very enamored of pirates and ships."

A tiny shiver ran down Theo's spine. How appropriate.

"My parents were worried I would run off and become a cabin boy or join a band of brigands. Because I liked to fight. And I've always been good with pistols. And a sword."

She could see Haven, standing on the deck of a ship with his imperfect nose, brandishing a cutlass, scaling the rigging and such or whatever it was that pirates did, in his lovely bare feet.

"Unfortunately, as I found out when I set out for Italy, my stomach doesn't share my love of the ocean. I get terribly seasick. I'm like Erasmus in that regard."

Theo laughed. "That is another truth, I think." She paused in her amusement, thinking of Erasmus and the discussion she must have with Haven about him. But she pushed the thought aside for later.

"And I loved that telescope." His gaze lingered on her. "I would look at the moon and imagine I saw a face, which my mother claimed was a hallucination brought on because I'd eaten an entire pie by myself. Apple, if that is your next question. I adore apple pie."

"I doubt there is any pie, my lord, which does not merit your attention. How old were you?"

"Nine." He shrugged. "Maybe ten. Coincidentally, it was the first time I found out my father had a twin brother. Erasmus announced his presence by riding up to the front door and falling off his horse, drunk. He'd come to beg money from my father and possibly to catch a glimpse of my mother. Whatever his reason, he was desperate enough to board a ship bound for England, at least. He stayed drunk most of the time he was here, which wasn't very long. Insisted on calling himself the Marquis de Haven. Which made no sense at all."

"Do you think," Theo said carefully, "he might have visited London for a time before he returned?" She was convinced that was the only way Erasmus could have seen or possibly met her father. Or seen her brother. The thought gnawed at her, begging to be explained.

"No. My father put Erasmus on a ship himself. Probably wanted to make sure his brother was gone. He went back to France with another sum bestowed upon him and some of my grandmother's silver, which we didn't realize until later. At any rate, I hope my telescope ended up in the hands of a young boy who was as fascinated by the heavens as I was."

Theo absorbed every word he spoke. The cadence of his rumbling tenor. The way he always sounded as if he'd just awoken. But mostly, Theo concentrated on the many truths her husband imparted to her. The parts of himself she suspected he hadn't shared with anyone else.

Haven reached out, tracing the spray of freckles up her chest with a forefinger, and whispered, "The Corona Borealis. It's a constellation. Your freckles are remarkably similar. I told Blythe that, you know. He never could remember the damned name."

Fire lit across the skin of her chest at his touch, flowing down across her breasts, peaking her nipples. The pull in Haven's direction, always present, tugged even stronger now. It was hard to concentrate on anything else but him. Even the fact that Blythe had stolen the idea that her freckles resembled a constellation from Haven failed to disturb her focus on the man before her.

"Is this studio your apology to me?" she murmured, catching his fingers with hers.

"Will Theodosia's Line of Demarcation finally be dissolved?"

"Possibly."

His lips brushed softly against her fingertips. "My greatest crime is for allowing you to think our enthusiasm for each other was commonplace. Something that any man with a cock and a willing woman could accomplish." His eyes shuttered closed for a moment. "It was not. What happened between us, my *feeling*—was only for Theodosia Louise Barrington, and no one else. As rare and beautiful as you are."

"Ambrose." She rubbed her thumb along his bottom lip, her heart squeezing tightly at his words. "I fear, my lord, that diplomacy is required for the dissolution of Theodosia's Line of Demarcation."

A soft, almost imperceptible sound of relief left him.

"Diplomacy?"

The notion had floated about Theo's mind since the day he'd come upon her in the park and had only grown stronger since. Her fingers itched for her charcoals. To have him at her mercy while she sketched out the curving muscle of his chest. The rough lines of his cheeks and jaw. The thought was highly erotic. "I want you to model for me." She lifted her chin. "I will accept nothing less."

"Is that really what you want? When you mentioned it before, I thought you were only being flirtatious." He pretended to examine her. "Have you hit your head?"

"No." Theo swatted at him, the slow burn working itself up her body making her shiver. "Because you remind me of Theseus," she said. "Surely Phaedra has mentioned the resemblance."

"Theseus?" Haven snorted. "I remind you and your sister of a Greek warrior?"

"No," she whispered, tugging gently on his hand. "The big feral tomcat who is chief mouser at Cherry Hill. I'll start with a charcoal sketch." She looked him directly in the eye and danced away, out of reach. "Take off your shirt."

❦

Ambrose should have guessed Theo didn't really think he resembled a famous Greek warrior but instead a feral tomcat. His feelings would have been hurt except he was far too aroused.

Theo marched to the shelf, shaking her head before crossing the room to one of her trunks. He hadn't emptied that one completely. It was full of notebooks and sketchpads. Her maid, a plump tyrant named Betts, had fought Ambrose mightily for those trunks, declaring that no one should touch them but Theodosia. And he knew why. One pad was full of nothing but drawings of an older man he took to be the late Duke of Averell.

Back bent, she clucked her tongue as she riffled through the trunk while Ambrose traced the slender line of her back with his eyes. Lovely, artistic hands fluttered about, pausing only to push the spectacles up her nose when they slipped.

He longed to have those beautiful hands skimming his chest. His thighs. His face. *Christ*, any part of his body would do. It pained Ambrose that she thought herself less than what she was; he found it confusing that such a beautiful, confident woman, a Barrington, no less, thought herself lacking in some way.

Theodosia was the most dazzling of all the stars in Ambrose's sky. Guiding him, like the north star, directly to her and no one else.

She searched through the trunk, finally standing with a pad and a piece of what looked like charcoal in her hand. Giving him a very pointed look, she said in a low, seductive tone. "Shirt. Off."

Jesus. The words shot straight down between his legs to his cock. He'd forgotten how bloody forward Theodosia could be. And how much he liked it. Especially when her bold behavior was directed at *him*.

He started to unbutton his shirt, a piece of extremely worn linen that could remain as one of Theodosia's paint rags for all he cared. "Will you be disrobing as well, Theodosia?" The hopeful note in his voice was difficult to miss. Sleeping beside her night after night without being able to touch her had been a particular sort of torture.

Theodosia didn't answer, only went to the stool and sat atop it, propping the sketchpad on the easel. "I'm going to do a drawing first. Using charcoal." She lifted the charcoal up in her hand to show him, using what he supposed she likened to an artist's voice. "Once that is finished, I might sketch it out on the canvas and then paint. Maybe. Or I'll use another sketch." The spectacles slipped down her nose again. If Ambrose didn't know better, he'd think she was leering at him.

Christ. "What about Theodosia's Line of Demarcation?" His voice was rough. "And *your* bloody clothes?" The entire lower half of his body grew taut with longing. The door to the studio was still open, though he doubted anyone would dare come up the stairs.

"I think you should recline. On your stomach."

"These breeches are terribly unforgiving, Theodosia. I should mention that." In fact, the leather had become painfully constricting.

"I've got my spectacles on." Her hand started to move across the pad. "I can see *everything* quite clearly." Theodosia shot him a look that was both lascivious and innocent at the same time. It was a potent combination, one that made Ambrose ravenous for her.

When he'd concocted his surprise for Theodosia, he'd thought the tour of her studio might end with her acceptance of his apology. They would dine together; the new cook was making fish in dill butter sauce *and* gingerbread. Then he meant to drag her upstairs and seduce her. The new bed and mattress she'd ordered had arrived this morning. Or perhaps they'd enjoy each other in a bath. *That* surprise was waiting in their room. A tub big enough for two.

God. The feel of her breasts with soap sliding over the nipples.

He lay down on his stomach with one hand above his head, much the same way he slept, and heard her feminine grunt of approval.

Hair fell over his eyes, obscuring his view of Theodosia who had started to hum while the charcoal flew across the paper. Her brow wrinkled delicately, pausing every so often to look at him, then immediately the sound of the charcoal against the paper would fill the air.

Ambrose, on the other hand, tried to stay still despite his *madly* throbbing cock.

Theodosia liked to tap her foot while she sketched, along with the humming. The tune was bawdy. Incredibly improper. There was no telling who had taught it to her. A strand of hair the color of burnished walnut fell over her spectacles, and she pushed it away, brushing her nose with an edge of the charcoal. Her eyes crossed as she looked at the smudge, nose wrinkling in consternation as she wiped at it. Which only produced another smudge.

Ambrose couldn't look away.

I'm in love with her.

The feeling came to him softly, not with a loud roar demanding his attention, but quietly slipping into the confines of his heart, whispering that one most important truth. He'd told himself wanting Theodosia was only lust. That claiming her was about justice for himself and punishing Leo Murphy. Saving his sister. Greenbriar. Even bloody Uncle Erasmus.

But it had never really been about any of that.

He rolled over. It was impossible for her not to notice his *admiration* of her talents.

Theodosia paused, her hand hovering above the paper. "You moved. Why are you moving?" Her eyes immediately dropped to the hard ridge pushing against the leather, widening in surprise as if she'd forgotten all about it.

His cock had *definitely* not forgotten about her.

Ambrose sat up and proceeded to take off his boots, tossing them across the floor where they fell with two loud thuds. He wasn't sure how he was going to get his breeches off without injuring himself.

Her hand fell back from the paper, the charcoal dangling

from between her fingers. "There is quite a bit of detail work involved when sketching or painting a person," she whispered. "All the lovely lines of one's form. Muscle and bone. I should probably come closer lest I miss something."

Bold. Brazen. Completely unaware of her appeal. How the very sight of her struck him dumb with the most unbearable longing and probably always would.

"Finally," Ambrose hooked his thumb in the top of his breeches, "we agree on something."

※

HAVEN CAME TOWARD HER ON BARE FEET, COMPLETELY naked. His desire for her would have been blatant even without her spectacles on. He didn't make any move to touch her, but the air in the studio grew thick, heavy with anticipation.

"Will you kiss me, Theodosia?" The soft words came close to her ear as Haven circled her with agonizing slowness, his breath buffeting against her neck.

The charcoal dropped from her fingers, rolling away beneath her skirts. Her knees wobbled, desire making her unsteady as she took in the large, naked male who so obviously wanted her. Theo's nipples pulsed against her bodice, hard and sensitive, begging for only a brush of his finger.

A hand skimmed down her hip, the barest pressure against her skirts as he moved behind her.

"Such a lovely neck." He inhaled at the base. "Lemons."

A sharp tingle shot down her spine, wrapping tightly around her waist, the tendrils sinking between her thighs to produce a dull, insistent ache.

Haven's hand lowered, his palm barely grazing the stomach of her dress before brushing with a featherlight caress further below.

Theo didn't dare move as sensation cascaded over the lower part of her body.

"No answer?" he murmured, his fingers tugging gently on the fabric of her skirts. "Will you kiss me?" He stood before her again, the warm spicy scent of Haven moving in the air around her.

Carefully, because Theo was shaking with want, she stood on tiptoe as Haven tilted his head down. At the brush of her lips with his, a low purr came from the depths of his chest.

"I know I mentioned that I would not be enthusiastic in my regard of your," Theo hesitated as the feel of Haven's tongue touched her ear, "person again, but I fear that is not the case. A lapse in my judgement, perhaps."

"You were angry." His mouth slanted, the line of hair covering his jaw spiking with copper as the light caught it. "Forgive me?"

Theo's palm slid up the warm skin of his chest, around the whorl of darker hair surrounding his nipples. She circled one peak with the edge of her nail.

Another purr came from him.

It was an odd sensation to be standing so close to Haven, fully dressed while he was not. He begged her attention like a great cat wanting to be stroked, and she willed her hands to move over him in exploration. Each touch of her fingers over the lines of his ribs to the curve of his buttocks elicited the most amazing noises from him. "I want to paint you like this," she whispered. "All shadow and light. Copper and amber."

He leaned in and slowly moved his tongue along her bottom lip before nipping gently. "You may do whatever you wish with me, Theo." He nuzzled into the slope of her neck, imperfect nose trailing up to her ear, tongue licking gently at the lobe. "Where do you want me?"

Theo tried to take a lungful of air and struggled. Her

entire body was flaring gently, desperate to be closer to his.

"Tell me." He pressed a chaste kiss to her cheek. "On my knees before you, your skirts raised?"

Her body arched toward his at the mere suggestion.

A graze of his teeth against her neck made Theo jump. "Bent over the sofa?"

"I—" Every word he spoke conjured up the most violently erotic images in her mind. The ache between her thighs was so fierce, Theo pushed her knees together to try to ease it. She looked toward the wall, noting with quiet horror that the door was wide open. Worse, she found she didn't care.

"I suppose you want me to decide." Haven pressed an open-mouthed kiss to her neck. Then his mouth fell on hers, hungry and hot with an urgency that met her own. She wrapped herself around him, his skin like molten silk beneath her fingertips. His hand tangled in her hair, pulling the pins away until the dark tresses swirled around them both.

The heat of him seared Theo through her skirts, stoking the ache burning between her thighs. Every thought except pleasure seeped away. All Theo could think of was Haven, the warmth of his skin, the way he kissed her. He half-carried, half-dragged her toward the poor sofa, which would be a great deal more battered when they were done.

He laid her down on the cushions, eyes so dark and fathomless, they looked black. One hand wrapped lightly around her throat, his thumb gently stroking her pulse, while the other pulled up her skirts.

I'm going to be ravished. Again.

He released her neck and sat back on his heels before her thighs, one big hand splayed possessively against her stomach, holding her in place. His fingers moved against her, gliding easily through her already wet, wanting flesh.

"I want those fucking pillows off the bed, Theo." Then, without further preamble, Haven leaned forward and pushed her knees up, entering her with one punishing thrust. He didn't move, giving her body time to adjust and accept him.

Theo could only gasp as her breasts strained against the confines of her dress, wanting his mouth, his fingers.

God, why hadn't Haven undressed her?

"Theo?" He moved ever so slightly, and a violent jolt shook down her body. The pleasure inside her was sharp. Waiting for the slightest push from him. She wiggled, needing him to move, but Haven refused, looking down at her with a raised brow.

Damn him. "Fine. Yes. Very well. No more bloody pillows. I promise. Unless I use one to suffocate you." A whimper left her. "Please, Ambrose."

He kissed her fiercely but with exquisite tenderness. "Fair enough." Then he proceeded to take her rather savagely on the worn sofa of the studio until the springs creaked in protest. Their joining wasn't pretty. Or romantic. Not even the stuff of the novels she so loved.

It was far more glorious.

The slap of their bodies as he took her filled the air, mixing with their cries of pleasure.

Haven rocked into her until her body hummed and writhed beneath his.

"Ambrose." Theo's head fell back as the first ripples of pleasure overtook her, arching her back and curling her toes.

"Don't close your eyes," he said, the restraint as his own release threatened to overtake him evident. He pressed his forehead to hers, slowing his pace. Tenderly, his lips caught hers.

Her body uncoiled, spiraling around his as stars burst before her eyes, lighting up the studio and the man above her. He groaned at the clench of her muscles, his face falling to the crook of her neck until there was nothing but the two of them. Bound together.

24

Theodosia's spectacles had stayed on during their entire delicious, inappropriate, middle-of-the-day . . . *romp*.

Ambrose eventually divested her of her clothing, afterward. Theo gave protest, stating they would only have to dress her again to go downstairs. Women's clothing was an exhausting process, she stated, thus the need for maids.

"I don't mind. Besides, there's a door on the other side of the hall which leads to the servant's stairs. No one will notice us. And the door has been open the entire time. I hope Rolfe didn't hear you screaming and venture up to check on you."

Theo giggled. Haven really was terrible. "Rolfe would never do so. He's very Pith-like. Pith never bats an eyelash at any of the Barrington antics. Takes everything in stride. I'm sure he's practicing fencing with Phaedra right at this moment." She turned to take him in. "Which you will be blamed for."

"Your sister is mildly frightening." Haven was gliding his fingers over the skin of one breast, watching with fascination as the nipple tightened and peaked beneath his ministrations. He pressed a kiss to the tip.

Pleasure twisted inside her once more. If she didn't think they'd eventually be missed, she would cheerfully stay here with Haven forever. But eventually he'd need food. A great deal of it.

His mouth danced against her neck. "I meant to seduce you after dinner."

"Did you?" Only Haven would think of food before seduction. "Were you going to ply me with wine?" Her finger trailed along his jaw, rubbing over his bottom lip.

"Gingerbread."

"I know. Rolfe told me."

Haven managed to appear offended and predatory all at the same time. Probably because his fingers were moving through the soft down of her mound, teasing her. "It was meant to be a surprise. I was going to share it with you. Maybe in a bath. After dinner."

A slight tremor ran through her at the light, seductive touch. "I might have known—" Her tone raised an octave as his fingers found the still-sensitive bit of flesh. His thumb rotated and pressed softly. "—your stomach would come before me," she breathed, opening her legs more fully.

Theo had never felt so wanton. It was incredibly freeing.

"Nothing comes before you, Theodosia." He pressed a kiss to the end of her nose. "Nothing." His fingers stroked until she whimpered against him.

"I think it wrong," a soft gasp left her, "for you to use sexual conquest in order to get me to agree with you."

"My methods," he kissed her lazily as her hips lifted, "are sound. I'm merely making a point."

Theo couldn't answer. All she could do was feel.

"I'm going to paint a very large picture in the drawing room," she told him much later as the sun was beginning to sink below the horizon. The entire household would suspect what they'd been doing all afternoon. She smelled of Haven. Every inch of her.

Haven helped her with her dress. He was very good at women's clothing.

"It will cover the whole of one wall," she continued. "A very large, complicated project." Theo wasn't going to ask permission. In cases like this, and with Haven in particular, it was better to just blurt out what she meant to do. They would argue about it later. And the idea had only just come to her.

"You're going to paint a picture on the wall? Like one of Granby's frescoes?"

"Yes. A large painting. On the wall."

"Why would you want to do such a thing?"

Theo stared at him over the top of her spectacles. "Did you not say I was in charge of decorating as I see fit? Making decisions and such?"

"I was talking about fabrics. Furniture." He pointed to the sofa, which looked worse for the wear. "Wall hangings. Besides, I thought you only liked to paint things no bigger than a book. Miniatures and such."

"I've decided I can handle something larger."

"You certainly can." He kissed her roughly.

"You're insufferable." There was no bite to her words. Indeed, she was struggling not to laugh out loud. "What I intend to paint will be magnificent."

"Will it at least," he tucked a stray bit of hair behind her ear, "be something I'll like? Not a scene from a ball with pompous lords and ladies?"

"I promise. Not so much as a hint of a fan or a gown."

Theo meant to paint the night sky over Greenbriar in varying shades of blues, the idea having come to her while Haven was telling her about his love of the stars, a love he'd shared with his father. She hoped it might ease some of the pain he lived with and remind Haven of a happier time. Hasten the forgiveness which he needed to give. She had witnessed what a lifetime of anger and bitterness could do; Leo and Tony's attitude toward the late Duke of Averell and their inability to forgive their father before he died had nearly driven a wedge between all the Barringtons. Both her brothers would live with a well of regret for the remainder of their lives. Theo didn't want that for Haven.

Which brought her to the next question.

"How did Jacinda become lame?"

Haven's fingers stilled against her cheek. "She fell." His features instantly shuttered.

Theo had already ascertained as much. "In the library?"

He stepped away from her, turning to look out the window. This was obviously a topic Haven didn't care to discuss, but unfortunately for him, Theo did.

"Our father, *while in his cups*," he spat out as if the taste of the words poisoned him, "knocked her off the ladder. I was . . . not here. He was such a bloody sot, he didn't even recall being in the library. And then he went and," his lips clamped tightly before inhaling sharply, not looking at her, "left Jacinda with nothing."

Not *me* or the *estate* but Jacinda. There was more to the story, but it wasn't the time, not with her body still humming gently from their afternoon together. She wondered if Haven's father had ever gone to Elysium. Lost a purse or two there while playing cards.

"Erasmus could barely stand." Haven shot her a hard look. "But at least he wasn't passed out on the floor while Jacinda wept in pain. Mrs. Henderson found them. But it was Erasmus who had the sense to summon a physician. My uncle isn't good for much, but he does care for Jacinda."

The image of Erasmus flashed before her. The way his lips had curled in dislike at his niece. Theo had to have been mistaken.

"After Erasmus visited when I was a child, when he fell off the horse in front of the house, my father mentioned my uncle at times to me, but never spoke his name in front of my mother. He considered Erasmus a lost soul. My father cared for him, but the brothers were not close, if they ever had been. At least, not until later." Haven turned away for a moment.

"When you were on the Continent."

Turning back to her, he ran a finger down the length of her arm. "My uncle claimed he had come to console my father. Said he'd heard of my death from the fairies." He gave a derisive snort. "Ironically, I was injured, but I can't imagine how Erasmus would have known about it. I'm fairly certain there were no fairies about when it happened to send him word. But with my temper, assuming I'd been killed in a fight wasn't much of a stretch." Haven's head tilted toward his shoulder where the scar she'd seen earlier shone stark white against his lightly tanned skin. "Set upon by thieves. I'm sure if they'd known how poor I was, they wouldn't have bothered."

Theo reached out, pressing her fingertips to his chest, desolation filling her at the mere thought of a world without Haven. "Possibly not."

A large hand covered hers. "Another one of my uncle's brandy-fueled hallucinations. If it matters, he also claims the fairies come and drink with him next to that tree he hides his spirits in." Haven's breath fanned across her cheek as he pressed a kiss to the tip of her nose. "We should wash up before facing the rest of the house."

Theo nodded, happy and at peace for the first time since arriving at Greenbriar. "You mentioned another surprise."

Haven kissed her again. "You'll see it when we wash up."

25

"Dear God. You've destroyed the drawing room."

A stray bit of hair fell across the top of her spectacles, and Theo puffed it away before twisting atop the ladder to glimpse Haven lurking in the doorway.

"How long have you been standing there?"

"Long enough." He did a poor job of pretending to be horrified. The weeks since their very passionate reunion in her studio had been filled with arguments over the repairs to Greenbriar, aspersions cast at her ability to correctly plan a menu—*always* have Mrs. Dottie make enough for six people, *not* four—the knowledge that Haven had purchased a tub big enough for two people, and a rather unfortunate mishap Theo had had with a blackberry bush because she'd forgotten her spectacles.

Theo was madly, *terribly* in love with the large male, covered in dirt, glaring at her from the hall. The feeling wasn't at all like her regard for Blythe, because she hadn't loved Blythe. "As it turns out, my lord, there is something I need to discuss with you."

Erasmus.

Two of her older miniatures had gone missing from her studio, along with her pastels. Jacinda had spent the better part of yesterday looking for one of the new books that had arrived from London. She'd thought to chastise Erasmus herself and had gone looking for him.

Theo took a step down from the ladder. She'd found more than she'd expected.

Erasmus had been standing in front of a cracked mirror in the back parlor. Haven's uncle had been talking to himself. Not unusual for a sot who had hallucinations and drank with fairies but—

Erasmus had been practicing his diction. There had been no hint of the quaver with which he usually spoke. No trembling lips. The sight had been disturbing, to say the least.

She'd backed away, all thoughts of confronting him disappearing, and had come directly to the drawing room to paint, all the while trying to decide how best to broach the subject. Accusing Erasmus of theft was one thing, suspecting him of —well, she couldn't very well have Haven condemn his uncle for practicing his diction, could she? Trying to improve oneself wasn't a crime.

"The destruction of my drawing room?" Haven moved into the room, crossing his arms across his chest, trying to intimidate her. Which never worked.

"*Our* drawing room, my lord. And there was nothing worth saving in here to begin with, as you well know." She pushed her spectacles further up her nose and gave his boots a pointed look. "You're tracking mud into the house. Mrs. Henderson will have a fit."

"I was visiting the pigs."

"Lovely. From pigs to me. What a compliment."

A dangerous half-smile lifted one side of his mouth.

"What is it you wish to speak to me about? As it happens, I've something to discuss with you as well."

"It's about Erasmus. Do you know where he is?"

"I just fished him out of the edge of the pond. Probably should have let him drown but for the expensive brandy he was clutching. Which he can't afford, not even with the allowance you've given him."

Theo bit her lip. "I meant to tell you about the allowance." She'd forgotten, in the midst of her newfound happiness and the love she felt for Haven.

Haven stalked closer. "It is no shame to be kind to others. I only wonder when some of that caring heart will be directed at me."

Wretch. He had her whole heart.

"I don't want to talk about my worthless uncle. What is this?" The moss-green of his eyes ran over her painting. "It looks like you just lobbed colors against the wall, hoping to create something."

"If you don't know, I'm not telling you." Theo had been working on altering the shades of blue toward the top of the ceiling, an arduous task and one Rolfe had been assisting her with. The outline of the constellations had been done, but from Haven's vantage point, it probably did look like she'd merely splashed paint in various directions. The bottom part of the painting would be the parkland surrounding Greenbriar. Furniture for the room, all chosen to complement the colors of the painting, was due to arrive by the end of the week.

Haven would see the finished drawing room first, while she was seducing him.

"You might need a physician."

Theo took her brush from the wall. "Whatever for?"

"I feel certain your eyesight has worsened." Haven came closer. "Am I as blurry as this bloody painting? Can you make it down the ladder without injuring yourself?" A shadow flickered across his features. He was remembering Jacinda's accident.

"You're being ridiculous." Theo came down the ladder completely, which was far shorter than the one Jacinda had fallen from. At worst, she might turn her ankle if she slipped off. "Erasmus—"

"Isn't important at the moment." He grabbed her, pulling her close to his chest. "I don't even care what you're painting."

"You've no appreciation whatsoever for art."

"I'm more concerned you've gotten paint on yourself." Fingers tugged at her skirts. "Probably underneath all *this*."

"Impossible," she whispered, thoughts of Erasmus and her unfounded, slightly ridiculous suspicions ebbing away at his touch. She wasn't even sure what her suspicions were. She would tell Haven later about her missing things and Jacinda's books. "How would I get paint there?"

He leaned over, nipping the side of her neck. "I should check to make sure you haven't any on your . . . person." Walking backward in the direction of the wall, Haven's face took on a predatory glint. "Come here, Theodosia."

"Are you going to inspect me for paint? Or did you interrupt me for another reason?"

"Yes, to both questions," he said, grabbing her hand. "We have roughly a quarter of an hour."

"For what, exactly?" The paintbrush trembled in her fingers as a soft ache pulsed at the apex of her thighs.

His answer was to turn her, pressing her back against the wall. He inhaled against her throat as his hands fumbled with her skirts. "I'll start with your thighs." Teeth grazed her throat. "Inspect them for paint. The idea came to me when I was with the pigs."

"Hardly," her breath caught as his fingers traced along her

slit, "flattering." This was one of the things she loved most about Haven, his completely unapologetic behavior about wanting to tup her whenever possible.

Today promised to be yet another delicious lesson in debauchery.

Fingers teased at her already aroused flesh. "Wet, Lady Haven. Were you thinking of me?"

"Perhaps," she whispered, "I was imagining the pigs."

"Naughty thing." His mouth brushed lightly against hers as the length of him pressed at her entrance. Lifting her, he hooked one of her legs over his arm.

Theo whimpered as he thrust inside her, the angle of his body touching some of Theo's very sensitive parts all at once.

"Wrap your legs around my waist." Haven lifted Theo higher, pressing her against the wall until she was pinned in place.

The paintbrush fell from her fingertips.

"Now," he murmured, taking her in full, deep strokes. "I must tell you that any moment, Mr. Barnaby is expected. He's come to dine. I believe he's bringing Mrs. Barnaby."

"The merchant?" Theo gasped. "Why?" Good lord, she needed to ensure extra places were set at the table. Inform Mrs. Dottie and Rolfe. She needed to bathe and change. Haven needed to—

A low moan left her mouth. She grabbed at his shirt, the smallest tendrils of impending bliss trickling down her limbs. "Why would you have Mr. Barnaby come to the house?" Haven, she recalled, through the intoxicating mist of her impending pleasure, had struck up a friendship with the merchant he'd met on their wedding night.

"Textiles, Theodosia. You gave me the idea with all these bloody over-upholstered bits of furniture."

He was very determined never to be impoverished again, not caring what anyone thought if he went into trade, no matter how quietly. "Comfortable," she breathed. "All the furniture is comfortable." The last word stretched out as he rotated his hips, hitting the exact correct spot.

"Oh, and one more thing." He began to thrust harder as his own pleasure approached. "I shut the door, Theo, but neglected to throw the lock."

Theo's eyes widened in horror even as she moaned at the wave of sensation battering her body. The deep sound of Rolfe filtered into the drawing room. Several sets of footsteps echoed across the tile of the foyer.

The moss-green of Haven's eyes darkened as he took her ferociously against the wall. His lips tilted in a smile just before catching hers, as if the possibility of being found by the Barnabys and Rolfe in a *very* compromising position constituted great fun.

Her climax roared through her, and Haven put his hand over her mouth, stifling the cry from her throat as she exploded in pleasure, legs shaking uncontrollably as her body writhed against the wall, even with Haven holding her in place.

A soft knock came at the door just as Haven stiffened, moaning his release into her neck.

"A moment." Haven's voice was rough. Out of breath. He pressed his forehead to hers, a smile still gracing his lips.

"Ambrose," she breathed against the damp tendrils of his hair. "Your timing leaves much to be desired."

"I'm sorry, I just—" He pressed a tender kiss to her lips. "I —missed you." Haven let go of her gently as her feet slid to the floor. He fixed his own clothing before seeing to hers, pressing another quick kiss to her mouth.

"Next time, hang on to this." He picked her discarded paintbrush off the floor. "You've gotten paint on your skirts."

Sometime later, as Ambrose glanced at his beautiful wife down the length of the large oval table which now graced his dining room, he found himself wishing Barnaby and his wife away before the second course was served.

Theodosia absently pushed up her spectacles before laughing at something Mr. Barnaby related. Light danced along the spray of freckles across one side of her chest. There was a tiny spot of midnight blue paint mixed in with those freckles, something she'd missed while making herself presentable after their interlude today.

What will I do when she leaves?

Fear punched Ambrose's gut. The thought was never far away, though in the last few weeks, he'd managed to push it so far into the recesses of his mind, the desolation only surfaced in the wee hours of the morning. The more time went by, the worse his anxiety became as he waited for his newfound happiness to be destroyed.

Averell would have written to Murphy of their sister's marriage, and enough time had passed that a reply should be forthcoming. One—or possibly both—of them was likely to show up at Greenbriar. Theodosia would know that Ambrose blamed her brother and Elysium for beggaring his father. That he'd threatened Murphy to take it all back one day. She would question the night she had been compromised as well as everything he'd ever said to her.

Barnaby turned his attention to Ambrose while Theodosia regaled Mrs. Barnaby with tales of her life in London. Mrs. Barnaby seemed starved for such gossip, hanging on Theodosia's every word. Theo was the daughter and sister of the Duke of Averell, and Mrs. Barnaby's eyes gleamed with ambition at the thought of their friendship.

He should tell her everything while he still could, before a letter or members of her family arrived. Confess to her what he'd meant to do and ultimately could not. Yes, he'd set out to use her, but compromising her at Blythe's had not been planned. Ambrose had taken the miniature only because it had broken his heart to know she'd painted it for Blythe and not him. He'd always wanted her. *Always*.

Pain snarled deep in his chest.

She won't believe me.

"Wouldn't you say, my lord?" Barnaby sipped at his wine.

"Agreed," Ambrose said to the older man, barely listening. All he could think of was how Theodosia had writhed against him as he had taken her against the wall. The saucy wink she'd given him before running upstairs to change.

And that life, *his life*, without Theodosia would be like that of a candle, struggling to stay lit during a storm, always sputtering, never, ever, to flare brightly again.

26

"Lady Haven? Where would you like the table?"

Theo turned to Rolfe and pointed to a spot just to the left of the window. "There, I think." The delivery of the furniture yesterday was the final piece of her renovation of the drawing room. She'd spent most of the morning with her stalwart butler moving about tables, settees, sofas, and chairs until they met her vision. Drawing rooms were meant to be grand, but Greenbriar's would also be cozy. Warm. Welcoming.

"'Tis beautiful, my lady." Rolfe, still holding the small table with delicately carved legs, turned in a circle to admire her work. "The midnight sky. The constellations. You are a true artist, if I may say so."

"You may, Rolfe."

Theo was immensely pleased with the look of the drawing room. Haven and Jacinda had been sternly warned away, and no one had been permitted entry until she was finished. The staff had been kept out by Rolfe, who was the only other person to have seen Theo's final touches. Only the sideboard remained empty. Erasmus had made off with the brandy the moment it had arrived. She'd had Rolfe lock the remainder of the spirits away.

After gently telling Haven about the theft of Jacinda's books and her miniatures, Haven had gone to confront his uncle yesterday, so furious, Theo had been concerned for Erasmus's safety. So Theo had followed, reminding her husband that Erasmus was a harmless sot.

His uncle had cringed at the sight of Haven, falling to the floor and scuttling away from his nephew like a terrified crab.

Theo had watched from her place by the door, determined to ensure that Haven didn't unintentionally harm his uncle. She pitied Erasmus. He unsettled her, but she didn't wish him hurt.

"My patience is at an end," Haven had said after berating his uncle over the theft. He'd turned away, shaking his head as he headed in Theo's direction.

"As it turns out, so is mine." Erasmus had stiffened, bleary eyes focused for once, and full of loathing. "Don't think, Ambrose," he had said in a hushed, smug tone, "that I don't know what you've done." Erasmus turned his head slightly, catching sight of Theo, who watched him from the door, and smiled—a thin, gruesome thinning of the lips which had made her misgivings about Haven's uncle seem not so wild after all.

Haven had stopped, turning back to his uncle. "What did you say?"

The hatred in his uncle's eyes disappeared, replaced with the vacancy Theo had become accustomed to. Erasmus started to sing. He rose and shuffled away, headed in the direction of the tree where Theo knew a bottle of brandy probably awaited him.

"Haven." Theo had taken his arm, meaning to finally tell

him that . . . well, there was something not right with Erasmus. Something beyond the obvious.

He'd shaken her off, a grim look on his face, before disappearing for the remainder of the day, only returning after she'd already gone to bed. Theo had awoken with the press of Haven's tongue between her legs before he'd taken her with an intensity that had frightened her. It hadn't seemed the right time to speak of Erasmus.

"Lady Haven?" Rolfe interrupted her musings with a nod to the position of the table. "Here?"

Theo turned her head, taking in the glorious room she'd created. "Perfect."

Everything was perfect, except for the tiny bit of dread which seemed to linger over her. It had formed immediately after Haven's confrontation with his uncle and refused to leave.

"Should I check to see when Lord Haven is expected?"

Theo nodded to Rolfe, smoothing her skirts. "If you please, Rolfe."

Haven had gone to the village very early this morning, pausing only to press a kiss on her forehead just as the sun rose. Something about the blasted pigs. He seemed obsessed of late with sows and piglets. He was due back shortly.

Jacinda and Mrs. Henderson had been sent to pick berries and wouldn't be back for hours.

Betts had dressed Theo in a gown of midnight blue in keeping with the color palette of the drawing room. The neckline was indecent. She wore her hair down, spilling about her shoulders. Spectacles, she left firmly perched on her nose.

The entire room, including herself, was spectacular.

Settling herself on the damask of her new sofa, Theo fluffed her skirts and waited for Haven to arrive. She loved him. If the painting in the drawing room didn't scream the words loudly enough to him, her seduction of his person would. Rolfe would ensure they were not disturbed.

Her butler, as if on cue, returned to stand before her, a packet of letters clasped in one hand. "Lord Haven approaches." A tiny smile lingered on his mouth.

Bless Rolfe. He'd had one of the newly hired grooms watching for Haven.

"Thank you, Rolfe. Is there a letter from my mother?" Theo pounded on the cushion to her left. It didn't look quite as plump as it should. She usually received at least one letter each day; from her mother, Olivia, Maggie, sometimes even Phaedra. Last week, she'd received an exceptionally long missive from Romy detailing her adventures with the Frost Giant in Italy and exclaiming over Theo's marriage to Haven.

There it was again. The ping in her brain. Italy. Where Haven had been set upon by thieves, and they'd tried to kill him for his purse. A gentleman who looked *impoverished*.

"From the duke." Rolfe handed her an envelope, bringing her attention back to the moment. "And one for Mr. Stitch from His Grace as well."

Theo frowned as she took the envelope. Her brother rarely wrote to her. Sometimes there were two or three lines added to the letters from her mother or Maggie, but nothing from Tony. Perhaps he'd written to tell her the Averell coach and footmen should come back to London, as it seemed he'd written to Stitch as well. It made sense. She'd already mentioned to her mother she was happy and planned on staying at Greenbriar.

Rolfe left her to her letter, going in search of Stitch.

Breaking the ducal seal, Theo started to read, expecting him to say he wished his coach back or possibly to share news of her brother Leo.

The letter did concern Leo. In fact, a note from him to her was tucked inside.

The paper crinkled between her fingers, the words blurring before her as she read Leo's note. A terrible sensation of dread blossomed inside her, finally bursting free. She thought it might be her heart cracking at the betrayal of everything Theo had thought to be true.

He lied to me.

Coldness set in as she placed the letter face down on the sofa, unable to look at it a moment longer.

Clasping her hands, Theo lifted her chin and waited patiently for her husband to arrive.

※

AMBROSE STOPPED AS HE CAME AROUND THE CORNER, seeing the Averell coach with the ducal coat of arms idling in front of Greenbriar. He inhaled sharply, nodding at Stitch as the driver came forward with a bow.

"The duke asked me to ready the carriage, my lord," Stitch explained, face absent of all expression.

"Has the mail arrived today?" Ambrose's mouth had gone dry. Murphy hadn't come to fetch his sister, nor Averell. He supposed he should count himself lucky, except Ambrose knew, with a horrible shredding sensation in his chest as he climbed the steps, that it only meant the news had come in the form of a letter.

His butler greeted him with a bow, questions hovering in Rolfe's eyes, though he was too well-trained to ask. "Lady Haven awaits you in the drawing room, my lord."

Once again, Ambrose knew that prick Leo Murphy and his pompous brother were going to take everything from Ambrose. And this time, it would be much more excruciating than simply impoverishing the Marquess of Haven.

I should have told her. Made her understand.

Ambrose walked into the drawing room, shocked for a

moment by the transformation of the space. Bloody beautiful. He prepared himself to dodge one of the recently purchased vases or knickknacks, but he should have known better.

Theodosia sat calmly, so stunning it hurt to look at her, a celestial body having fallen from the heavens to grace the drawing room. There was nothing left of the flirtatious, slightly empty-headed young lady, ripe for ruination, whom he'd met so long ago.

No, not empty-headed. Theodosia had only refused to see her own value. Stumbling about blindly to attract Blythe's attention. Instead, it was Ambrose who'd been drawn to her. Seeing the look on her face, she might prefer Blythe now, after all.

Her shoulders were stiff. Chin tilted upward not in defiance but with disdain. There was no warmth for him in the swirling blue of her eyes. Only a flash of the wound he'd inflicted. His last hope that Leo Murphy had forgotten the Marquess of Haven evaporated.

How ironic. He'd lived for years wanting Murphy to remember him.

He approached the wall, unable to look away from what she'd painted. For him. He'd never told her he loved her. He should have. Theodosia would never believe those words, not now. And she had returned that love. The proof was before him.

The night sky above Greenbriar, the same one he'd seen outside the windows of the studio he'd given her upstairs, was depicted across the long wall facing the door. The stars looked exactly as they had on the untold evenings Ambrose had spent with his father, picking out the constellations. Dreaming of the moon and stars while his father instructed Ambrose how to navigate using the heavens.

He and his father would share pie and drink cider.

Ambrose would tell him all about his day, the rocks he'd collected in his pockets. The frog he'd brought for Mother, though she wasn't at all impressed.

The wall was stunning. Magnificent. Far more than Ambrose deserved.

Theodosia wore midnight blue, matching the sofa she sat upon, an opened letter next to her. Even from where he stood, Ambrose could see the seal of the Duke of Averell. He took a step closer, pained when her slender form fell back slightly as if his touch would soil her.

"It's magnificent," Ambrose said. "*You* are magnificent."

"Did you want me the moment I spilled ratafia on you or only after you realized I was Leo Murphy's sister?"

A fist clamped down on his chest—the pain of his heart breaking. "Theodosia—"

"Answer my question, Ambrose."

"It's complicated," he said softly, taking a careful step in her direction, afraid she would run from him. "Please let me explain."

"All this time." Her words held such an acrid note, hardly sounding like Theodosia at all. "You had me believing—" She looked down at her lap before raising her chin again. "You made me believe you wanted *me*. But that wasn't the case at all. *You* wanted Leo Murphy's sister."

"I didn't lie about wanting you."

"Only everything else." Her words were sharp. Cutting. As if the last few weeks had never happened.

"One had nothing to do with the other. I fell in lov—"

"Don't you *dare*. Do not say it." Theodosia trembled slightly, blinking as if to stop from weeping, something he'd never seen her do, not even when Lady Blythe treated her with such scorn. "You promised to be honest with me."

"I did. I am. You know how I feel about you." He pressed a palm over his chest, directly above his heart. "You *know*."

Theo's gaze flicked over him, chilly and uncompromising. "You never told me Elysium was where your father beggared himself, Ambrose. Never explained to me that he gave away everything you held dear so he could play dice at the club my brother owns. Wasn't that a truth you should have told me?"

"My father didn't give it away," he shot back. "Your brother coerced him into it." He was angry now too. Incensed that one letter from Leo Murphy far outweighed the nights spent in his arms. The way they'd worked together to rebuild Greenbriar. The love Ambrose *knew* lay between them.

He took a step forward. "My father would *never* have gambled everything away, especially not my sister's dowry, without someone drawing him along. I'm sure he made the perfect mark. Grief-stricken. Wealthy. Easy to manipulate. Your brother is a monumental prick who delights in destroying bits and pieces of the aristocracy because he will never belong to it. My father is doubtless only one of Murphy's victims, all because your brother can't tolerate being a low-born bastard."

Theodosia didn't even flinch at Ambrose's snarling temper. Instead, she smoothed down the fabric of her skirts.

"My brother's illegitimate birth in no way diminishes who he is or my love for him. He is a businessman. You behave as if Leo incited your father to drink and gamble away everything but his title. Edmund Collingwood," her eyes narrowed behind the glass of her spectacles, "was a sot and a very poor gambler. Liked whores as well, I'm told."

Ambrose thought he might snap in two. He backed away from her, horrified by this repulsive conversation. One he'd prayed never to have.

"He was only too happy to sign away your inheritance, Ambrose. The only inducement he needed was found at the bottom of a bottle of scotch. A truth you refuse to see but one I'll acknowledge."

Even as angry as he was, Ambrose admired Theodosia's steel. Her absolute loyalty to her brother and her family. He just wished she felt a bit of that loyalty for him.

"I am not sure how you managed to be in the study at exactly the right time, nor do I wish to know. Maybe you and Blythe conspired together." She gave a shrug. "I suppose when faced with both myself and my sister at Granby's house party, you couldn't decide which one of us would do. I suspect Granby claiming my sister deterred you, so you sought out second best."

"You are not second best, Theodosia." A wash of agony hit him in the chest, pushing aside his anger and frustration. "You are first, last, and always for me." His voice broke. "Please—"

A contemptuous laugh came from her as she stood, ignoring his outstretched hand. "I'm leaving, Haven. I cannot bear to be near you right now." She purposefully took off her spectacles and tossed them carelessly on the sofa. "I can't stand the *sight* of you. I was much happier before everything was made so clear to me." She bent to pick up the letter, careful to stay out of his reach.

Ambrose reached out and took hold of her elbow. The anger between them made it difficult for him to breathe. He wanted to lock her away until she listened to him. Let him explain.

"At least take your bloody spectacles, Theodosia," he growled. "You won't be able to see. You'll trip and—"

"Grope some unsuspecting gentleman?" she whispered in a falsely flirtatious manner. "Dear God." She leaned in purposefully so he could see down her bodice. "I hope so."

Ambrose released her, temper flaring again at her words. "You would do well, Lady Haven," he hissed, "to remember that this will not be a marriage of distance or one where you take lovers. That has not changed. Nor will it."

"Oh, dear. Fight a duel over it. I beg you." Theo strode from the room, her skirts swirling about her ankles. "Goodbye, Ambrose. Enjoy the painting and my dowry."

27

Theo was learning to play faro. She'd become quite good at it. Enough so that she was winning. Either that or Duckworth, one of her brother's dealers, was intentionally letting her win. Either way, it was an excellent way to amuse herself. Pass the time. Not think of Haven.

Once, it would have been drawing or painting which she'd gravitated to in order to soothe herself. But lately, Theo would start out with the intent to sketch a dog, for instance, and moments later it would be Haven. Haven naked walking out of the pond he liked to swim in. Haven asleep on his stomach, one foot sticking out of the sheets. Haven talking to Jasper the pig farmer who, as it turned out, was a lovely man.

Theo wobbled on her stool as longing for her husband struck her.

Dammit.

"Anything wrong, Lady Haven?" Duckworth peered at her with concern.

"Nothing at all." She gave him a broad smile. "I was only wondering if Duckworth was your real name."

The dealer leaned in. "Unfortunately, it is."

Theo laughed and tried to pull her thoughts from Haven. A difficult task. Thus, the need for faro. She'd learned how to stroll among the tables at Elysium until she found a game that looked promising, confidently sitting down at any table she wished. Sometimes Tony joined her when he wasn't working the floor, but usually, it was her sister-in-law, Maggie, who served as her companion. Sometimes the Dowager Duchess of Averell appeared in glittering skirts of gray. Mama liked dice.

It was true. Married women had all sorts of freedom, especially if they possessed an estranged husband who preferred the country.

It had been several weeks since Theo had returned from Greenbriar, arriving at the Averell mansion ensconced in her brother's lavish coach, deposited on the doorstep like some horribly overpriced package. The gossips weren't surprised by her return to London, given the start her marriage had had, especially Lady Blythe. Theodosia, long the odd Barrington, now appeared to be the most scandalous one.

Everything in London had taken on a dull, gritty sheen since she'd returned from Greenbriar. And it wasn't because she'd left her spectacles in Haven's drawing room and refused to consider getting another pair.

Plain and simple, she missed him. Dreadfully. The day her brother's letter had arrived, Tony, behaving far more wisely than she'd thought him capable of, had not explicitly ordered her to return home. He'd only said that it was time Stitch return the coach to London. It was Theodosia's choice whether she wished to be in it.

I didn't know what else to do.

The shock of Leo's note enclosed in Tony's letter had left Theo sitting on that stupid sofa, unable to breathe. Neither of her brothers had any reason to lie to her, though Papa had always told Theo there were several versions of the truth. She thought the advice especially pertinent in this instance.

'I barely remembered the Marquess of Haven until I got Tony's letter.' Leo had written. *'Determined to drink himself into an early grave. Always asked for the most expensive French brandy. His son did ask me to stop extending him credit, but the marquess laughed it off, decrying his heir as privileged, lazy, and all too likely to bankrupt the family on his own.'*

Theo tapped the table for another card and smiled up at Duckworth. Staring at her cards, she barely saw them. None of Leo's letter made sense to her. Haven was the furthest thing from lazy, though possibly in his youth he might have been. Before he went to Italy.

'When the son, now your husband, returned after inheriting, he did threaten me. I replied in kind. I showed him the papers with the signature of the late marquess. He'd signed everything over to me, what little that was left. His daughter's dowry, which he said she wouldn't be needing since the useless girl is lame. I may be a bastard, Theodosia, but I have three sisters and Olivia, all of whom I love. He was deeply in debt to me, but I drew the line at taking that poor girl's dowry. The marquess insisted.'

Jacinda spoke of her late father with affection, albeit with a great deal of disappointment. Edmund had been wracked with guilt over Jacinda. Why would he have punished her further? Addictions to drink and gambling could change a person for the worse, Theo supposed, but the idea that Edmund had caused his daughter's accident then intentionally left her penniless?

Brandy. French brandy.

"There you are. Shall we call it an evening?" Tony stood before her, blindingly handsome, oblivious to the greedy stares of several ladies fluttering about the tables. He stuck out his arm to offer escort. "If you win much more, I might have to call you out for cheating."

"I think Elysium can afford the loss." Theo grinned at him and scooped up her winnings. "I'm ready to return home."

"I agree. I'll be thrilled when Leo shows his bloody face again. I wish he'd hurry up about it."

The entire family knew Leo was chasing Lady Masterson in New York, though he claimed to have gone there on a business venture.

"Has he caught Lady Masterson yet?" Theo asked, taking her brother's arm. "I feel certain he won't return until he does."

Tony shrugged. "I've no idea. He doesn't mention her in his letters, only the investments he's been making and directions on how to run Elysium. Since he hasn't returned, I'll assume things aren't going exactly as he wishes." He led her through Elysium to the waiting Averell carriage outside. "Even your current predicament couldn't wean him from his pursuit."

Tony rarely spoke of her marriage. Never used her husband's name. His favorite way to refer to Haven as of late was the *parasite*.

He handed her into the waiting carriage and crawled in behind her. "Truthfully, I'm ready to seek my bed. If one more bloody idiot thinks I'm Leo, I may be forced to commit violence. As if Leo would ever dress so tastefully," Tony huffed. "Those ghastly waistcoats he favors hurt the eyes and are an affront to finely tailored gentlemen everywhere."

"He just likes a bit of flash." Her brothers looked very much alike, so much so that people often confused one for the other, especially from a distance.

"I can't imagine anyone mistaking us. Those waistcoats are a dead giveaway."

"Leo is much more fun," Theo said with a laugh.

Tony scowled at her. "I'm delightful. And I have a ducal accent."

The smile on her face froze. *Diction. Erasmus had been practicing his speech.* Sounding very unlike his usual, rambling self.

But Haven's uncle was incompetent. Sweet, in a sot sort of way. His worst offense was stealing money for drink.

"Is something wrong?" Tony peered down at her.

"No, it's just—" Leo hadn't wanted to take Jacinda's dowry, but the Marquess of Haven had forced him to. He'd called his lame daughter worthless, according to her brother. As angry and unforgiving as Haven was toward his father, he still insisted Edmund had loved Jacinda. Haven refused to believe his father would have deliberately gambled away everything he had, including the money set aside for Jacinda, without inducement. He blamed Leo for luring his father into drunkenness and poverty. It was his whole reason for wanting to compromise Theo.

She took a breath. Because it *still* hurt.

Despite Haven and his sister, even their father before he drank himself into oblivion, all thinking Erasmus was terrified of the ocean, it might not even be true. Had he really been living in France? Couldn't he have come to England whenever he wished, possibly impersonating his brother, knowing Edmund was at Greenbriar? Haven wasn't in England. Who would have known differently?

Leo wouldn't have. Especially if Erasmus was smart enough to take Edmund's signet ring, and she thought he might have been. Wear his clothes. Speak like him. *Be* him.

Theo gave her head a little shake. She was being fanciful.

"Are you thinking of the *parasite* again? You realize Leo will never accept him. There's bound to be a fight of some kind."

"Stop calling him that." She elbowed Tony. "He—perhaps set out to compromise me to get back at Leo." She looked up at her brother with certainty. "Haven loves me." Theo knew it to be the truth now that the shock of her brother's letter had worn off. It didn't excuse Haven or—

"Dear one." Tony ran a hand through his hair and shook his head. "I know it may have seemed that way. But, well, you are beautiful. Any man might want to . . . what I mean to say is, that isn't love." He waved his hand around as if at a loss for words.

"I'm not an idiot, Tony. I know the difference." So did her heart.

"You thought Blythe cared for you as well. Forgive me if I don't immediately embrace the idea of you and Haven. He did set out to compromise you for dishonorable reasons."

"He did but I'm not thinking of Haven, or rather, I am. Did you know Haven has an uncle?" She looked at her brother. "His father's twin."

Brandy. Leo said the Marquess of Haven had always requested French brandy. But Edmund had been a scotch drinker. Even Mrs. Henderson had mentioned that to her.

"A twin?" Tony scoffed, shaking his head in disbelief. "A secret twin no one knew a thing about. In London, where you can't even sneeze without someone commenting?"

"Erasmus didn't live in England. I know it might seem a little—"

"Addled? Mad?"

"Yes, but I think it was Erasmus who dealt with Leo, not the Marquess of Haven. Erasmus pretended to be his brother."

Tony burst into laughter. "Theo, sweetheart, do you hear yourself? This isn't one of those novels you and Olivia like to read. Even if what you speculate is true, what possible reason would this twin—"

"Erasmus."

"—Erasmus have for bankrupting the estate? Especially if

his brother was supporting him? Would seem to be rather foolish, wouldn't it?"

Erasmus had called her brother a bastard. Theo assumed he'd meant Tony, but he'd been talking about Leo. And the insult was literal. Because he'd *met* Leo. As far as meeting her father, Erasmus could have seen him at any time over the years. Because she doubted he'd spent all his time in France. Nor did she think, any longer, he was the simple-minded sot he pretended to be.

"Don't you see the flaw in your logic?" Tony nudged her. "Look, if you wish to return to Haven, you don't need to make an excuse. I know you imagine he cares for you."

"One minute." Erasmus had told her exactly why he'd do such a thing. "He was the younger twin by one minute." She looked over at Tony. "Don't you see? He was riddled with jealousy over the fact that his brother was the marquess and married to the woman Erasmus loved."

"Oh, Theo." Tony shook his head. He didn't believe her. "Every word is more ludicrous than the next. Haven is simply not that interesting. Nor his father. I grant you the tale is a rather entertaining one. Perhaps you should write rather than paint."

It didn't matter what her brother thought. Haven had tried to tell her he loved her, right before she left him. He *did* love her.

And she was right about Erasmus. She just didn't know what to do about it.

28

"My lady, Coates wishes to speak with you."

Theo looked up from her book, though she'd barely managed to read a page. She was still ruminating about Haven's uncle and what she should do about her suspicions. She'd thought of nothing else all day yesterday and had written several letters to her husband, unsure what else she could do, but had yet to send them. Her imaginings, in the clear light of day, seemed just that, despite the overwhelming evidence to the contrary.

Overwhelming may be too strong a word.

The fact remained, she had no proof. No one would believe Erasmus had bankrupted the family on purpose because it didn't make sense for him to do so. Even Theo thought it was a rather idiotic thing to do even if you were half-mad. There was no way to prove he'd impersonated his brother. And for all she knew, Haven's father had developed a taste for French brandy when he gambled. It was no sin to like brandy.

"Lady Haven." Coates stood at the door, hands clasped, a worried look on his broad face.

"Hello, Coates." She waved him in. "Is something amiss?"

"No, it's only—" He glanced at Pith, then back to her. He looked down at his clasped hands.

"Pith, would you bring me some tea, if you please?" Theo gave the butler a pointed look. Coates had something to say, and he wouldn't, not if Pith was listening.

The butler bowed, glaring at Coates, a subtle reminder to mind himself around Theo. Which was ridiculous. Coates would never step out of line.

The footman visibly relaxed as Pith left. "I'm sorry to disturb you, my lady. But something happened last night, and I must make you aware of it." He looked away for a moment and wet his lips as if struggling over how to tell her.

"It's all right, Coates. Go ahead." She nodded, encouraging him to speak.

"As you know, my brother works the door at Elysium most nights," he said in a rush, glancing down at his boots.

"I do."

"Well," he started, cheeks pinking. "Sometimes when I have a night off, I visit my brother at Elysium, and I was off last night."

"Is that what you came to tell me? I assure you it isn't the most terrible thing in the world. The duke won't mind, as long as you don't make a habit of it, and it doesn't interfere with your brother's duties."

"Begging your pardon, Lady Haven, but that isn't it. Last night, I was with my brother, and Lord Haven's uncle appeared at the door. He didn't see me, not at first. He was raving something awful. Demanding entry to Elysium."

Theo's fingers shook slightly. "You're certain? It was Lord Erasmus?"

"I am. Begging your pardon, my lady, but he smelled of brandy. Said he was the Marquess of Haven. And—well he didn't sound— " He struggled for the word, probably not wishing to offend her.

"Dimwitted?"

Coates nodded. "Told my brother he'd have his job for refusing him entrance. Said he knew Mr. Murphy, that they were old friends. His membership would be reinstated because he was the Marquess of Haven and he'd soon be coming into a fortune. He was dressed very fine, my lady. Even had a walking stick. When I stepped out from behind my brother, he started shaking something awful and ran off."

There was something else. Theo could see it in the footman's face.

"What else, Coates?"

His throat bobbed. "I don't even wish to tell you." He reddened further. "He tried to hit me with the walking stick before he ran." Coates bit his lip. "Said to tell you, my lady, that you'll make a lovely widow. He was well in his cups. Could be just the ravings of a man whose had too much to drink. But my brother and I both thought you should know."

"This was last night?" What if Erasmus had already gone back to Greenbriar? What if—

She looked up at Coates.

"Yes, my lady. After midnight."

Her brother wasn't here. He'd escorted Maggie, Olivia, and her mother to an outdoor gathering at Lady Fulton's. Phaedra was somewhere. Practicing with her wooden sword, most likely. By the time Tony returned or she sent word, it could be hours, and Theo wasn't sure there was time to spare.

I was right. Very satisfying. Unless Erasmus had already made her a widow. There wouldn't be anything satisfying about that.

"Coates." Theo stood and addressed him. "Fetch Stitch and the coach. I'll need you to accompany me to Greenbriar. We must inform Lord Haven of what has occurred."

"My lady?"

Erasmus *might* just be a drunk spouting nonsense. Or he could be a calculating lunatic who meant to harm her annoying husband. And Theo couldn't allow that to happen. Because if anyone was going to suffocate her husband with a pillow or pinch his nose when he snored, it was going to be her. Erasmus better not lay a hand on Ambrose. Not so much as a quivering finger.

"Immediately, Coates. There isn't any time to waste."

29

Theo paced outside the small coaching inn they'd stopped at to change horses, frowning at the way the sun was dipping lower in the sky. The sense that she must get to Haven immediately had her walking in circles, growing more anxious by the moment. What if she was too late?

No one at Greenbriar suspected Erasmus of anything worse than petty theft so he could buy himself a bottle. Not even Haven thought his uncle capable of plotting his demise.

Theo tapped her chin with her forefinger. He had fooled everyone. Even her. He'd had the audacity to ask her for an allowance, sing his ridiculous songs, and pick her violets, all the while planning to kill her husband.

I'm coming, Ambrose.

Bloody idiot didn't even know he was in danger. Theo's only consolation was that Erasmus on his own was unlikely to do much damage. He *was* still a sot, though a very devious, malicious one. But he could have hired someone. As he'd done in Italy. Because she was fairly certain that Erasmus was behind the attack on his nephew. Which is why he'd gone back to Greenbriar because he'd assumed the attack would be successful. And told everyone who asked that the fairies told him his nephew had died.

Fairies my—

"My lady, we are ready." Coates appeared next to her, probably wondering why she'd been circling the courtyard like some crazed chicken for the better part of an hour.

"How much longer, Coates?" Erasmus *could* wield a pistol. Probably, depending on how much he'd had to drink.

"Not too much longer." The footman looked up at the sky.

Or slit Haven's throat while he slept.

"Tell Stitch to drive faster."

※

AMBROSE SAT OUTSIDE ON HIS NEWLY RENOVATED TERRACE, admiring the recently trimmed row of hedges in his garden, and took another sip of his mildly expensive wine. The sun was setting low, hanging over the edge of the trees as it sank into darkness. Soon, the stars would come out, filling the sky above his head with their brilliance, very much like what was depicted in the drawing room.

Not one bit of it interested him.

He took another sip of the wine. There weren't enough bottles in all of England for Ambrose to drown himself in. *Finally*, Ambrose understood some of his father's grief. Why he'd started drinking. Theodosia wasn't dead, not in the way his mother was, but she was gone all the same.

Each morning, when his fingers crawled across the mattress, searching in vain for her slender form, Ambrose considered riding to London to fetch her. The smell of paint no longer suffused the bedsheets. Nor lemon. Yesterday, he'd gone up to her studio and taken out one of her sketchbooks to look at. In her haste to be away from him, Theo hadn't packed any of her things here, nor had she sent for them. She'd only taken her maid.

Ambrose took that as a sign of hope.

The pad was full of sketches of her father, the progression of his illness apparent in the drawings. He could make out Theodosia's grief in every brush of the charcoal. Saw the water stains of her tears blurring the edges of the paper. Another sketchpad held drawings of her sisters. Her mother. Several of the duke. One page revealed Leo Murphy, flawlessly handsome with a smug grin on his lips, staring up at Ambrose.

He'd stared at that face for a long time, allowing the anger to ebb and flow over him. Theodosia loved her brother.

Even if Theodosia forgave him one day, and he prayed she would, she would never give up her family. And if Ambrose didn't put aside his anger—

Leo Murphy was likely guilty of many questionable things; he had to be in his line of work. But he hadn't made Edmund Collingwood a drunk. Ambrose's father had managed that all on his own. Acceptance of his father's failings was painful, but also necessary. He had to believe the evidence his father's behavior presented and put the past behind him, as difficult as that may be. It would do no good to continue to blame Murphy.

Because he loved Theodosia. Every half-blind, clumsy, brazenly improper, artistic bit of her. He probably had from the beginning.

After she left him without allowing him to explain, something that infuriated Ambrose even though he knew the fault was his, his temper had slowly faded. Barely hours after the Averell coach had rolled away, Ambrose was left with an enormous hollow feeling in his chest. A gnawing emptiness that would not be assuaged. The very worst sort of hunger. He'd always be starving without Theodosia.

Ambrose had shut the drawing room the very day she'd left, threatening Rolfe with bodily harm if anyone so much as dared step inside.

Rolfe, to his credit, hadn't so much as flinched at the threat.

Ambrose, to his everlasting shame, couldn't allow anyone else to see what Theo had painted for him. At the very corner, tucked near the windows, was the outline of a man and his son. Watching the stars together outside Greenbriar. A message meant for Ambrose alone.

And I let her leave.

A small growl left him. He sat down on one of the stone steps and took the bottle of wine he'd brought with him, refilling his glass.

Jacinda had been devastated by Theo's departure. She had only recently started speaking to Ambrose again, and when she did, it was not without censure.

'What did you do?' Her delicate frame had shaken with unshed tears once she'd found out Theodosia was gone, pushing away any attempts by Ambrose to explain himself.

A hand crawled across his chest, pressing a palm against his heart. He was surprised the bloody thing was still beating.

Ambrose wore himself out to the point of exhaustion every day, traveling among his tenants and addressing their concerns, trying not to think or feel. He tried to focus on his family being made whole again, taking back everything Murphy had taken from his father. Meeting with Barnaby in Warwick to talk about the textile mills he no longer cared about. Watching as crates of books arrived for Jacinda and then seeing his sister burst into tears at the sight. Eating the dishes carefully prepared by Mrs. Dottie, barely tasting the food.

A shame really. Mrs. Dottie was an excellent cook.

His uncle, thankfully, kept to himself after Ambrose tossed him a small bag of coins. He hadn't seen Erasmus in days and idly wondered if he'd drowned in the pond.

Ambrose would check tomorrow.

"Hell." Draining his glass again, he resolved to go after Theodosia. Control his temper and swallow his pride in regard to her brother. Apologize to the entire family including that fucking butler who hated him.

What mattered most to him was Theodosia. First, last, and always.

※

THEO NEARLY JUMPED OUT OF HER SKIN AS THE COACH finally pulled up in front of Greenbriar. Briefly, she took in the freshly painted front door. The two pots full of bright red flowers which stood on either side in welcome. Exactly as she'd instructed.

I must remember to thank Rolfe.

Coates had barely opened the door when Theo leapt out. She marched up to the door with purpose as Rolfe opened it. Surprise showed on his stoic features.

"Lady Haven."

"In the flesh. Where is Lord Haven?"

Rolfe took her cloak and kept pace beside her. "I'm not certain, my lady."

"Have you lost my husband, Rolfe?"

"No, my lady. But Lord Haven . . . wanders in the evenings. Mostly no further than the terrace, where he takes a nightcap."

"Wonderful. Coates and Stitch are outside. Have you seen Lord Erasmus?"

"No, my lady."

Well, that at least was good news. Still, Theo marched into the drawing room and went right to the sideboard. Scotch, the kind Haven favored, sat next to a bottle of expensive French brandy. The brandy told Theo that at the very least, Erasmus hadn't been here long enough to steal it. Perhaps she'd beaten him to Greenbriar. Her hand grabbed the brandy bottle by the neck.

But it would be best to be prepared.

Just in case Erasmus was lurking about.

***

Ambrose put down the bottle of wine as the shuffle of footsteps met his ears. For a moment, he thought it might be Jacinda. She liked to berate him about Theodosia around this time every evening. It had become something of a nightly ritual. But there'd been no thump of a cane. Nor was the tread heavy. So not Rolfe. Nor Mr. Henderson, though he did shuffle somewhat. The stale smell of brandy and unwashed clothing met his nose.

"Hello, Uncle." Ambrose didn't turn around. "Looking for coin? I was growing concerned that I'd have to fish your body out of the pond."

A small, impotent whine came from behind him, and Ambrose turned, lifting his brow at the sight his uncle presented. Trembling. Half-drunk. Pistol quivering in one hand. Rather interesting. Eramus looked more likely to shoot his own foot off than Ambrose.

"Is that thing even loaded?" He took another swig from the bottle, nodding in the direction of the pistol.

Honestly, Haven hadn't given his uncle much thought as of late, considering he had more important things on his mind, like how the fuck he was going to retrieve his wife. But when he did consider Erasmus, it was to remember the words his uncle had hurled at him when Haven had found him stealing for what seemed the hundredth time.

'I know what you did.'

He hadn't mistaken the words nor the hatred in them. It had given Ambrose something else to consider besides Theodosia.

"The pistol is loaded, you worthless whelp." Erasmus raised his arm. "And I'm so close it's unlikely I'll miss."

"Now, why would you want me dead, Uncle?" A ridiculous question. Ambrose was fairly sure he knew the answer.

"This is my home." The pistol shook. "My estate. It should *never* have been yours to begin with. Now that you've married a fat Barrington dowry, I want it back."

"That isn't exactly how all this works, Uncle." Ambrose took another lazy sip of his wine. "You reek of brandy, by the way."

"I never cared for you in the *least*, Ambrose. Or your tragically lame sister. I should have pushed the ladder harder. Now I'll be stuck with Jacinda. Your wife will insist she be cared for. And I, her adoring uncle, will have to ensure she is comfortable."

His fingers tightened on the bottle. The thought had crossed his mind that it had been Erasmus and not his father who had knocked Jacinda from the ladder, especially in light of recent considerations. Jacinda had said they'd both been in the library with her that day. But his father had *admitted* to accidentally pushing the ladder. And Erasmus had been stricken, according to Mrs. Henderson. All an act, that much was becoming clear. "My father—"

"Believed whatever I told him." A smile crossed his uncle's thin lips. "Poor Edmund was prone to blackouts when he had too much scotch. Made him forget all about how he gambled away the family fortune at Elysium. Couldn't even recall that he went to London so often. Or that I did."

Ambrose sucked in a breath. Impossible. How had Erasmus managed it?

I wasn't here.

"You have no idea how wonderful it was to be addressed *properly* as the Marquess of Haven instead of as the brother no one remembered Edmund even had. When we were younger, your father and I used to change places all the time, and no one was the wiser. I learned to imitate him, you see. After a time, he didn't care for it." His brow furrowed. "Matilda knew after—well, after that *one* time. I don't think she ever told Edmund."

Christ. "You pretended to be my father with *her*. My mother."

"I loved Matilda. I just wanted to *be* with her. Once. He got to marry her. Sent me away because I loved her too. Incredibly unfair."

Ambrose felt sick to the very bottom of his stomach. How had he never guessed? Never looked in his uncle's direction? "You hated my father."

"So *very* much." His uncle's lips twitched to form a sneer. "Edmund took the title. Took Matilda. I was left with *nothing*. All because of *one* minute." Spittle collected at his lips. "When she died trying to give that greedy prick another child, I knew it was finally time to act. Edmund was stricken with grief and guilt. I popped in every so often to commiserate with him. Help him through his sadness. Scotch helped. Gambling. Whores. The only thing we disagreed on was cards. I preferred dice."

His uncle was insane. Not harmless. Or sweet. But completely mad. "It was you at Elysium. But why? Why would you beggar him? He gave you money. Supported you—"

"I finally decided that if I couldn't have it, he shouldn't either. And it was such delightful fun, Nephew. Spending your inheritance on whores and dice. The things they'll allow at

Elysium." He smacked his lips. "I adored demanding Leo Murphy extend my . . ." A giggle. "*Credit*." The pistol waved wildly. "I demand you extend my credit, Murphy," Erasmus said in a voice sounding remarkably like Ambrose's father. "You never guessed. You weren't here. How did the streets treat you in Venice, Nephew?"

Ambrose glared at him. Erasmus had tried to have him killed. Hoped he was dead. And then Jacinda had had her accident. Perhaps he meant to kill them both. No one ever suspected Erasmus of doing anything other than being a sot. Not even his father. A forgotten piece of Collingwood history Ambrose had inherited along with Greenbriar, the title, and his father's debts. *How long* had Erasmus been slipping in and out of the estate pretending to be Edmund? How many of the servants had even known his father had a twin?

"You aren't terrified of the ocean, are you? Nor seasick."

"Not a bit. We went sailing as children once. I ate too many sweets and became ill. I let everyone believe it was the terror of the sea," he thundered in an imperious voice, once more sounding like Ambrose's father, "because I didn't want to get in trouble. I never bothered to correct anyone. It was easier for everyone to assume I was weak."

A terrible thought occurred to Ambrose. "Was it you I argued with that day, or my father?" It was that argument that had driven Ambrose from his home. Estranged him from his father. A relationship that had never been repaired. The pain and regret never left him.

"Me!" Erasmus let out a laugh at his prank. "And you *never* guessed because you'd forgotten I even existed. Perfect Ambrose. So much his father's son. Such a bloody hothead. It was hilarious when you stomped about, blaming Murphy and Elysium for your ills. And as much as I enjoyed watching you twist in the wind, wearing your worn boots and a perpetual look of worry, I was much relieved when you married Theodosia. My plan to bankrupt Edmund might have been somewhat short-sighted. Sometimes my emotions get the better of me. But you, Nephew, exhibited such *deviousness* in ruining Murphy's sister so you could get back the wealth I so willingly gave him. I never knew you had it in you." He shrugged, and the pistol waved yet again. "I think Murphy may have actually felt bad for taking everything, but he was far too greedy to say no. Except Jacinda's dowry. He didn't want to take that. Eventually, he came around. I can be very persuasive."

Ambrose wondered if he could grab the pistol before Erasmus fired and was fairly sure he could.

"Did you kill my father, Uncle?"

30

Theo's fingers curled around the neck of the brandy bottle. She stopped, seeing a shadow on the terrace, one too rounded to be her husband.

"Me!" She heard the word, slightly muffled, through the doors leading to the terrace.

Erasmus.

Rolfe was no longer behind her. She'd asked him to send Coates for the constable. There were footmen around, though. Somewhere. But Theo didn't want to tip off Erasmus by summoning them. He might startle and shoot Haven.

She hefted the brandy bottle. She *really* disliked Haven's uncle, regretting every bit of coin she'd ever given him. Preying on her sympathy. Trying to sell her miniatures. Attempting to kill her husband.

Theo opened the door to the terrace quietly. The two men before her never even looked in her direction as she slid onto the terrace. Theo, much like her sisters, was very good at playing bowls. And while tossing a brandy bottle wasn't *exactly* the same, she thought she could manage. Though it was hard to see. If there was ever a time Theo truly wished she had her spectacles, it was now.

"Heavens, no." Erasmus sounded offended. "I may have detested Edmund, but I'm no murderer. He choked in his sleep." Haven's uncle made a face. "A heavy dinner, far too much wine, and a whore. You, Ambrose, will be my very first murder."

Not if Theo had anything to say about it. She crept closer and placed her feet in the correct stance. Tossing the brandy bottle at Erasmus was probably the best she could manage. It would be enough. Haven would do the rest. Even now, though she could barely see him, Theo suspected he was coiled up like Theseus, ready to strike a large rat.

"Lucky me."

"No, I'm the lucky one. I will finally have the title I deserve. Marquess of Haven. You've already brought me a fortune and pissed off your wife. She'll be told the same thing as everyone else. You shot yourself cleaning your gun."

"No one will believe for an instant that I can't clean a gun properly. Or that I was doing so while outside on the terrace."

"Everyone knows your despondency over Theodosia. No one will think it an accident," Erasmus said sadly.

Theo pressed a hand to her heart. Haven had been *despondent*. She *knew* he loved her.

Focus, Theo.

She crouched, swinging her arm as if she were about to toss a bowl.

"You've been mooning over her for weeks. I am sympathetic, having lost my own true love. I'm doing you a kindness, Nephew. Erasmus raised a trembling hand, attempting to aim. "Now, hold still if you please."

Theo tossed the bottle, wishing she had something clever to say to Erasmus as she did so. The bottle swung over his head, the neck clipping his ear before it disappeared into the darkness of the garden with a loud thud.

Dammit.

The distraction was all Haven needed to leap at Erasmus. He easily took the pistol from his uncle, who screeched like an owl at his nephew's assault. Haven punched him once, hard, in the nose, and Erasmus fell to the terrace, blood seeping through his fingers. He turned to look over at her.

"Theodosia, you're here." There was wonder in his voice.

"I am. I came to save you. From him."

"I suppose I should count myself fortunate you could see well enough to discern who was who and I wasn't hit with a brandy bottle." He held out his hand, reaching for her, before turning back to his uncle.

Theo went to him without hesitation, peace filling her at the feel of Haven's strong fingers curling around hers. They could discuss the particulars later.

※

"I suspected it was him," Jacinda said.

Theo looked up from her seat in the drawing room as they waited for the constable to arrive. Hearing the commotion on the terrace, Rolfe had rushed out along with one of the recently hired footmen. They'd taken the sobbing Erasmus down the hall to the small parlor, ironically the same room Theo's trunks had once been locked in. Jacinda, hearing the commotion, had come down the stairs, giving her brother a wide-eyed look before hugging Theo.

Now, Haven's sister sat across from her in the drawing room, sipping on a cup of tea procured by Rolfe.

"What do you mean you suspected him? Why on earth wouldn't you have said anything to me?" Haven was pacing about like a caged tiger, threatening to wear holes in the new rug Theo had purchased. "How, Jacinda? I didn't."

"You weren't *here*, Ambrose," Jacinda stated. "And I didn't suspect him at first. Why would I? I'm not even sure I knew I had an uncle until he showed up at Greenbriar while you were gone. Before Uncle Erasmus officially arrived, Mr. Henderson kept babbling about seeing Lord Haven down by the tree. You know, the one where our uncle eventually took up residence? One night, he came in to tell Mrs. Henderson that his lordship had sworn at him like those soldiers who followed old Boney. Napoleon is who he meant. Mr. Henderson fought with Wellington in his youth."

"I'm familiar, Jacinda."

"He was speaking French," Theo said. All the energy rushing through her earlier in her anxiousness to get to Haven had faded and was quickly being replaced with exhaustion. "I take it your father did not speak French. Nor was he, I suspect, overly fond of brandy."

"No. And there were times," Jacinda said, "when I was certain father was upstairs, but I'd see him walking out to that tree." She shook her head. "Erasmus was here on and off and I never knew it. Not then, anyway."

A knock sounded at the door, and Rolfe's broad shoulders appeared. "My lord, the constable has arrived."

Haven nodded and went to his sister. "Go up, Jacinda. We'll talk more in the morning."

She set down her cup, hobbling over to Theo and taking her hand. "Thank you for rescuing my brother."

"I didn't need rescuing," Haven replied. "I had the situation in hand. All she did was toss a brandy bottle. Poorly. She was just as likely to hit me."

Theo didn't mind his snarling. She'd felt the way his fingers had gripped hers, as if he were afraid she wasn't real and would disappear. He was probably still worried she'd leave, which partially accounted for his mood.

Jacinda pressed a kiss to Theo's cheek. "I'm glad you're home, Theo." She limped toward the door, her cane thumping along the floor. Pausing, she cast a narrow-eyed glance at her brother before drifting out into the hall.

"My lord." Rolfe was still standing patiently. "The constable."

"I'll be along in a moment, Rolfe." Haven waved his hand at the butler. "A moment."

When she and Haven were alone again, he took her hand in his, rubbing his thumb along her fingers. "Don't leave." The intensity of his gaze on her deepened until the moss of his eyes was nearly black. He turned her hand over, pressing a kiss to her wrist. "Please."

"I won't, Ambrose. I promise." Theo had no intention of leaving.

"I am profoundly happy you are here, Theo." He pressed her fingers to his heart. "Wait for me. I'll be up in a bit." He dropped her fingers and walked to the door. "And don't even think about putting up Theodosia's Line of Demarcation."

31

Theo watched the flames dance across the room as she waited for Haven, considering all they needed to say to each other. She'd had a lot of time to think about her marriage. How it had begun and how she wished it to proceed. The betrayal was still there, but it was muted by a sense of feeling loved. So many things spoke of it. The studio Haven had made for her. Remembering she hated mushrooms. Insisting she wear her spectacles. Logically, there wasn't any way for Haven to have known she would paint a half-naked miniature of herself nor bestow it on Blythe. He *had* tried to get her to leave the study. Although he could have tried harder.

Did it matter any longer whether he had taken advantage of the situation?

She loved Haven. Forgave him. Believed him. He loved her, and while he hadn't said the words, Haven had shown her in dozens of ways before that terrible day when her brother's missive had arrived. In his eyes, Theo flared brilliantly. Such a feeling was worth fighting for. Cherishing. No matter how it began.

The sound of footsteps came toward the door. Haven. She knew what he sounded like.

He came into the room, peering at the bed to see if she was still awake.

"Hello, Ambrose."

The bed dipped as he sat, eyes intent on her, devoid of his usual annoying comments. "I was afraid you wouldn't be here when I came up." The words were hoarse as if they'd sat in his throat for days.

"I promised you I wouldn't leave. And I could see you perfectly well, by the way," she said in a saucy tone. "Or at least enough to notice which one of you was Erasmus."

"You realize you didn't hit him."

"I clipped his ear." She frowned slightly. "At least I think I did."

His hand, warm and slightly calloused, cupped her cheek. "I missed you, Theodosia." The low rumble whispered over her. "So much."

"In addition to mushrooms," she whispered, "I do not care for turnips. That is my truth. Now tell me yours."

"I did plan to compromise you, just not at Blythe's." He pressed his forehead to hers. "Thought about when I should do it. I had several opportunities, and dear God, Theodosia, if any woman was begging to be ruined, it was you."

"You are doing a poor job at apologizing." She looked away, the pain just as sharp as it had been when reading her brother's letter. "I had hoped for something better."

"Just listen." He brushed her lips with his. "I also wanted you the moment I saw you. *Only* you. I thought it fated that you were Murphy's sister. A way of some higher power finally tipping the scales in my favor. A woman I desired who was also the solution to my problems. But I didn't take the miniature from you that night to compromise you."

"Then why?"

"I—" His voice grew thick with emotion. "I could not bear the thought of Blythe—or any other man—having you. I wanted it to be *me* you had painted it for. I wanted you *in spite of* you being Murphy's sister. Had I not felt so deeply for you, I would have compromised you and taken your dowry without a second thought. I planned to be that ruthless. But in the end, I couldn't. You can thank Lady Blythe for our marriage. And our wedding night, I just assumed—"

"Because of my enthusiasm?"

"Yes. Even you must admit, Theo, that most young ladies wouldn't immediately take their husband's cock in their mouth before being bedded for the first time. I assume you either read about it or witnessed it. Somehow." He lay down beside her so they faced each other.

Theo felt warm and secure next to Haven, the gravelly sound of his voice soothing her.

"Elysium," she blurted out. "I saw—" Theo felt her cheeks warm. "I snuck onto the second floor with Romy while Leo was otherwise occupied. I opened a door and witnessed—" She paused and cleared her throat as an image of she and Haven possibly doing that flashed before her. "Both parties seemed very pleased. So I thought you meant for me to do it."

"You neglected to mention that." He drew his fingers across her cheek, their noses almost touching.

"Just as you neglected to inform me that you blamed my brother for the ruination of your father. I find that more vitally important than whether I saw a woman put a man's—"

"Cock," he supplied helpfully.

"I understand why . . ." She hesitated. "I don't like it, but I do *comprehend* why you sought to compromise me. But—"

A tremble ran through her as he pressed a tender kiss to the slope of her neck.

"You know, Ambrose, that your anger was directed at the

wrong man, don't you? My brother is hardly a paragon of morality, but even he draws the line at stealing dowries."

"I do. And I plan to beg humble forgiveness."

"I doubt you can do that. Be humble. Your pride won't allow it."

"Very well, I will at the very least *appeal* to the duke, tell him that I have come to realize the truth and ask him to reconsider his blatant prickish behavior—"

"I appreciate you apologizing to my family," she interrupted. Haven might never get on with either of her brothers, but at least she wouldn't have to worry about them coming to blows over dinner. "What will you do with Erasmus? Impersonating a marquess must be some sort of a crime. My brother is a duke. So is Granby. Surely they can both ensure justice will be done."

"He'll be a guest of the constable for the next few days. After which Erasmus will be going to Australia. I'll write to Estwood in the morning. He has property there. I'd rather not drag this matter out. No one remembers my uncle, and I'd like to keep it that way." Haven had started to nibble down her throat in the most distracting manner.

"I see." The word crested upward as his hand cupped the underside of one breast. "I didn't realize Erasmus had any aspirations to visit Australia."

"Neither did he." He toyed with her nipple. "Stay with me. Always."

"Do you promise," she murmured, her pulse fluttering in her neck, "that going forward, we will have honesty? Not to be wretched. Impossible. Difficult."

"I can promise you honesty." The grip on her breast became possessive. "But I can't offer you *any* of those other things. I will always be impossible. Blunt. *Wretched*."

"You're ruining it," she whispered, though he wasn't, not really.

"But I can offer up my heart." His voice grew raspy and rough as he pressed his lips against her throat. "Which admittedly isn't my best feature, but it belongs to you, nonetheless." He turned her head and brushed his lips gently against hers. "You have *never* been second best. Never odd. Never to me. In my sky, *you* are the brightest star, dazzling me with your brilliant light."

A tear ran down her cheek and she wiped it away. "I suppose that was acceptable groveling."

He ran a finger along her jaw before pressing his forehead to hers. "I *love* you, Theo. If you believe nothing else, I beg you to believe that."

EPILOGUE

The Duke of Averell frowned down the long table gracing the dining room, his gaze alighting on the sight of the *parasite* demolishing a plate of food as if he hadn't eaten in days.

Tony was in a bit of a foul mood. There was nothing quite like arriving home from Lady Fulton's tedious affair—which he'd been forced to attend—only to be told by Pith that Theodosia was not at home. His sister had taken off in a flurry for Greenbriar, claiming she must rescue Haven. Immediately. Apparently, Haven's uncle, in addition to being a spectacular sot, was also intent on murdering his nephew. According to Pith.

The entire affair, of which Tony had not yet wholly heard, was outlandish and sounded like the plot of one of those novels Theodosia liked to read. Twins impersonating each other. Gambling away the family fortune. A nefarious uncle who lived in France. In the end, all of it had turned out to be true.

It did not mean Tony was in any mood to welcome Haven with open arms.

Parasite.

First that giant block of ice Granby and now Haven. His sisters truly had the very worst taste in husbands. Tony glared in Haven's direction as if doing so would make him disappear.

The slight ping of a fork against a plate turned his attention from Haven to the end of the table. Tony's duchess wiggled her brows, dark eyes flashing with caution.

"*Behave,*" she mouthed to him.

"*Never,*" Tony mouthed back. He'd deal with Maggie later. In the privacy of their bedroom. Saucy thing.

Phaedra, just to his right, giggled.

Good God. There wasn't any telling who or what Phaedra would bring home one day. His youngest sister, closest to him in personality, was probably destined for scandal. She'd taken to helping him with some of the paperwork at Elysium, asking far too many questions about the inner workings of the gambling hell and pleasure palace. When she wasn't tagging behind him, Phaedra was torturing the poor gentleman Tony had engaged to teach her fencing.

An indulgence he was sure to regret one day.

"To what do I owe the pleasure," Tony said, finally deigning to speak to Haven, "of your dubious company?"

Haven and Theodosia had appeared just two hours ago, jumping out of the Averell coach. Two valises told Tony they planned on staying at least for the night.

The Marquess of Haven's jaw hardened before he stilled and gave Tony a blatantly forced smile, full of false submission and nearly well-hidden dislike.

"Business of a personal matter, Your Grace. And Theodosia wished to make a proper farewell to her family before we return to Greenbriar."

"I see." Tony took a sip of his wine. It appeared their estrangement was over.

Tony saw his sister move slightly and Haven's resulting

wince. They glared at each other for a moment, and he thought a fight might erupt. But then Theodosia smiled and pushed her spectacles back up her nose.

Haven regarded her in adoration, or what passed for such a thing on his rough features. He always appeared to have just left a tavern fight. It seemed Maggie was right, as she so often was. Haven and Theo were a love match. He supposed he'd have to tolerate the *parasite* for her sake. He wasn't sure how Leo would feel.

"Stop scowling, Anthony," his stepmother, the dowager duchess, admonished him, a small smile on her lips. "Haven is beginning to grow on me," she said in a low tone.

"Much like Granby, Amanda?" Tony speared a carrot from his plate. "I was hoping Pith would do us all a favor and poison both of them. Perhaps he is only waiting for the holidays to bestow such a gift on me."

"Anthony," his stepmother cautioned. "Please don't give Pith any ideas."

Phaedra giggled again.

Haven, a small frown marring his features, had doubtless heard their exchange. He paused in his devouring of the excellent meal, fur ruffled like the tomcat Phaedra claimed him to be. At the moment, Tony could see the resemblance to Theseus.

"I have something I would like to discuss with you after dinner, Your Grace."

"Of course." Tony gripped his knife, wondering how good his aim was. "I look forward to it."

Leo would be very displeased when he returned.

※

THANK YOU FOR READING **THE MARQUESS METHOD**. I hope you enjoyed the story of Theo, Haven and one very inappropriate miniature. If you did, I'd so appreciate a review. Reviews keep me writing.

CLICK HERE FOR THE WAGER OF A LADY available for pre-order and arriving in 2022.

Georgina, Lady Masterson, is keeping secrets.

Wed to the elderly, sickly Lord Masterson, Georgina's dreams of romance are dashed by the reality of her situation until she meets the wickedly attractive Leo Murphy.

Murphy, owner of Elysium and the bastard son of the Duke of Averell is *everything* Georgina's husband is not.

One night with Leo changes Georgina's life forever, putting her in a precarious position. Compromised both in heart and body and terrified for her future, Georgia reaches a decision.

One that Leo Murphy will *never* forgive her for.

Keep reading the next in the series **THE WAGER OF A LADY.**

The Beautiful Barringtons start with a chance meeting between a very jaded Duke of Averell and the beautiful lady's companion he falls in love with. Claim your FREE copy of **THE STUDY OF A RAKE** and read the love story of Amanda and Marcus.

Wait…have you read THE WICKEDS?

Alexandra Dunforth didn't plan on creating a scandal. She's just trying to avoid the marriage her uncle has arranged. But one chance meeting with the infamous Marquess of Cambourne and suddenly Alexandra finds herself kissed, nearly set on fire and she's gained the attention of the biggest rake in London. **CLICK HERE TO READ WICKED'S SCANDAL.**

Visit www.kathleenayers.com for a complete list of my books, news on releases and **two free books!**

AUTHOR NOTES

The idea of Theo painting a naked self-portrait for Blythe came after seeing a picture of *Beauty Revealed* by the American miniaturist Sarah Goodridge (1788-1853). Ms. Goodridge was well-known in the early 19th century for her portraits of politicians, particularly Daniel Webster. Goodridge and Webster were longtime friends and possibly more though the nature of their relationship has never been clearly defined. What is known is that Goodridge gifted *Beauty Revealed*, a miniature of her naked breasts, to Webster. There is a fascinating article about Webster and Goodridge if you care to read more. https://medium.com/the-collector/a-shocking-miniature-and-a-mysterious-connection-762689f7c054

I went down the rabbit-hole in looking at the history of eyeglasses and optometry (a term that wasn't used until the end of the 19th century). Jane Austen wore spectacles (she had a tortoise-shell pair) prescribed by a London oculist. But by the early 1840's (when The Marquess Method takes place) spectacles with varying types of magnification were being mass-produced and sold. Check out this link if you want to read more about Jane and her spectacles. https://www.journals.uchicago.edu/doi/pdfplus/10.1086/692020

Winsor and Newton (where Theo gets her artist supplies) opened their doors in 1838 in London. I learned so much about how paint was stored, artist boxes (Theo's is based on one I found listed at an antique dealer) watercolor, walnut oil...I could go on and on. Winsor and Newton really did invent glass syringes for paint storage in 1840 (up until then paint was stored in bladders). They have a wonderful website (and are still in business) which I encourage you to look at if you're interested.

The demand for miniatures was dying out by the mid-19th century when a new art form came into existence – photography. The invention of the daguerreotype (1839) meant people didn't need to carry a portrait in their pocket, they could have an actual picture of their loved one. I like the thought of Theo moving from miniatures to photography, despite her eyesight.

ABOUT THE AUTHOR

Kathleen Ayers is the bestselling author of steamy historical romance and an avid romance reader since she was a teenager. Kathleen likes her heroes a little damaged, her heroines feisty and her endings happy. When not writing Kathleen is most at home in a pool or the ocean (with or without her husband and son) swimming with her dogs, learning how to grow a perfect tomato or attending a wine tasting. Drop her a line anytime at kayersauthor@gmail.com.

Sign up for Kathleen's newsletter:
www.kathleenayers.com

Like Kathleen on Facebook
www.facebook.com/kayersauthor

Join Kathleen's Facebook Group
Historically Hot with Kathleen Ayers

Follow Kathleen on Instagram
https://www.instagram.com/kayersauthor

Printed in Great Britain
by Amazon